Provided

by

Measure B

which was approved

by the voters in

November, 1998

Published by
Algonquin Books of Chapel Hill
Post Office Box 2225
Chapel Hill, North Carolina 27515-2225

a division of
Workman Publishing
708 Broadway
New York, New York 10003

Printed in the United States of America.
Published simultaneously in Canada by Thomas Allen & Son Limited.
Design by Anne Winslow.

Grateful acknowledgment is made to the following magazines, where
portions of this book, in substantially different form, first appeared: *New
Delta Review, The Carolina Quarterly,* and *Buzz: The Talk of Los Angeles.*

This is a work of fiction. While, as in all fiction, the literary perceptions and
insights are based on experience, all names, characters, places, and incidents
are either products of the author's imagination or are used fictitiously.
No reference to any real person is intended or should be inferred.

Library of Congress Cataloging-in-Publication Data

Wilson, Wayne.
    Eddie and Bella : a novel / by Wayne Wilson.
        p.   cm.
    ISBN 1-56512-297-6
    1. Poets—Fiction.   I. Title.
PS3573.I4758 E33   2001
813'.54—dc21
                                        00-062070
  9 8 7 6 5 4 3 2 1
First Edition

Eddie & Bella

Also by Wayne Wilson
Loose Jam

Eddie & Bell

A NOVEL BY WAYNE WILSON

Algonquin Books of Chapel Hill

This book is for Sarah.

ACKNOWLEDGMENTS

I'd like to offer my heartfelt thanks to the following people: for unfailing encouragement during my frequent Sloughs of Despond, my agent, Faith Childs; for believing in this book for the same reasons I did, my editor, Kathy Pories; for cogent responses to various incarnations of the manuscript, Michael Byrd, Kem Nunn, Dalit Waller, and the late Matt Clark (whom I miss to this day); for truly humbling generosity way beyond the call of friendship in setting aside their own writing to read, reread, and comment on this project since its very inception, Michael Griffith, Nicola Mason, Dave Racine, and Josh Russell; and for all of these things as well as advice, patience, and love, Laura Saltz.

I brought a heart into the room,
But from the room, I carried none with me.

—John Donne, "The Broken Heart"

Eddie & Bella

Raphael

Though it's after the lunch rush the booths at Fritatta & Fugue are still crowded with customers nursing coffee. Raphael figures they're talking about the Panama invasion. Nodding to the regulars, he makes his way briskly through the smells of cumin and clove to the kitchen, where a Cambodian kid in a Megadeth T-shirt pushes rattling trays of coffee cups through the dishwashing machine. The back door is open. Outside, the eucalyptus trees toss in the wind. Raphael checks the schedule, makes sure everybody's shift is covered for the next three weeks, calls in the wine order. While he's on the phone the cook slinks through the back door, reeking of pot smoke. "There you are," says Raphael. "Maybe I'm wrong but you don't seem exactly weighed down by your responsibilities. Do I have to remind you that Hilary—

Hilary and I—are going to be depending on you while we're gone?"

The kid rubs his mossy goatee. "Kind of late, ain't she?"

Raphael gropes for a cutting rejoinder but it's true. By now Hilary should be back from Monterey. Faced with the cook's smirk Raphael feels oddly embarrassed. He frowns, then tells the guy to worry about his own punctuality and hands over the spare keys. Raphael makes himself a cup of mint tea and takes one of the empty seats at the counter. Hilary has posted a new sign over the steam table: WHEN THERE IS A TASK TO BE DONE, WE "ARE" THAT TASK. Why isn't she back? What could be that compelling about the Forum on Total Quality Management in Alternative Business?

The cook sticks his head out of the kitchen and tells Raphael to pick up the phone by the register. It's Hilary.

"Babe," says Raphael. "You're home."

"Not really. I'm at my sister's."

A premonition of catastrophe bursts within him, an icy flare like the first instant of an earthquake, and sends him sifting through a jumble of women's faces, trying to factor them into dates and alibis. He hears the distant clang of a railroad signal and glances out the front windows; beyond the field across the street a freight train crawls past the industrial park. "Hil, what's going on here?"

"I want you to tell me about Bella," she says.

The horizon turns upside down. For a second it's as if the train, the industrial park, and the spine of hills beyond are reflected in the surface of a lake. "Who have you been talking to?"

"Someone who cares for her very much."

"Oh, give me a break—not that dork she used to live with. The carpenter? Managed the co-op?"

"Vern isn't a dork, Mr. High-and-Mighty. He has his own furniture design company in Albuquerque. And for your information there's standing room only at his Tao of Excellence presentations."

Raphael swivels on his stool and watches the skinny new waitress. Wearing black tights and a short plaid skirt, she carries a coffee urn from table to table through pools of lemony sunlight. "Mister Personality, we used to call him."

"Don't be so negative."

"What are you talking about? This is not negative. This is seriously concerned. I'm holding two nonrefundable tickets to Cabo San Lucas and you call from Monterey to grill me about some woman I haven't seen in years. What do you expect?"

"I learned a lot from Vern."

"Like what—Buddhist cabinetmaking?"

"You think you're so smart. You told me Bella was dead, Raphael. You told me she was dead and all you had to remember her by was that coin and blah-blah-blah and I bought you the necklace and you *wear* it, Raphael. You've been wearing it for *years.*"

"Hil, this is history. Literally. We hung out for a while,

we broke up. I mean, it was a painful part of my past, and, I don't know, it's possible that I did misrepresent things. So, OK, guilty as charged, whatever. I'm happy to talk about it with you. But can't the discussion wait till you get back?"

"I'm not sure when that's going to be."

"You're not *sure?* What am I supposed to do with the tickets?" Behind him he senses a sudden lull in the drone of voices, as if each customer has stopped talking in mid-sentence.

"You do what you need to do," Hilary is saying. "It's not like this is the first time you've lied to me, Raphael. And I need to think stuff over. Issues of trust. Because the way I feel now I don't even know you."

Her declaration sounds rehearsed. People have started talking again but Raphael can't figure out if it's his imagination or if they're really shooting him amused glances. "Indeed," he hears himself say, then hangs up. Clinging to the register are five yellow stickies, messages of increasing urgency reminding Raphael to call Poughkeepsie Insurance Solutions. Blindly he cashes out the drawer.

Outside it's still cold, for California, anyway—nearly twelve long summers here have thinned his blood—but the wind has died and the pepper trees that line the north end of the parking lot barely rustle. The new waitress is sweeping hibiscus petals off the sidewalk. Squinting into the sun, she stands there with the broom and watches Raphael walk to his car. "You and Hilary must be so

4

psyched," she says. "Three whole weeks in Cabo. That's like my most awesome fantasy."

"There's no reason it has to stay one," says Raphael. "Daphne, right?" From behind his sunglasses he registers her goofy smile of assent and realizes with a pang how young she is. Past the pink hair, lip ring, and tattoos, the curves of her face shine, as if lit from inside, with the simple perfection of a seashell. "Put it out there, Daphne. You can make it happen."

"I guess. Is Mexico close to Panama?"

"Not close enough to worry about." When she kneels to pick up the dustpan he lets her mute appeal ripple over him. "Refresh my memory," he says. "You're a potter, right?"

She looks up, her smile reflecting not the gratitude he'd expected but a kind of sly triumph, which vanishes so quickly he thinks he must have imagined it. "No," she says. "A photographer. But it's a beautiful art. Ceramics, I mean."

"Beauty," he says, "is the beginning of terror."

Raphael drives downtown, dodging the hordes of Christmas shoppers. He makes the bank deposit and finds a parking space across the street from Mitchell Park. Beneath a flapping hand-painted banner that reads U.S. KEEP YOUR DIRTY HANDS OFF PANAMA, there's a crowd of shouting Latinos. Smears of brassy music blare from a loudspeaker. Somehow at the end of the eighties the crowd's theatrical outrage seems dated and clownish. Raphael sits behind the wheel of his gray Civic, trying to exorcise the specter of Bella watching fireworks from his roof. He finds his hand under his sweater, touching the *I Ching* coin that hangs from a silver chain around his neck. From an ice age ago. Why had he told Hilary that Bella was dead? It had been a stupid move. A pointless move. A kid's move. As he locks his car and heads toward the gym some men in mirrored sunglasses yell at him in Spanish.

WHEN HE MET her he was twenty-two. He'd come to San Luis Obispo in 1978 and rented a room in a ramshackle house across the tracks from the Amtrak station. Five nights a week he waited tables at an Indian restaurant and a year after the Diablo Canyon nuclear power plant blockade he helped cater a party in the hills overlooking Morro Bay. It was a housewarming for Meredith, a Louisiana girl who'd moved west with a windfall inheritance and fallen under the spell of a sixteen-year-old Bengali guru.

"Life in the Fast Lane" blasted from the speaker columns and the deck was jammed with tanned people, their Birkenstocks and bare feet shuffling on the redwood planks. A couple of naked little girls ran back and forth, provoking waves of lazy laughter. The sun scorched Raphael's neck as he helped set up tables. He poured himself a beer and started dipping tofu skewers in a glass of marinade. Every time he glanced up at the serving line he seemed to confront some woman he'd slept with. A florist. A landscape architect. An English instructor from the community college. Even one of his roommates, a shiatsu masseuse. They shot him meaningful looks over their paper plates and he wished he could erase each of those encounters —blunders, every one, he knew that. But how were you supposed to say no to those soft pleading expressions? What did these women get from him anyway? What kept them coming back?

When a couple of lawyers asked him to play Frisbee he grabbed his glass and went into the kitchen. It was cool and dark and in a far room he could hear the rattle of clothes in a dryer. As his eyes recovered from the dazzle of the sun the shadows resolved into a woman with a red bandanna over her dark curls facing out the window that overlooked the deck. "Hi," he said. "I'm Raphael."

"Yeah," she said, without turning from the window. "The poet. I know all about you."

He was pretty sure her accent owed something to New Jersey. She faced him and he saw that she was older than he—probably in her late twenties—with dark skeptical eyes and a long nose.

"Don't be too sure," he said.

She lit a cigarette, blew out the match, and squinted at him through the smoke. "I know you don't like Frisbee."

He slipped the elastic from his ponytail and tossed his

hair. "I don't really get off on games. Frankly I'm not into this whole scene." He gestured with his glass at the naked little girls outside. "I mean, look at those two. Talk about a class act."

"Are you always this generous with your opinions?"

Raphael cocked one finger. "Let me guess," he said. "You're from another country."

"Yeah. It's called Philly."

"Funny—I would have guessed Czechoslovakia."

She sighed. "Spare me, OK?"

Meredith came into the kitchen carrying two tiny dresses, a limp hibiscus over one ear. "Hey, Bella," she said. "I see you've met Raphael."

"Yeah, he's explaining class to me."

"Really?" Meredith held out the dresses. "Washed and dried. I believe I got most of the popsicle off."

Raphael emptied his glass in one gulp, realized too late that it was the marinade, and an instant later found himself doubled over the sink, gagging up safflower oil and garlic.

"You must be a terrific poet," said Bella. Raphael heard the sticky lisp of her thongs as she took the dresses out to the deck. "Darshon, Sage!" she shouted. "Time to get dressed, girls."

"Isn't she great?" said Meredith.

"She's a jerk," wheezed Raphael as he wiped his mouth with a paper towel.

"You hush. She needs a lot of support. Her old man is in jail because of the blockade." She frowned. "The word is, he and all the other protesters are being tortured."

By sunset a lot of people—the ones with Subarus and Mazdas—had left; those who remained didn't look as if they were going anywhere for a while. A skinny woman with long hair and protruding ears brought out an acoustic guitar. While she tuned up, Raphael stood at top of the stairs and watched the fog roll in. The railing was wet. Below him tight yellow halos knobbed the lights along the docks and he could hear the hollow knock of boats at anchor, the pulse of the distant surf. In the driveway below, Meredith blubbered to Raphael's boss, a dour silver-haired Hindu. "The Maharishi is my savior," she said. "He's teaching me how to live."

"If such a boy was giving me spiritual advice," said Raphael's boss, "I would certainly spank his bottom."

The woman with the guitar was singing about plutonium when Bella appeared beside Raphael, carrying her younger daughter on one hip. "You know what's pathetic?" she said. "Someday this is what we're going to mean when we talk about the past."

HE'D PLANNED TO work that night on some revisions for an upcoming reading at a local bookstore but he couldn't concentrate. Drinking the marinade—what was wrong with him? He never blew it like that. He ended up staring at the acacia outside his window, sipping root beer—a secret vice—and tapping his head with a felt-tip pen. Around midnight he glanced at the manuscript before him and saw that the top page was covered with column after column of Bella's name.

Raphael was still burping fumes of safflower oil and garlic the next afternoon. One of the cooks showed him a newspaper article about the Diablo Canyon protesters. They'd been released and it was revealed that the allegations of torture rose from the guards' refusal to pass out extra blankets. He was polishing wineglasses when Bella came into the restaurant accompanied by her daughters and a pinched-looking guy with a sparse red beard.

"They tortured our dad," said the older, dark-haired girl when Raphael brought menus to their table.

"Indeed," he said.

Bella turned to her companion. "This is Meredith's friend. That poet I told you about."

"How Bohemian." The guy glanced at Raphael over the top of his menu. "Big fan of Gwendolyn Brooks, are you?"

"Well—"

"I didn't think so. Where are you from anyway, Newark?"

Bella put down her menu. "Jesus, Vern, do you have to be such a toe-tag?"

The girls were giggling. "Meredith says he's a scamp," said the older one, pointing at Raphael.

"Hey, you two," said Bella. "Cool it, OK?"

"Scamp, scamp, scamp," chanted the younger sister.

THE WEEK BEFORE his reading Raphael stuffed his daypack with flyers—*From Santa Cruz–Sioux. Local poet Raphael will read from his Urban Sutras*—borrowed a roommate's ten-speed, and pedaled out Broad Street, no hands, his lanky shadow skimming the pavement. As he coasted through the railroad crossing, some girls in a VW convertible slowed down and whistled. He found the co-op behind a Circle K. Out front, Vern was building a fence around the herb garden; he answered Raphael's greeting with a curt nod. In the shade of a ragged eucalyptus the girls sat on either side of a tethered goat, sucking popsicles. A boom box on the sidewalk played a tape of someone speaking with an Indian accent. Inside, Bella was stocking vitamins.

"*Ploughshares* keeps asking for one of my urban sutras," he told her. "But the art-commerce thing makes me really uncomfortable." After posting a flyer he pointed to the photo taped to the cash register: a bloated dark-skinned boy smiling with supreme self-satisfaction as he sprayed rich-looking white folks with rose-colored water from a squirt gun. It was the same picture Raphael had seen on Meredith's refrigerator. "I see you're into the Maharishi too."

"Afraid not." Bella nodded toward the door. "Vern's in charge of spiritual progress." Hammer blows echoed outside and Raphael could hear the drone of the guru's taped lecture, Vern's admiring laughter. "Not again," muttered Bella. "How many times do we have to hear this?"

"You're too sophisticated?"

"Sophisticated enough to know you don't find inner peace by asking Santa Claus."

"You don't find it if you stop looking, either."

"Don't you ever relax? You sound like a used-car salesman."

She was a loser, he told himself as he rode away with his cheeks burning, exactly the kind of woman who smoked, the kind you'd expect to let her kids run around naked, and he decided to put her out of his mind.

AMONG THE LOCALS milling around in front of the Third Eye Bookstore he spotted Meredith and her new boyfriend, James, a black Vietnam vet who ran a managing insurance agency. He slapped Raphael's palm as Meredith held up a slim paperback: *Blood Lemons* by Sioux. "Sooks is wonderful," she said. "Her work is really spirit-filled."

Raphael shrugged. "I really don't get off on publication."

"Look here, Big Time," said James. "Maybe you can help me out. What it is, I need a new name for my business. Scorpio Solutions is kind of dated. And we're going to open up branches all around the country. Cleveland, Atlanta, New Orleans—you name it. I'm looking for something that suggests nationwide."

Raphael thought for a moment. "New York Solutions?"

"Too obvious."

"Poughkeepsie?"

James tapped his nose with a long forefinger. "Right on, right on, right on."

Then Raphael saw Bella making her way through the crowd in what looked like a Ukrainian peasant outfit. The late sun was behind her, that wild hair irradiated with red light, and when he met her eyes he couldn't look away. Vern was right behind her.

James snorted with laughter as the couple walked up. "Fresh from Monday night folk dancing," he said. "I'm surprised you can still boogie, Slick, after all that torture."

"That's an enlightened remark," muttered Vern and ushered Bella into the bookstore.

James elbowed Raphael in the ribs. "Get your eyes back in your head. Mister Personality is pretty territorial."

They sat three rows behind Vern and Bella. Sioux, a spindly woman with wine-colored hair, began by taking a dozen lemons from a shopping bag, passing them out, inviting the audience to experience them. Their texture, odor, sexuality. After putting them back in the sack she began to read. Five minutes later Raphael had tuned her out, though he appeared the soul of attentiveness. Trolling the bookstores and coffee shops of Harvard Square years ago with a clumsily annotated copy of *Sonnets to Orpheus* and testing the child of light routine on girls with names like Courtney and Magda, he'd mastered the sage nod, the knowing chuckle. Sioux droned on and on in a singsong voice while Raphael tried to will Bella to look at him. Every so often one of the other women would dart a sidelong glance at him. But not Bella.

When it was his turn he stood behind the lectern, conscious of nothing but her face, and read "The Hound of Satan." There was scattered applause when he finished. Afterward, facing down the indignant murmurs, he cut into the line of people waiting for Sioux to sign their books. "I really like the way you place line breaks," he told her.

"Is that a fact," said the poet in a dead voice.

Raphael thought he heard Vern laugh. When he went outside it was dark and the wind smelled of jasmine with a coppery tang of the ocean. Behind him the bookstore door opened and closed on a shrill gust of chatter and a moment later he smelled patchouli. Bella's shadow appeared beside him on the sidewalk. "Interesting," she said.

"Initially," he said, "I think of each poem as a chunk of wood." He held out his forearms, palms up, as if supporting a massive log. "It dictates its own form. And this is the sort of stuff I've been doing lately. Kind of experimental."

"The thing is, I don't think Satan would have a collie."

Raphael explained that the dogs' narrow skulls were

like tight shoes, squeezing their brains, making them stupid and vicious. "Look it up," he said, as she walked off laughing.

He was watching her and Vern pull away in a battered green pickup with one taillight when James and Meredith stopped to chat. "Still down on publication, Big Time?"

"Hey, this whole moon-menstruation theme is dead. About what you'd expect from someone who can't handle line breaks."

James looked amused. "She shut you down?"

"Come on. I mean, *Sioux?* Her name's probably Helen Crump."

"You guys," said Meredith.

THAT SPRING HE danced with Bella at a benefit concert for the Abalone Alliance. A local band, Jungle Wrought, was playing—three men in flowered shirts and bell-bottoms, a couple of women wearing wraparound skirts and espadrilles that tied at the ankles. The bass shook Raphael's spine, and bodies swayed all around them like seaweed beneath an ocean of blue smoke. From across the room he could see Vern watching them with a look of barely restrained fury. "I don't understand that guy," said Raphael. "What's he got against me anyway?"

"I'd think you'd be used to it by now."

"Used to what? What did I do?"

"You're doing it now."

When the music ended Raphael followed her to the bar. "You've got me all wrong. How about if we meet someplace? Just to talk."

She sipped her tequila and gave him a brief sad smile. "I don't think that's such a great idea."

"Why not?"

"Because I don't even know you."

"That can change."

"Come on," she said, "stop instigating."

But she finally agreed to meet him the following evening for a drink. "Just one," she said and named a bar in Pismo Beach. He found the place down the block from a sorry-looking carnival. A row of choppers gleamed near the entrance. Inside, the bar was dark and drafty, fireplace stuffed with trash, no toilet paper in the one bathroom still boasting a door. A hangout for the chronically unemployed, felons, musicians, old freaks drinking up their drywall pay. Raphael felt as if he'd never left home. Through the back door he could see dune buggies roaring up and down the tar-stained beach. He'd been nursing a long-necked Bud for twenty minutes and was just about ready to leave when Bella stepped into the lounge wearing a red cloche hat. A couple of bikers looked at each other across the pool table and raised their eyebrows. When she sat down Raphael handed her a copy of *The Duino Elegies.* "I'd like you to have this," he said.

"Listen," she said, after her third glass of burgundy, "does this poetry business really mean anything to you?"

"It means I can bear witness."

"To what—how many times you get laid?"

"You can leave anytime, Bella."

"I'm sorry. It's just that I can't afford any magic moments with you. I've got a good thing. Why should I blow it? You know I've got this commitment to Vern, right?"

"Are you in love with him?"

"I don't know." As she stared into her glass, candlelight flickered on her hair and wove lacy shadows across her face. "He tries so hard. Maybe I'm trying to find out what love means."

"Who isn't?"

"Poor baby." Bella reached across the table and with one finger traced a vein along his forearm. Her foot grazed his shin and hot lobes of desire spiraled slowly down some axis deep within him.

"Really, when I saw you at the reading this longing, this *yearning* spilled out of my heart like warm honey. I'm *serious*."

"The sad thing is, I almost believe it."

A couple of days later he borrowed Meredith's Mazda and drove to the co-op as Bella was closing up. "Why?" she said when he asked her to go for a ride.

"Come on. What do you say?"

"Well, as long as it's a short one. I have to pick up the girls."

They drove up the coast to Cayucos. Bella found some country station and sang along in an off-key voice. They parked at the end of a dirt road, facing the ocean. Before them tufts of beach heather shuddered in the wind. Inky clouds scrolled across a cold red sky. Raphael cracked his window and the rank smell of kelp mingled with Bella's patchouli. It seemed the very scent of possibility. "It's like this," he said. "I'm walking through these dark woods and find an abandoned farm. I go through the empty rooms and pick up a newspaper from 1932, yellow and brittle like old leaves, then head out to the barn—can we turn off the radio?"

"The better to hear you with, my dear?"

"So I step into the dark. It smells like hay and there's a hole in the roof with dusty sunlight slanting down through the broken boards. A woman moves into the light. It's you."

"Don't think I'm not on to you," she said. "Because I am. You're instigating again."

"Then how come you're here?"

"You don't know how to play Frisbee, do you?"

"What are you talking about?"

"I'm *tawkin'* about, if you want to keep passing for the complete California boy you better do something about that accent. That afternoon at Meredith's—when they asked you to play Frisbee? It was like watching somebody's wig slip." Her hand was on his arm. "Listen, I'm the last person who should be teasing you. Sometimes I look at these impossibly healthy people all dusted with golden light and I feel like I just got off the boat."

Raphael was quiet for a while. Then he leaned forward, sighed, and rubbed his eyes. "You know the American Dream?"

"I've heard of it."

"Well, till I moved here I didn't even know Frisbee *had* rules. It was another rich kids' thing. I grew up playing half-ball. We lived in a dump that smelled like Lysol and rancid salami. In the winter we'd heat water on the stove once a week and take baths in a plastic wading pool. There wasn't a book in the house." It was dusk now and over the rush of the surf he could hear his heartbeat. He turned to stroke Bella's cheek. "You feel like a shadow."

"Take it easy now."

"You're telling me this doesn't seem like a good idea either?"

"I'm telling you," she said, "that it never seems like a good idea."

Her kiss tasted of tobacco and wine. The upholstery was chilly but she wedged the hat under her bottom and Raphael didn't even try for the expression of Vedic bliss he usually brought to such encounters.

"The girls," she sobbed afterward. "I was supposed to pick them up an hour ago. And the *hat*. Vern bought it for me at the craft fair."

Raphael was no stranger to women's tears but he was rattled anyway. And as he held her there in the phosphorescent glow of the dash lights it suddenly came to him that all those snowy nights so long ago as he'd trudged home to his apartment back in Central Square it was this troubled woman's face, her eyes lambent with sorrow, he'd been looking for in the windows of the passing buses. "I know what it's like," he'd said without the faintest idea of what he meant. "I know what it's like."

ALL THOSE YEARS, all those memories, fading like old bumper stickers. With little recollection of how he'd gotten here, Raphael finds himself in his aerobics class. On the sound system Julio Iglesias sobs an up-tempo version of "O Holy Night." The instructor, a burly Asian woman in mauve tights, lets out yips of feigned enthusiasm. Raphael spots himself among the sweating ranks reflected in the mirrored walls and suddenly discerns what looks like a faint gray film over his hair. Maybe it's just the fluorescent lights but he can't shake the feeling that everyone else notices too and he leaves early. Despite the abbreviated session his legs are trembling. Sparks of pain singe his knees. Slipping into a drugstore, he grabs a bottle of natural deep brown *Nice 'n Easy* and a newspaper. On the front page is a photo of a grim-looking President Bush pointing to a map of Panama. *Every Other Avenue Was Closed* read the bold red headlines. His sudden ripple of vertigo is simply stress, he decides. No big deal.

Retracing his steps toward the park, he passes Book Galaxy, where the Third Eye used to be. *The Language of Wood,* Sioux's latest, is in the window. She's done all right —for a fraud. Won prizes, appeared on PBS a few times. A success story, he supposes, that calls into question his own vocation as a poet but surely he can be forgiven for putting that on the back burner while making a living. Up the street two wizened old hippies unload a truckload of Christmas trees, and as Raphael walks by, the astringent scent takes him back to the cramped sunless streets of home in Revere, Massachusetts. His brother and the other local vets, long-haired spooky-eyed guys shivering on the corners in their field jackets. The cold-water flat over Fat Tony's Sub Shop where Raphael lived with his broken mother and two waspish sisters. The wretched boredom of Mass at St. Theresa's.

He has to talk to someone. He thinks of all those messages from James. At a phone booth Raphael consults Information, then heads out of town on a back road bordered by oil derricks. He listens to the news on the radio. Operation Just Cause is a success, says the president. Casualties are low. Everybody's happy. Raphael picks up the freeway in Pismo Beach and drives south past the poppy-spattered bluffs overlooking the ocean. Long ago he'd asked James to define a managing insurance agency but all he can remember was that there was essentially no product and it made a lot of money—which, along with James's veteran status was cause for a lot of aggrieved head shaking among Meredith's friends. Raphael gets off the freeway in Santa Maria. Across the street from a field of oil derricks stands an imposing two-story structure of black glass. POUGHKEEPSIE INSURANCE CONCEPTS reads a sign by the parking lot entrance. WE'VE GOT YOU "COVERED!" Inside, a robotic young woman with glossy blond curls speaks into a phone and a moment later James comes down the hall in a three-piece suit, rubbing his hands. "My *man*. Fast-talking, slow-walking Raphael. The cat with the million-dollar smile. The word is, you're looking for a job."

"What are you talking about? I've got a job."

"But how long, Big Time? How long? That's the question." In his office James sits behind his desk, leans back in the chair, presses his fingertips together. "You still writing those poems?"

"I'm surprised you even remember me."

"*Remember* you? How much did I lend you to bail that woman out of jail? Seven hundred bucks? Now that was one qualified chick."

Raphael breaks into a sweat. "Didn't I send you a check?"

James laughs into his fist. "You know, you trip me out, Big Time. I like the way you carry yourself. Yes, you sent me a check all right. But it bounced. So let's just say you owe me one." He spins in his chair as Raphael tells him about Vern and Hilary, the cook's leer, the customers' malicious glances. Bella. In the parking lot outside, a spindly black kid wearing a metallic blue hard hat and an orange jumpsuit is talking to a couple of blond girls. As Raphael watches, the kid turns a nimble pirouette, one leg flexed like a stork's, then sinks into a split. "We were all a little messed up in those days," James is saying. "I mean, look at Meredith. Gives all her money—I'm talking about a seven-figure inheritance—to that little gook and ends up running a greasy spoon down there in the swampland. I told her. I said, 'Girl, if that fat little creep's got the key to wisdom I'm George Peckerwood Wallace.' So what if Hilary's got her lip out? You want to manage her restaurant the rest of your life? Now you take me. I could have just stayed in Louisiana. Sold strawberries alongside the highway. Tended bar like my cousin. But a man got to stay on his toes. Think about it. Maybe it's time to move on."

"What should I do about Bella?"

"Do? What's all this got to do with you? Nothing, that's what. Did you tell her to Dixie-fry her life? No? Look here. Sooner or later all of us get our hearts broke. Could be a man, could be a woman. Could be a war, you understand what I'm saying? It's just a question of time till we find out we don't matter."

"That's a pretty grim way to look at it."

"There it is."

WISPY CLOUDS SPIRAL westward, dragging faint shadows across the fields, as Raphael drives out Johnson toward Hilary's place, a lavish spread nestled against the brown hills. What, he wonders, does Bella look like now? When had she given him the *I Ching* coin? How come he's still wearing it? Why out of all the women in his life had only she discovered that he was ticklish? How long has it been, honestly, since he's written anything and where have the nights gone, the nights he'd lain abed fighting for breath against the sheer weight of all the gorgeous things left to say? How long since his last confession? And what difference does it make now?

He and Bella had bought an old Volkswagen bug from Meredith and rented an apartment in a two-story Victorian near the university. As Raphael turns into Hilary's driveway his inner eye fills with the image of Bella on a long-ago Fourth of July. They'd spread their sleeping bags on the roof. Down the street a radio blasted the shrill chorus of "Surrender" and red fireworks sputtered against the sky. A string of muffled thumps, distant applause. Bella stood naked beneath a branch of the camphor tree that sheltered the roof, her body in shadow except for a crescent of rose-colored light outlining one hip. Raphael crawled across the tarpaper to kiss the back of her knee. "When I touch you," he whispered, "it's like swallowing stars."

She stroked his hair. "Why me?"

"Why did I fall for you? I guess I couldn't help it."

"You couldn't *help* it?"

He knew he'd screwed up, though he wasn't sure how. "I just meant that it's strong," he said hastily. He put his arms around her waist. "My feeling for you. Irresistible. What's wrong with that?"

"So this is some kind of reflex? You're telling me you're with me by *default?*" She shook her head. "How could I have been dumb enough to think someone would love me for myself? Let *go* of me."

"You don't understand," he said and she jammed an elbow into his cheek. The night splintered into red streaks. He pulsed back to full consciousness and found himself flat on his back. He was alone.

The next day he went to work with a black eye. "This is what you are getting," said his boss, "for associating with scofflaws."

By then Raphael knew Bella was buying coke but whenever he brought it up she would either start crying or call him a toe-tag and tickle him into shrieking hysterics. She started working cocktails at the Golden West. A customer gave her a huge marginally housebroken mongrel named Dudley. Before long the walls and carpets had soaked up his gamy odor. Dudley's fur hung in the air like a fog; before showering you had to dig plugs of it from the drain.

The Volkswagen broke down a couple of times a month, generally when Bella drove out to Los Osos to pick up the girls. There were towing bills. Repair bills. Raphael was working six nights a week and it still wasn't enough. The November rent check bounced. After sitting for twenty minutes in shamed silence one morning while the landlady pounded on the door and Dudley barked himself hoarse, Raphael called his brother back in Massachusetts and asked for a loan. In his voice he recognized desperation.

That December Bella, having told Raphael that she was helping Meredith paint her kitchen, totaled the car on the way back from a party in Paso Robles. She was arrested for drunk driving. James lent Raphael the money to bail her out and turned him on to a repossessed Valiant with a shower curtain taped over the rear window. The court gave Bella the choice of losing her license or attending Alcohol Awareness classes. Raphael drove her to the first session. As he looked around at all the desperate people with their JCPenney clothes and sad haircuts he knew he wanted out. It wasn't just the smoking or the cocaine and quaaludes or the drinking or the kids or the dog or Vern; beyond all these was an inexorable devouring darkness. True, for the first time in his life he was writing every day, scribbling page after page and filling trash bags with the results, but if this was the price of inspiration he was ready to pass.

In the winter of 1980, at a memorial service for John Lennon, he first saw Hilary. Jungle Wrought was packing up after a set of lackluster Beatles covers, and Hilary, a young auburn-haired woman in a black sundress, was talking to some men in business suits to the left of the stage. The day was windy with a blinding blue sky, the Mission foaming with greenery, and she kept reaching up to fool with her gold hair pick; her curves would shift beneath the fabric and as Raphael shouldered his way through the men around her he could feel the surges of brute desire. "Strange day," he said when he was standing beside her. "So beautiful. And yet so sad."

"It's a terrible tragedy," said Hilary.

The tinny rattle of abused machinery had been grinding its way into Raphael's awareness, growing louder and louder, and when snickers broke out around him he looked past Hilary to the street. There was Bella, driving the girls back out to Los Osos. The Valiant wallowed past in a cloud of black smoke; Dudley's head poked through a hole in the shower curtain that covered the empty rear window frame. "Yeah," he said, pausing to mold his expression into one of wry melancholy. "And tragedy's something I'm becoming pretty familiar with. Someone very close to me just died."

Hilary, who was down from Monterey to close the deal on the storefront for her new restaurant, Fritatta & Fugue, talked for a long time, brow furrowed as if she were trying to remember a complex script, about Total Quality Management. "TQM might even help you get over your grief," she said. "The thing is, everybody thinks it's just for business but we can apply these dynamic strategies to our own lives too."

"I've never thought of it that way," he said. "I'll bet most people are so knocked out by your glamour and all that they don't give you credit for this kind of insight."

Hilary blushed. "You're just saying that."

"You know," he says, as if suddenly overwhelmed, "it's uncanny. You're the very image of this woman in a villanelle I just roughed out. A Modigliani portrait that comes alive, with her own subjectivity and all. Look, I have to know, is this just me? I mean, it's like we're treading water, only it's not water, it's this, I don't know, hidden guilty river god of the blood and then all of a sudden our feet touch. Whew! Do you know what I mean?" As they walked to her Volvo he let her know that he was ready to move up from waiting tables. And though he honored the principles of Total Quality he had to admit that he wasn't all that familiar with its actual practice.

"Well," said Hilary, "if it works out I wouldn't mind teaching you."

"It might take a while. I'm a slow learner."

She gave him a placid smile. "That could be interesting."

And Raphael saw the years ahead falling like a choice

hand of cards into his palm. All those sweet sweet plans he'd made in his room above Fat Tony's, reading *Letters to a Young Poet* night after night as the sign outside washed the ceiling with lavender light—those plans were working out after all. He was safe.

HE CHECKS THE answering machine. Hilary still hasn't called. He showers, lathers his hair with *Nice 'n Easy*, rubs lotion on his hands and face. Raphael is pretty sure that everything will blow over as usual. But even so, around three he breaks down and dials Hilary's sister to see what's going on. Lee has never warmed to him, especially since the name business. A week or so after moving in with Hilary, Raphael's brother had called about that old loan and asked for him by his birth name. At first Hilary was totally freaked out. *Eddie? Your name is Eddie Hoffa?* He explained that Raphael was his spiritual name, which satisfied her. But not her sister. *His Holiness,* Lee still calls him. *Pope Eddie the Last.*

It's Lee who answers the phone. "News flash," she says, "you're not kids anymore. Rise and shine, guys. There's a real world out there."

"I'm aware of that. I manage your sister's restaurant, you know."

"Manage, right. You're nothing but another leech."

"Can we discuss my shortcomings later? Right now I've got to know if Hil's coming back in time for our trip or not."

"Don't make me laugh."

"Will you at least give me some idea of what's going on up there? What's this geek been telling her anyway?"

"Use your powers of imagination, Your Holiness."

"Lee, Bella and I had something but it just didn't work out. How does that make me such an ogre?"

"You told Hilary this poor woman was *dead,* for crying out loud." Lee shuddered audibly. "There's such a thing as sisterhood, buddy. And if I were you I'd be gone by the time we get down there."

"My pleasure," he says. It occurs to him that his position may be a little precarious. For sure, there will be an accounting. At the very least explanations, difficult ones, will be required. Still deep inside him there's something shining, something pure—how many times has he been told that? Isn't it by piecing together such instants of reflected light that you see, as it truly is, your life? What else do you have to go on?

THEY'D SPLIT UP on election night. Though Raphael didn't get off on the media, he was watching the returns while Bella sat across the kitchen table from him, chain-smoking Camels. "Nobody's ever blown me off before," she said. "Nobody."

"That's not what's happening," said Raphael. "We simply have a different economy."

"Thanks, Mr. Insight. I can't believe I'm hearing something so fatuous from the guy who—a different *economy?*

"Look, I don't need any more lateral movement. I'm trying to get my work done. Of course I know you think it's just a hobby."

"What do you call it?"

"A vocation."

"You would. I wish I could think of someplace else to go. I can't hack one more evening of folk dancing." She glanced at the TV. "And on top of everything else people are actually voting for this clown."

"What do you want? Four more years of Carter? We're still getting bomb threats at the restaurant because of the hostages. Everybody thinks we're Arabs."

"If you voted I'd be worried."

"It's all semantics anyway. Politics is a word."

She stared at him for a moment, then looked away, shaking her head. "I must deserve this. I must have, I don't know, driven a tow truck or something in a former life. What kills me is that I came out here to find something."

"So did I."

"Well, what we got was each other."

"Don't be lugubrious. I meant everything I said."

"Are you kidding? You told me you loved me."

Raphael looked at his hands. "Who knows what that means?"

"Right," she said with a bitter laugh. "I'll tell you what. It feels really terrific to get dumped for a Rhodes scholar like this . . . this chick with the restaurant." She crushed out her cigarette in a wedge of cold pizza. "I can't even think anymore. I could probably straighten myself out if I could just slow down and think. But I can't."

"Bella—" He reached over to touch her hair and she jerked away.

They were sitting there in silence when a sepulchral voice from outside called Bella's name. Raphael followed her to the window. Out in the driveway where her boxes were stacked stood Vern and the girls. Vern's face was taut behind the fringe of beard. Bella went stumbling down the steps with Dudley slouching behind her and tried to push past them. "Don't look at me," she said.

Vern put an arm around her. "Honey," he said, "it's OK now. Everything's OK."

They started carrying boxes down the driveway toward Vern's pickup. And Raphael imagined himself running after Bella, pleading with her to stay. *Wait,* he would shout, *it can't be over yet.* It would have been the natural thing, the right thing, the perfect thing to do. But he just stood there. He could still hear Vern talking. Off in the dark Dudley barked once.

Days later the house still smelled of patchouli. In January Meredith told him that Bella had left Vern and taken the girls to Israel.

By now it's clear that Hilary's not going to call. He digs out his notebooks and glances at the abandoned poems. The last entries are ten years old.

Yams = hams.
Blowjob from Miss Professor Block. Crows on hay bales?
Guy shines his shoes.
We stumble into knavery.

Lifting his gaze from the notebook, he brings back Professor Block, a tall woman with prematurely gray hair. She'd attended a conference in Santa Barbara and he'd picked her up at the airport early one morning. Just west of town she'd untied his drawstring pants and bent to his lap. He remembers the hay bales—*golden cubes faceted with black square shadows,* he'd written—in the fields beside the highway, her muffled bleats of delight, though years after the event his concern that someone would read these notes and posit that she'd been a man seems a little silly.

He calls the café and asks for Daphne. He hears the hiss of the broiler, footsteps, then, over some old Dan Fogelberg tune on the tape deck, the cook braying her name. Raphael takes the phone out to the deck. On the wood before him slug tracks glisten in the sunlight. He catches a breath of jasmine from the vines braided through the trellis. *Politics is a word*—had he actually said that? Someone picks up the phone. "This is Daphne."

"How would you like to go to Mexico?"

While waiting for her to drive out he thinks back to the last time he'd seen Vern. It was at Meredith's bankruptcy party. The teenage guru had fled to Bogotá with his followers' savings, and Meredith was losing the house. By then James had moved out. A Doobie Brothers album was on the turntable. Raphael could hear someone hopelessly retching. Between the stereo and barbecue, Mister Personality, grim and rabbinical in the light of the coals, stood slugging down Sauza. From the kitchen Raphael could hear the drone of manic conversation broken every few seconds by explosive snorts and whinnies. Presently Meredith emerged in a cloud of pot smoke, her nostrils rimed with coke. Jungle Wrought's bass player, a tall guy in a white sport jacket, stood sniffing behind her. "Lord word," she said. "Where are all the happy people? There are happy people, aren't there?" She put her palms over her ears and squeezed. "Will somebody please *answer* me?"

Raphael was about ready to leave when "What a Fool Believes" ended with a ripping squeal; he turned to see Vern fling the album into the darkness below the deck. "Sponges!" screamed the carpenter. "You're nothing but a bunch of poisonous sponges! You'll die and you won't even know you've been alive!"

"Hey, bro," said the bass player, "don't you think that's a little radical?"

Everybody laughed. Raphael looked past Vern and the

haggard, addled faces of the crowd, past the new houses and the highway, to the harbor trembling with starlight, and his mood curdled into sadness so heavy that he tasted bile. Before he knew it he'd stepped over and taken Vern by the arm. "Come on," he said. "Don't let these creeps laugh at you."

Vern's eyes widened. "You—" he said. "You *cannibal.*"

Raphael saw the punch coming in time to duck. Vern hooked the bass player. The guy grabbed his nose and dropped with blood squirting between his fingers, down the front of his jacket. A woman in a black jumper clubbed Vern with a beer pitcher. His eyes rolled back. When Raphael went down the steps four or five men with perms and Hawaiian shirts were slamming around the deck behind him, throwing drunken punches. He took his time. A woman who ran a sourdough bakery downtown was waiting for him in her car but his knees were shaking and he knew it wouldn't hurt to make her wait a little longer.

"SOME NERVE," SAYS Daphne. "Calling you a cannibal. You don't even eat meat."

Raphael, having taken one of the Rohypnols she brought along, sits on the deck with a tattered manuscript of "The Hound of Satan," watching the sun drop behind Bishop's Peak. Daphne strokes his temples. To the east the windows of the scattered ranch houses blaze gold and it's chilly enough to see his breath. He doesn't care. The pill has loosened his tongue and after praising Daphne's photographs—poorly focused studies of various pierced body parts—he starts in on Hilary. "Now that she's talked to her sister she's got it in her head—yeah, right there, Babe —that I've betrayed her somehow. That's what I get for using metaphor."

"The whole thing's so bogus," says Daphne. "I mean, it's none of my business but as far as I'm concerned Hilary don't really appreciate you. Like, God, your poem was awesome."

"That means a lot to me," says Raphael. "It's the sort of material I've been drawn to lately. A little experimental, I suppose." He tells her how moved he is by the scent of her hair.

"It's a tar-based shampoo," she says shyly.

Suddenly Raphael feels supremely confident. He hustled his way out here and he can hustle his way back, it's no big thing. "Indeed," he purrs. As the shadows stretch across the fields he flashes Daphne a groggy smile. "Ever since you've joined us," he says, "I've been meaning to—you know, when I'm near you it's like swallowing stars. I have to find out—is this just me?"

She takes so long to reply that for a second he wonders if he's lost his touch. Nevertheless, with confidence born of long practice he nuzzles her throat.

"Did you want to do anything else?" she asks in a small voice.

He leads Daphne upstairs, goes into his routine, blissful expression and all. How young she is, all bones like a Persian cat, but he keeps forgetting who she is; whenever he tries to focus on her face Bella's ghost flickers before him like a stained-glass saint with grief-stricken eyes. "I think," he says, after a while, "that it's your diaphragm. I'd just as soon be alone now."

As the room fills with the scent of jasmine Daphne goes to the window and puts in her earrings. "It's not anything to panic about," she says. "And how about that moon? Just like some cosmic light show."

Raphael watches the ceiling. "Just like," he says. Daphne's car keys jingle and he senses those soulless eyes turned his way.

"You're not suckering out on me, are you? I mean, we're still going, right?"

There's a proprietary edge to her voice that he hasn't heard before and doesn't much like. But it's a little late to start playing manager now. "Of course," he says.

"So how about if you pick me up at the café tomorrow after my shift?"

When he agrees she clomps down the stairs in her combat boots. He lies there without moving until he hears her ancient Fiat pull out of the driveway and buzz off toward the road. Her acrid girlish smell clings to the sheets.

In the dark hours of the morning the telephone awakens him, dry-mouthed and queasy, from a dream: a school burning in some tropical slum, screaming dark-skinned children with their hair in flames. When he picks up the receiver he hears only pulsing static but he knows someone is there. "Come on," he says. "Who is it? What's this about?" His voice is cracking, querulous, and it scares him. Over Daphne's scent the smell of jasmine is so potent he's afraid he'll choke. As he climbs out of Hilary's bed his knees creak. He pulls on some shorts, heads downstairs, and flings open the front door. On the deck fat mottled slugs ooze across panels of moonlight. Raphael stands frozen with one hand on the doorknob, staring across the dark fields toward houses outlined with Christmas lights. The *I Ching* coin is a wafer of ice against his chest.

He's pretty sure he can sweet-talk his way out of this. But what if he can't? Say he does pick up Daphne at the café tomorrow, how will he face down all those smiles, those smiles of satisfaction and smug pity? Forget it. But he has to make a move. What, though, if everybody can tell?

Bella

A caravan of idling Winnebagos stretches across the toll bridge from Mexican customs all the way back to where Bella fidgets behind the wheel of her rusted Falcon and waits for the Rohypnol to kick in. She's on her way home from San Hilario—one of those towns where the phones don't work and even the kids carry weapons—and the yammering boys trotting up and down the line of vehicles with paper flowers keep reminding her that she promised to pick up presents for her daughters. Jewelry for Sage, *milagros* for Darshon. It's the week after the Panama invasion. Among the casualties were some kids from San Hilario attending a missionary school in El Chorillo. It's not a great time for souvenir shopping

On the seat beside her a shoe box stuffed with cocaine and Rohypnol throbs like a smashed finger.

Some boys pound on her door; when she rolls down the window a frigid desert wind blows their voices into the car like frantic black bats. *You like? You buy?* One kid passes her two toxic-looking bouquets. His ratty smile is like a reflection and Bella has to fight to keep from looking away as he grabs her money. His fingers are mottled with dye. *You go to jail, Señora.*

The RVs ahead wobble in the exhaust fumes. When she tries to focus on a weathered red feed store across the river the picture explodes into pastel nettles and for a bad moment she doesn't know where she is. Bella closes her eyes till the pieces fall back into place. She's been up for two days. An hour or so out of San Hilario the Falcon had suddenly been swarmed with hallucinatory wasps the size of avocados. True, they'd vanished by the time she'd wrestled the car off the highway but all in all she's had better mornings.

Jaimie was supposed to meet her at the *farmacia* in San Hilario. The plan was, they would take care of business with a doctor from Boquillas del Carmen. Afterward Bella would drop Jaimie at the river, then pick him up on the Texas side. But he didn't show. She ended up making the deal herself in pidgin Spanish while boys in *Ghost Buster* T-shirts prowled the street outside with automatic weapons and the doctor and two cronies in powder-blue leisure suits watched her with hot penitentes' eyes. The flavor of breakfast —a chorizo taco and three cans of warm Tecate from a roadside stand—swells inside her, a massive bubble blown from stale grease.

When the RVs begin to move she takes a deep breath and turns on the radio. *"Casa Loco!"* screams a reverberant voice. She keeps telling herself that she knows what she's doing. She's said that before, though, and by the time Mexican customs is only a few car lengths away the oil light is flashing and the weight of everything she's not thinking about is squeezing hard. Just as she's trying to remember how she acts when she's straight, the Rohypnol gives her a playful little stroke. Her stomach settles. "Mercy," she says.

The guards with their stern yearbook poses look as if they're just out of military school. They glance disdainfully over the car—the interior festooned with dog hair, the girls' schoolbooks strewn about the backseat—pausing only to inspect the sticker on the back window; it's an eye superimposed on the palm of an open hand, something Darshon bought years ago in East Jerusalem. Once the guards wave Bella through she realizes that she's been holding her breath. Ahead, the last Winnebago pulls away from U.S. customs and crosses the border into Presidio. All of a sudden she can smell herself, this brassy odor like a courtroom in the afternoon.

An old customs officer in a green uniform peers into her window. Bella flashes her scrip for insulin, gives him the diabetes story. The guy's handlebar mustache twitches.

"Well, Miz Kipper," he says, "maybe you ought to stay away from that sweet stuff."

"I was doing a little sight-seeing too," she hears herself say, as if reading somebody else's lines. "Enjoying the scenery."

The man takes off his sunglasses and looks across the leaden river and the patches of green scabbing the flood-plain. "Would you mind stepping out of the car?"

In an instant so brief it seems a memory she sees the spokes of the steering wheel through her hands; as she gets out the image floats before her eyes—phosphorescent bones, webs of flesh. The pavement is icy beneath her bare feet.

The officer leans forward with a puff of tobacco and leather to kiss her cheek. Loud barking laughter comes from the office behind him. "Get it, Pops," somebody shouts.

"Happy birthday," he says, handing back Bella's license. "Now wear your damn glasses."

SHE PICKS UP oil and automatic transmission fluid, then parks behind an IGA to reward herself with a couple of lines of cocaine. The medicinal taste blooms at the back of her throat and she jolts right through the Rohypnol buzz to the threshold of an unassailable conviction that Everything Is Going to Be All Right. Once Jaimie moves the shoe box there will be money again, lots of it, enough to start over, move to, say, Vermont, put the girls in a private school, open a café or a bookstore. *"Es muy fresca!"* screams the radio.

She plugs *Hank Williams' Greatest Hits* into the cassette player and zips north. Pretty soon the tires are buzzing, the sky coming at her nice and smooth, and the flutter of the paper flowers in the backseat fans her back to Israel with the girls in the early eighties. Dimona, a development town in the upper Negev. From the windows you could see hills scoured down past the bones, black bedouin tents, a few dinged-up Mercedes sedans, some camels. The very light seemed to promise second chances, and her memory of those first few months always evokes the childhood scent of lilacs. She tries not to think about it too often, though, because sooner or later she'll come to the part where one thing led to another and It Hadn't Worked Out either.

The sun is already low. A glaucous membrane of cloud veils the lower half of the sky and lightning crackles over the Chisos. Before her the town rises from the desert and the next thing she knows she's stopped at the single traffic light. Taped to the wall of a boarded-up video store is one of Jaimie's posters: HEAD SURGERY: A NIGHT OF POLITICLE COMEDY WITH DR. R. KANE WISDOM. She eases past the Shell station, Gilda's Mexican restaurant, and pulls into the Hi-Way Inn lot. There's a three-wheeled chopper angled in front of the office so she parks between a Volvo sporting a

Bad Brains bumper sticker and a Chevy van with *El Servicio Particular* airbrushed on the side panels. When she turns off the engine the Falcon sputters and shakes. Over the wind she hears muffled barks from the office, the steady thump of a cranked stereo. Not showing up in San Hilario —that's a pretty radical lapse, even for Jaimie. Right now, though, she's too tired to muster even a show of righteous anger, too tired for anything but relief that she's home. She imagines herself melting like hot wax through her seat, dripping between the springs.

"Slide It In" blasts from the speakers as she steps inside with the shoe box. Near one window a couple of dim-looking boys in Rasta hats and baggy shorts watch her and pretend to talk to one another. A tiny kid in diapers lies on the couch, sucking a pacifier and staring at the ceiling. Slow-dancing with a drummer who calls himself Swamee Dave is Bella's younger daughter, Sage, who, along with her sister, is supposed to be in class down the highway in Marfa. When she spots Bella she steps away from the guy. In the weak light her hair is the color of pencil shavings. Over by the counter Jaimie has one arm around a red-haired woman with spiderwebs tattooed down one shoulder. They are vacuuming Bella's dog, Dudley. The three of them—Jaimie, the woman, the dog—stare at Bella with the same accusing gaze. It's as if she's interrupted some ceremony, though what unholy ritual would call for a mongrel sheepdog, a vacuum cleaner, and music by Whitesnake is beyond her imagination.

"Hey, girl," says Jaimie as the song ends. His arm slips from the red-haired woman's shoulder and he turns off the vacuum. "This is Angel. She drove all the way from Alpine to help me get rid of this bad boy's fleas. And I bought you a present," he says and smoothes his beard over his shirt-front. Angel laughs as he shoves a half-empty fifth of gin into a gift box and holds it toward Bella. "Happy birthday, Homegirl."

"Jaimie—where were you?"

"OK, I have to explain about that. I all of a sudden had an audition for this club in Del Rio, etcetera, etcetera. Why—did you run into any hassles?"

"Like you care."

"Hey," says Angel, "you got the time?"

"Wait," says Jaimie, "you're talking about do I care?" His face stalls between expressions as he tries to register chagrin and deep concern. "You know I loved you since the first time I saw you. Remember? Coming out of that laun-dromat in Akron, holding your hair on top of your head like a hat? I swear to God," he says, his voice melting into an operatic sob, "if anything had happened to you I would have gone down there and wasted the whole town." He steadies himself against the counter and holds out the gift box. "Come on, I bought this, right? I mean, I *purchased* this bad boy for you." He wipes his mouth with the back of his hand. "Hey, I knew everything would go off all right. What do I always say, girl? You're the coolest."

"Casa Loco," says Bella.

"How about this," says Jaimie. "I been envisioning a totally new routine, right?" Adjusting an invisible microphone, he beams around the office. "You know how to start the revolution? You make the return envelopes in the utility bills too small for the invoices. But seriously, folks, how many of you are from Philly? Yeah? Tough shit."

Everybody laughs except Bella. When she'd met Jaimie, back when he was dealing to all the bar bands in Cleveland, she'd thought he was dangerous. And it seemed clear then that dangerous boys were the safest bets of all: On one hand you were unlikely to stay with them out of inertia and on the other there was no way you'd fall for their threadbare jive. As it turned out there were problems with that line of reasoning. Anyway it hadn't taken long to figure out that Jaimie was not so much dangerous as simply too scattered to think more than five minutes ahead. Now, listening to his jailbird flummery, she's amazed at what a hurry she was in to get here. How many men, how many cities, how many addled mornings in sunlit kitchens? She looks around at the figures struck like unfinished statues in the shafts of orange light slanting through the blinds. "Tell me," she says, "how do you spell *political?*"

Swamee Dave and the two boys make booing noises.

"For your information," says Jaimie, "you don't need a Ph.D. to lead a rich interior life."

Bella takes the bottle from him and tosses the shoe box onto the counter. As Jaimie roots through the baggies she swallows a mouthful of gin. "I'm in hell," she says.

Angel hooks her thumbs in her hip pockets and thrusts out her chest. "Hey," she says again, "you got the time?"

"Up yours," says Bella. Something pops behind her eyes and she finds herself leaning against the counter, holding her lip. She tastes blood. The angles of the room are all wrong. Through an aurora of blue spots she sees Swamee Dave and the two boys holding the thrashing red-haired woman by the arms. "I'll cut her!" screams Angel. "I'll cut that stuck-up *huera!*"

The others stare with big wet eyes; they all look nuts. The kid in diapers starts to squall. Dudley crawls out from beneath the stereo as Sage comes to stand next to Bella. Bella can feel it—something in this room wants to swallow them.

THE TV IS on in the girls' cabin. Darshon lies in bed, reading *The Count of Monte Cristo.* Her face shines with sweat. Wisps of dark hair cling to her forehead. She looks gravely over her book at Bella. "You're bleeding," she says.

Sage grabs a pen from the nightstand, sprawls next to her sister, and starts drawing lines along her forearm. "Angel slugged Esmeralda," says Sage.

"Will you stop *calling* me that?" says Bella. "And don't write on yourself."

Sage keeps drawing. "Why?"

"Because it's tacky." On TV some jowly old trio is singing "Five Hundred Miles." It's Peter, Paul, and Mary. The audience is made up of graying jokers dressed like academics, all of them dabbing at their eyes with handkerchiefs. Bella sits on the bed and touches her daughter's face. "You're hot."

"She passed out," says Sage. "Then she started, like, puking up all this yellow junk with pieces of eggplant in it."

"It was awful," says Darshon. "The sky cracked open and wet black things crawled out. And I heard a voice. It was pounding from the sky like a million hammers and it said, *Little girl*—"

"You forgot to eat again," says Bella. "Didn't you?"

Sage puts down the pen and starts switching channels with the remote. "Jaimie says all she needs to do is take some speed and sit in the sun."

Bella goes into the kitchen. She fills the ice pack and puts it on Darshon's forehead. Outside a big rig whips past; in the expanding hush Bella hears Whitesnake hammering away again, a door banging in the wind. Holding an ice cube to her lip, she opens the door to the adjoining cabin she shares with Jaimie and looks at her things. Her clothes, a few books, a stack of cassettes, Darshon's collages. On the wall opposite the window an egg of red sunlight wobbles on the plaster. Through the waning glow of the last lines of coke she sees herself dragging the girls from one snake pit to another: Akron, Detroit, Atlanta—in and out of school, living on peanut butter and apples, sleeping in the car— and now this town where the wind blows all the time, bare-assed kids roam the dirt streets, and on summer afternoons you can hear rocks crack in the heat. Suddenly it's as if the room is thick with smoke and before she knows it she's stuffing everything she owns into plastic trash bags. She knows what she has to do.

IT'S DARK WHEN Bella turns into a gas station in Van Horn. Sage follows her to the phone booth. She faces the interstate with her jacket whipping in the wind while Bella calls the girls' father in Albuquerque. After a stiff silence Vern asks if she has a cold. She tells him everything's fine, that she just left Jaimie.

"Which one is this now?"

"The one who vacuums the dog, I guess."

Sage groans and turns around. "Mom, he was *using* the upholstery attachment."

"Bella," says Vern, "what are you holding out for? Isn't this getting a little old? You've been doing this for ten years."

"They weren't all bad. We've had our moments, the girls and I." She watches Darshon and Dudley get out of the Falcon. Wearing the sleeping bag like a cape, Darshon walks the dog through the halo of yellow light surrounding the gas pumps and stands beside her sister. The girls stare at the phone booth—cinders, small pale strangers from whose eyes every trace of childhood has been burned away—and just looking at them makes Bella's throat ache. She closes the door. "Look," she says, "I was wondering if they could come stay with you for a while." In the background, over the clink of dishes, she hears Luanne, Vern's wife. *Ask when she's going to pay you back for those girls' braces.* The phone is muffled for a second.

"I suppose," says Vern when he comes back on the line. "But I would have thought you'd want them to go to your parents' place."

"I don't need to deal with my folks right now."

"You said everything was fine."

"Yeah, well, I need to regroup. I mean, I thought I was doing OK and then before I knew it I wasn't. That's the thing about having a strange life. As soon as you decide to change, funny stuff starts happening. Sometimes there's nothing around me. Nothing on top, nothing underneath. You get the idea?"

"Are you on something?"

"Now?"

"Listen, the girls are always welcome. There's never been any question about that. Even if they can't seem to leave fast enough whenever they visit."

"This is only temporary," she says. "I just need a little time to get organized."

"How could you let this happen, Bella? I'll never understand how someone as smart as you consistently ends up with such boneheads." Vern's voice has been growing steadily quieter and now he's whispering. "Like that bullshit artist you left me for back in California. That—that *poet*. What if I told you he's still up to his old tricks?"

"Really? What did you hear?"

"Listen to you. What a glutton for punishment. It's pathetic."

"I'm sorry," she says. "What can I tell you, Vern?"

"It's up to you," he says, his voice normal again, "whether the glass is half empty or half full. Why can't you be happy?"

"Maybe when it comes to happiness my goals are pretty modest."

Vern sighs and asks if she needs money. She says no, tells him she'll call as soon as she puts the girls on a bus, and hangs up. If there was a room where she could go and close the door, just close the door, that would be heaven. In the car she plugs in the Hank Williams tape, then gets back on I-10.

"You forgot my ring," says Sage. "You forgot both our presents. And I'm *hungry.*"

"Stop your whining."

"For how long?"

"I dreamed I saw the greatest horses," says Darshon. "The most beautiful horses in the world, running across the sky, and I tried to catch them but I couldn't."

"I'm losing my mind," says Bella.

THE WINDOWS OF the bus depot restaurant are still painted with snow scenes and wreaths. Next to the parking lot runs a row of picnic benches shaped like oil derricks. "Look over there," says Darshon. "Camels."

"New rule," says Bella. "No camels. No voices. No horses in the sky." Her fingers are swollen and when she gets out she feels the wind between her ribs. Her feet are freezing.

"Mom," says Sage, "where's your shoes?"

"I can't think of everything, OK?"

Inside there's a foyer where a white-haired Mexican woman sells newspapers and flowers. Bella glances at the *San Antonio Sun* headlines and heads for the women's room. In the stall she stares at the words inked across the door in loopy cursive: *A broken heart is like a nefphew with assma.* She keeps thinking about the headlines but the notion of Noriega trapped in the papal embassy by soldiers playing bad music provokes no bright ideas about how to break the news. She finds the girls sitting in a booth under a pair of steer horns. "Happy birthday," they say. Sage hands her a bouquet of roses; her hands are mottled with ink, the lines along her forearm knitted into a spiderweb. Darshon passes Bella a square tile covered with feathers, bones, scraps of barbed wire, paint, tiny medallions shaped like arms and legs. At the table across from theirs three women with bleached beehive hairdos and bolo ties lift their wineglasses in a toast.

Bella nods back, then turns to the girls. "Look," she says, "the timing is never going to be great for this but how would you feel about visiting your dad? It wouldn't be for long—what's so funny, Darshon?"

"This is a grimace of *pain*. I worked for *months* on your present and now you want to get *rid* of us."

"Keep your voice down, will you?"

"Dump us off on Luanne the Buddhist?" says Sage. "I don't think so."

"Don't make this any harder than it already is," says Bella. "No one's dumping you off. This would just be till I get something together. Anyway your dad's a Buddhist too."

"So's the kid," says Sage, sliding down in her seat. "All they eat is seaweed and peanut butter. And Dad would never let me get a tattoo."

"What?" says Bella. "Who said—"

"We *belong* to you," says Darshon.

A boy in a cheap suit, angry pimples around his shirt collar, approaches their table. "Howdy," says Bella. "I seem to have lost my appetite but you can see what these guys want."

"Ma'am," he says, "we can't offer you all service until you put on some shoes. It's procedure."

"Don't do this to me," she says. "I mean does anybody around here really care if I have shoes on or not?"

"Procedure's procedure, lady."

"Procedure, my ass."

"Mom," says Sage, by now slumped almost below table level. "You're blowing it."

Bella is working herself up for a major scene when she realizes that everybody in the place has stopped talking to watch her. She heads back out to the parking lot, where the Falcon is still making weird noises. She smells scorched metal. In the trunk she finds a pair of Jaimie's rain boots. She slides behind the wheel and puts on her glasses. On the other side of the picnic benches there's an abandoned garage, and in the moonlight she makes out INJECTION MOLD TOOLING stenciled over the mechanics' bay. She drinks the last of the gin, then tosses the bottle out the window. She's kept a little of the Mexican stash for herself and she's trying to do a line off a pocket mirror when Dudley whimpers. Bella looks up to find three or four huge knobby creatures looming out of the shadows on the other side of the fence. They study her with bored contempt. After a moment Bella closes her eyes and searches through the pulsing layers of fatigue for some kind of landmark. Dudley barks frantically. She opens her eyes and sees the camels loping off through the chaparral. What are they running from? A dark-haired woman with a fat lip, wearing a sweatshirt over a peasant blouse, nose to a mirror? *The sky cracked open and wet black things crawled out.* As she gets out of the car it hits her with a cold rush that this isn't somebody else's life and her head keeps right on going till she's looking down at the lot from what seems like several hundred feet, time spinning out beneath her in a long gelatinous string, then whipping her back with a snap that almost knocks her to the pavement. She leans against the door and sees the years ahead, a sad highway with no rest stops, spooling off like a ribbon of tin toward a horizon unbroken by a single rock or tree.

She shuffles through the dining room in the rain boots. There's a sign over the cash register: PLEASE DO NOT FEED THE CAMELS. The table is empty and the pimpled kid tells her the girls have locked themselves in the women's room. One of the ladies with beehive hair stands in the hallway by the telephones, shifting from one leg to the other. Bella bangs on the door. "Come on, you two—other people are waiting."

"Not till you promise," says Sage. "Not till you promise to take us with you."

"Come out and we'll talk about it."

"Promise!" yell both girls at once.

"They want to stay with their mama," says the lady with the beehive hair. "Now I suggest you promise them whatever it is they want before I pee my britches and you have a nervous breakdown."

"Nobody's having a nervous breakdown."

The woman smiles and takes off her glasses. Her eyes are pale blue. "Then what do you call it, honey?"

"Assma."

IN THE BACKSEAT Darshon sings "Puff the Magic Dragon."

"Where are we going?" says Sage.

"East," says Bella.

"Yeah, but—"

"*East,* OK?" She checks the rearview mirror and sees Darshon feeding Dudley a hamburger. Tumbleweeds bound across the road, pale in the headlights, and ahead a half-moon hangs low over the black scallops of the mountains. She's up to eighty. Her hair whips her eyelids. Paper flowers rustle around her feet. She can't stop wiping her nose.

"Esmeralda?" says Sage. "Somebody told me you have great hair."

Bella's heart gives an absurd leap. "Who?"

"A fly on the toilet seat."

Bella can't help herself and pretty soon all three of them are giggling like idiots. "What a couple of twerps," says Bella. She stops laughing when she sees the cop drift up behind them in the right lane. He moves to a car's length from the taillights—Bella tries to remember if they work or not—and stays there. Then as the interstate winds into the mountains the Falcon starts slipping out of gear.

As she approaches the first crest the shadows of the hills fall away and for a few seconds she sees nothing but the muddy pink wash of the sky; then the lights of Fort Stockton reel out of the darkness below her and the Falcon is coasting, back up to sixty, lurching in the gusts of wind. Bella squints down hard on the white line and chews the insides of her cheeks. Her pulse bangs in her ears. Her bones hurt.

The road goes up again. The oil light flickers. Traffic streams past them up the grade. A few cars flash their brights. Bella pins the accelerator to the floor and lunges against the wheel as the speedometer needle wavers from sixty down to fifty-five, then fifty, then forty-five. Pickups hauling boat trailers sweep past her in the center lane. The Falcon finally evens out at forty. When Bella cracks her window the whine of the tires rises to a shriek. Ragged strips of roof liner flap behind her and she hears exhaust smoking through the holes in the muffler, splattering off the pavement. It has to be faced: The car is falling apart. Dudley lets out a long quavering howl, then another. He doesn't stop.

The cop is still right behind her. Bella slugs the steering wheel. "Get off my ass, joker." Sighting down the parallel streaks of red and white before her, she sees more hills silhouetted against the city lights.

"I don't want to go to jail," says Sage and starts to blubber.

"Then I'll tell you what, Miss Fly-on-the-Toilet-Seat. A miracle is what we need here. Because there's nothing else I can do."

Darshon leans forward and puts her hands on Bella's shoulders. Her fingers are hot. "I can feel the stars," she says. Her voice trembles with exaltation. "I can feel them pulling us."

Dudley falls silent and Bella brings back the memory of a bus trip from Haifa with the girls—it could have been the week Muddy Waters died. Around sunset they stopped at a crossroads south of Beersheba to drop off a chubby Hasidic man and his little boy; now the image of the two scooting down the dirt road, side curls bouncing, toward some rust-colored roofs glows in her chest, a hot oval. Darshon's fingers burn through the sweatshirt. Over the faint pumpkiny scent of the roses, Bella smells lilacs. Her feet are suddenly warm. The Falcon is up to fifty-five. She feels hollow and light and safe, as if they are sailing unerringly homeward through the night, and it comes to her that she's not that old, that maybe she can do something with computers and then she and the girls will be a real family —when people see them coming they'll say, *Here come the Kippers.* That's how it would be. "Now," she says, "where are my accusers?"

Tears spill down Bella's cheeks as the car's angry racket blurs into a spectral chorus. They are in the hands of God.

Chubb

Meredith came back from California broke, humbled, and reconciled to the faith of her childhood. Her hair was dusted with gray and Chubb wouldn't have complained if she'd put on a few pounds. But he couldn't deny that she was still one fine-looking woman. So it didn't come as that big a surprise when only a few months after scraping up the downpayment for Boudreaux's Chicken Shack she married Sonny, a local boy with little more than a year left of his army enlistment. It was a modest ceremony, right after Mardi Gras. Chubb still keeps a picture on his nightstand. Sonny is wearing his Class A's; Meredith stands beside him in a blue silk dress, holding a bouquet of daylilies. Both smile at the camera, tickled to the point of rapture at their luck in finding each other. The reception was held at Boudreaux's, where Chubb so gorged himself on meat loaf, mashed potatoes, and pecan pie that he got stuck in a booth by the ice cream freezer. Sonny, his expression innocent of anything except concern, freed him by unbolting the table from the wall.

Chubb was genuinely grieved when on day one of the Panama invasion Sonny fell out of a chopper to his death. Right away every bird dog in the parish was itching to step into his shoes but Meredith never took off that little ring and as the months went by and her wedding picture remained next to the register they got the idea. It's been eight months since Sonny's death in Panama and since then she's run Boudreaux's Chicken Shack by herself, a sad pretty woman whose clothes often look as if she's slept in them. Chubb entertains at Boudreaux's on weekends. Often on Tuesdays or Wednesdays he'll drop by between business calls for a couple of drafts, shoot the bull with Meredith, play the jukebox, maybe scarf a little. Besides chicken, Boudreaux's features meat loaf, boudin, catfish. What have you.

WEDNESDAY AFTERNOON CHUBB'S working on a fried catfish plate. Down the counter from him, Meredith sits in a stained Tabasco sauce T-shirt, drinking wine with Baby Toy. Now Baby Toy, she's big and round with curly red hair. Dyed, is Chubb's guess. But that's all right. She thinks she's looking pretty good. And so does he. Just like a queen of old. Of course Chubb goes for a big-legged woman. Before everything got turned around, the two of them, Chubb and Baby Toy, would do the do a couple of times a week, his place, usually, slats of light on the floor, a fan buzzing in the next room, no lies, no promises—sweet and easy, like a chord with no third.

Chubb goes out to his car for some Tums and sees Lonnie from the Mobil station turning off the highway in the tow truck. He's hauling a gray Civic with California plates. Somebody's in the cab with him. He bounces across the tracks and drives past the square. Chubb goes back into Boudreaux's and after a while he hears the chatter of Lonnie's air gun.

Enter this tall young joker with a suntan. Blue polo shirt, sandals. He stands there in the doorway by the cigarette machine, flipping back his long hair. "So," he says, "how's it going, Meredith?"

She claps one hand over her heart and drops her glass on the floor. "Lord Word," she says. "*Raphael?* What are you doing here?"

"Just passing through," he says. "Sort of. Car trouble. And it's Eddie. Actually."

Meredith looks as if she's just reached for her wallet and found it gone. "What's Eddie?"

"Well," he says, "Raphael was my spiritual name. One I chose myself." He realizes that everybody's staring at him. "I guess that sounds kind of strange to you guys. But it's quite common out west."

"Eddie?" says Meredith. "Do you mean to tell me that all those years I didn't even know your name?"

"Come on, it wasn't all that long. Honestly, I don't understand why this comes as such a shock."

Meredith goes behind the counter and pours herself some more Gallo. Her hands shake. "I have a different life."

"So do I."

"You seemed pretty happy with the old one."

"Obviously not happy enough. Hey, remember—"

"I don't want to remember. Can't you respect that?"

"Well, excuse me. Thanks for the warm welcome."

Baby Toy watches him head out the door. "Now there goes one long tall drink of water."

Meredith pats the hair at the back of her neck. "I knew him out west back in the seventies," she says. "He's a poet."

"Yum," says Baby Toy.

THURSDAY AFTERNOON CHUBB comes in to set up his PA. It's right after a thunderstorm. The ceiling fans are going full blast, chains jiggling, both doors propped open to catch the breeze off the cane fields. Meredith is wearing a plaid sundress and she's washed her hair. She, Baby Toy, and Tasha, the waitress, fill napkin holders and watch *The Young and the Restless* on the TV behind the counter. Tasha's a scrawny college dropout with a black cat tattooed on one shoulder, about twenty-five rings in her face, and so much eye shadow that she looks to Chubb like a raccoon.

Enter Eddie with a bunch of pink roses. "Look," he tells Meredith, "I didn't come here with any ulterior motive."

She puts the flowers in a pitcher. "I never said you did."

"Well, it's imperative that you understand that."

Imperative. This kills Chubb.

Eddie orders an iced tea, then makes Tasha take it back because it's got sugar in it. "That Lonnie guy says I need a new trans. Even if I could afford it I'd have to wait at least a week for the parts. And that's if I'm lucky."

Meredith turns off the TV and sits back down at the counter. "So what are you going to do?"

"Right now I don't have a clue."

Lonnie comes bustling in, wiping his hands on a rag, and orders a draft. "Sorry to interrupt the funeral," he says. He pushes back his hat, and his scalp shines moon-pale through the little bit of hair he's got left. "You can always sell your vehicle to Chubb here for parts. He's got his own little old dealership. Think about it." He finishes his draft and goes back to work.

"This is a nightmare," says Eddie.

"Come to the dance tomorrow night," says Baby Toy. "Come to the dance, California, and check out old Chubb. I guarantee you'll hear more poetry than you could ever imagine." She winks and Chubb almost chokes on that funky smell blowing off the cane fields.

"Indeed," says Eddie. "Sounds great."

"Count your blessings," says Meredith and fans herself with a menu. "And thank God for that breeze. Wouldn't this be a wonderful day to relax in the shade with a book?"

Baby Toy runs her tongue around her lips. "Book, nothing," she says. "You need a man."

Chubb is stunned when Meredith falls out laughing. It's a magical sound, like hearing somebody chording a piano through an open window, and it's been a long long time since Chubb has seen whole Friday night crowds hush for a second upon hearing it, as if trying to place the tune. "Baby *Toy!*" says Meredith as soon as she can talk. "Shame on your mess."

Baby Toy smiles modestly and looks at her nails.

As soon as Chubb gets up to fool with his PA, Eddie flips his hair back again, gives Meredith a sleepy smile. Baby Toy, it occurs to Chubb, isn't sad enough for Eddie, and the broken places don't show. When she goes to the ladies' room he hears Eddie whispering to Meredith. "That fat woman—I think she's trying to pick me up."

"You hush," says Meredith.

"Hey, I honor big women."

Chubb's heard enough. Just because he's husky doesn't mean he's not hip. And this dude's not looking for a woman; he's looking for a home. Anyway it's time for business. Tasha's trading in her Tempest on a Riviera and Chubb has to run her over to his place. At this particular time he's driving a '56 Seville. Lake Placid blue and built like a tank. Chubb holds the door for Tasha, then squeezes behind the wheel. He heads out of town and turns onto the gravel road that follows the levee. "What do you think?" he asks Tasha. "Would you say this Eddie's good-looking?"

She takes off her headset. "I'd say he's a tool. Him and his tea. *I don't do sugar.* Changing his name. Talking through his gonads."

"You should have heard Meredith yesterday. *Get out of my life, bird dog.* Shut him right down."

Chubb owns a mobile home near the river, out by the old Jewish cemetery. Back under the willows, past his used cars, lie rows and rows of tombstones, a good half of them broken, circled by a rusty iron fence overgrown with wisteria. Sometimes in the fall when the cane fields are burning he'll sit out there and pick old Doobie Brothers tunes. The whole time he'll hear bones rattling around in the shadows behind him like a roomful of old ladies knitting. Don't get the wrong idea. His life's a drug-free zone now. Once it was pot, pills, the needle, what have you. A lost highway leading straight to Memphis, where he spent six months in a hotel with no electricity on the wrong side of Beale Street, squeezing scag out of used cotton balls. But that's all behind him. He parks between a couple of pecan trees and Tasha's old car. Along both sides and across the trunk of the brick-red Tempest naked women are airbrushed under the road scum. On the hood, giant black letters spell out La Pistola. Somewhere along the line the column shift has been swapped for a Vise-Grip.

"I might could fix him for you," says Tasha when they go inside.

"Do what?"

"Conjure." She pats her little backpack. "Snag a pair of his drawers, put them in a bottle. Bury it upside down and it's Snuff City."

"I don't play that noise, Tasha."

"How about just a little Hot Foot spell? Or Cast Off Evil?"

"No, ma'am."

"Chubb, people have put their faith in these rituals for thousands of years. Centuries, even. This is medicine in its true sense—not that bogus patriarchal squat you get in hospitals. How can you let yourself be so brainwashed? You're as bad as Baby Toy."

"You shouldn't be bad-mouthing her."

"No? You should hear what she says about you."

"I doubt it." He opens a can of condensed milk and chugs it down. Tasha stays inside when he goes out to feed the dogs. It's getting hot. The clouds are breaking up and a thousand suns flare in the windshields all around him.

Meredith pulls up in that green Plymouth Chubb sold her; it bucks and rises about six inches on its springs as she and Eddie and Baby Toy climb out. Tasha stomps down the porch stairs in her paratrooper boots and crosses the yard with barely a nod to anybody.

"We were kind of wondering," says Eddie, "if you'd be up for a trade-in."

Chubb frowns as he watches Tasha drive off in the Riviera. "I don't do imports."

"Now, Chubb," says Meredith, "I know good and well that's a lie." She follows him up the stairs and pushes past him through the screen door. Baby Toy is right behind her. Chubb smells something burning. In the kitchen Meredith wrinkles her nose. "Are you still letting those dogs sleep in here?" She opens the bedroom door and there in the middle of the floor are three burning black candles, each shaped like a man's private place. Each bristles with straight pins. "Lord word, Chubb. What do you think you're doing?"

"Hold on—"

"I see it," says Baby Toy, "but I don't believe it."

Meredith looks sick. "I don't even want to know what's going on here."

"Will everybody just hold on a darned minute? Let me rethink this Civic business."

"Don't bother," says Meredith, and goes back outside. On the porch she turns and faces him through the screen.

"Chubb, I am *so* disappointed in you. You know what the Bible says? It says a sorcerer shall be damned."

"Now, listen—"

"*Damned,* Chubb."

He watches them drive back toward town. "That's all right," he says.

ON THE WAY to Boudreaux's Friday evening he's trying to come up with a song as urgent as the words on a tombstone when he spots Meredith's Plymouth parked in front of the Gas Lite Motor Inn, where Eddie's staying. The young Salvadoran gardener edging the lawn waves when Chubb drives past. When the kid was shopping for a truck he and his two little girls came out to Chubb's place and under that ratty straw hat—what would have been called a sick lid back in Memphis—his eyes were not exactly scared but quick and ready. And Chubb knew that if he hadn't seen it all he'd seen whatever it takes to run a man out of his own country and put him to cutting lawns in hundred-degree heat for a trashy bunch like the ones who run the Gas Lite. Just to feed his children. Where's their mama? South of the border somewhere, six feet under, is Chubb's guess.

Tasha's Riviera is parked behind Boudreaux's. In the kitchen Chubb unpacks his guitar, the old Gibson Hummingbird his father had played. Once his father had opened for Old Hank himself at some high school gymnasium in Bogalusa. As Chubb tunes up he's steady thinking about

Eddie and Meredith over at the Gas Lite. But pretty soon there's a good crowd out front, his local fans plus some soldiers, and then it's time for his show. Chubb does a lot of Roy Orbison. Make no mistake, Chubb's no impersonator and his act certainly isn't one of these darn *tributes;* still if he had but one wish it would be that he, Chubb, had written "Only the Lonely." Other than that, besides his originals, his repertoire is mostly covers. Stone country: Old Hank, George Jones, Merle, Ernest Tubb, what have you.

Eddie comes in halfway through the first set. By then Chubb's got the whole place rocking. Over the dancers' bobbing heads the ceiling fans whip fumes of crawfish boil and sweat and wine and perfume into a smoky meringue. Man, this is living. After his break, Baby Toy shows up with her Lafayette friends, a bunch of trash from Jefferson Street, all of them loud on wine. She's wearing a new black halter top and a short pink skirt, bright red lipstick, and dangly earbobs. "Oh, hello," she says. "You going to dedicate a song to me, Chubb?"

"It depends," he says, playing it cool. "It depends on what you're doing after the show."

"I have plans," she says. "And anyway I wouldn't want to take time away from your extracurricular activities."

"Do what?"

She nods toward the cash register where Meredith's got that pitcher of pink roses next to Sonny's photograph. "When's the last time you bought me flowers, Chubb?"

"Girl, why don't we just spare ourselves a lot of misery and not have this discussion?"

She gives him a look. "That might be best." During the second set she spots Eddie dancing with Meredith. "Hey, California," she hollers. "I know what room you're in. How about if I just come over there and get you? How about that?"

"Anytime," he says. He smiles at Meredith and lets his eyes go all soft and hot.

Anytime. This kills Chubb.

That night his room still smells of whatever Tasha was burning along with those candles—High John the Conqueror oil, she says, but it smells like mothballs to Chubb. And as he lies in bed the pictures keep coming. No matter what he does he can't push them away. Here's how he sees it. At some lonesome dreadful hour Eddie wakes up and hears a car door slam out in the parking lot, then the slow steps of a big big woman coming across the gravel. The doorknob squeaks. Eddie looks up as the door swings open. And there's Baby Toy in a green silk nightgown. For a second she just looks at him. Then she crosses the room and pulls down the sheets. Eddie wants to run for it but he can't. His heart's going like crazy. When she kneels on the bed the mattress sags almost down to the floor. She doesn't say word one, just runs her fingers up across his ribs and back down his belly. She sucks in each breath with a mighty hiss. Eddie weeps bitter tears as Baby Toy's fingers close around the evidence.

"I got you now," she says.

SUNDAY CHUBB TRADES his Seville for a '55 two-tone Buick. Red and white. Dynaflow. He likes a solid ride. That night there's a Creole tomato festival across the river, and fireworks pop against the sky as Chubb drives to Boudreaux's. Down the counter from two lady soldiers— Vietnamese girls in camouflage fatigues—Eddie sits next to Meredith. She's wearing a black short-sleeved blouse, white slacks, high-heeled sandals. Toward the end of the show Chubb does "Only the Lonely," what his father would have called a real belt-buckle polisher. Eddie and Meredith sit it out.

When the last set's over Chubb is bushed. It seems like years since he's slept. Out in the parking lot the smell of sweet olive sticks in his throat and the last of the fireworks hangs over the river like an umbrella painted with stars. He's too whipped to drive so he climbs into the backseat of the Buick and rolls down all the windows. A couple of drunk soldiers stumble from car to car, asking for jumper cables. Somewhere a woman's trying to sing "Ooby-Dooby." He stretches out the best he can. Chubb closes his eyes and remembers watching from the school bus window as Meredith, a long-legged girl with sunlight glazing her dark braids, followed her long shadow up the dirt road between the cane fields toward her parents' house. Then Chubb sees himself, a husky boy in bib overalls, sitting on his father's porch with a Sears Roebuck guitar on a Sunday afternoon, listening to Sonny Boy Williamson on King Biscuit Time out of Helena. As he nods off he dreams he can hear a harmonica going, *Help me, help me, help me.*

Voices wake him and when he peeks over the seat backs who does he see but Eddie and Meredith sitting on the hood. "Come on," Eddie is saying. "Do you really think I'm that one-dimensional? Your pal Chubb obviously does."

"He's just being protective," she says and touches his shoulder. Chubb lies back down. "We go back a long way. He used to be very spirit filled, you know. Which is one reason I find this witchcraft stuff so upsetting. I guess he thinks he has to look out for me. Protect me against boys like you."

"Well, spirit filled or not I'm afraid he's wrong. Things have been happening to me that I don't understand. I was in the area and it seemed important to see you again. And not just because my car broke down."

"You know, if you're really stuck for money I could give you a couple of weeks' work while Tasha's on vacation. That's if you don't mind waiting tables again."

"Why are you so nice to me, Meredith?" His voice sounds different.

"Because you're one of the Lord's lost children."

"I wish I had what you have."

"Faith? It's there for you too."

"I can't make myself believe in something that doesn't exist."

Meredith laughs. "You haven't changed a bit."

"How would you know?" He's talking through his nose again. "Back in California I wasn't really free to tell you how I felt."

"Eddie, I'm not sure I like where this conversation is going. What do you want from me? The past isn't some piece of wedding cake in your freezer. I mean, I'm happy to give you enough work to help you get your car fixed, fine. But you have to be realistic."

"Please don't take this wrong," says Eddie, as if he just can't help himself, "but your beauty and grace have always overwhelmed me."

"You are such a *scamp*," says Meredith. "Time to get you home, boy." But Chubb can tell she's not really mad and Eddie's going on and on about Rembrandt and Renoir as her heels click off across the pavement.

Back home that night Chubb lies in the dark with his guitar, picking out a mess of blues. He still smells Tasha's oil and before he knows it he's seeing the pictures again. He sees Eddie over at the Gas Lite, an empty bottle of champagne on the dresser, a plastic glass holding a pink rose. Meredith comes out of the bathroom in nothing but a Disney World T-shirt, brushing her hair, watching him with scared eyes. And Chubb understands that this is what people mean by perdition. He puts down the guitar and presses the sides of his head till the pictures go away. Why is a man born to see such things?

THE NEXT EVENING he's driving back from town with a deep-fried turkey leg when he spots Eddie trudging alongside the road toward the Gas Lite. Up ahead a road crew is mowing grass. Chubb pulls over and pops the passenger door. "Get in."

"You've got a pretty interesting act," says Eddie. Up close he doesn't look so young; in fact he's a little too old for his clothes. "Have you ever thought about trying for a somewhat broader audience?"

"Broader? I'll tell you what. Once I did a show for a bunch of colored folks down in Lettsworth and I'm here to tell you they dug it just fine. I sing them the way they're meant to be sung—urgent. And it ain't nothing but the blues."

"I see," says Eddie. He looks bored.

"I got to ask you," says Chubb. "You're obviously one of these guys can get any woman he wants—"

"Hey, you think that's some great blessing? Having every woman you meet want something from you? Especially when you don't know what it is? I mean, you think you're having some great conversation and all of a sudden you realize she's looking at you like you're, I don't know, a big *pie* or something. How would you like it?"

"Never mind about all that. Why don't you just change your name again and leave Meredith be?"

"What's your problem, Chubb? I'm down on my luck. I'm in a jam. That's all. Is that some big crime around here?"

"Let me put it to you like this. You can walk a log over

a creek and you'll be just fine till you look down. Only I'm not talking about any particular creek. I'm talking about destruction."

"This parable is supposed to illuminate something about Meredith?"

"You tell me. You're the poet."

For a second Eddie watches the road crew. "I know things got weird for her in California. I know things got real bad. I know—"

Chubb feels sick to his stomach. He slaps the wheel. "Don't tell me about it. I don't want to hear it. You'd never understand this, never in a million years, but it used to be, every time I closed my eyes I'd see her floating over a forest of men's hands."

"Well, the last thing I want to get involved in is some rural—some local—psychodrama. Hey, things got weird for me too. Did it ever occur to you that nobody comes back from there without losing something?"

"Maybe. But you ain't going to find it here."

"What am I supposed to do—walk to New Orleans? Find me a car, Chubb, and I'll leave tomorrow."

The sun flashes between the trees, and the sweet smell of cut grass fills the car like sorrow. "I can live with that," says Chubb.

IT'S LATE AFTERNOON the following day when he picks up a new batch of posters over in Monroe. Under his picture it reads *Chubb—Country Music's Big Man*. He figures there's no point in putting it off so he drives into town. Tasha's old Tempest is in the bay at the Mobil station; Chubb's already put in a new battery, which should get Eddie to New Orleans, but Eddie—or more likely, Meredith—is having Lonnie check the car out anyway. Out front Meredith's talking with Baby Toy. Chubb parks by the Dumpster and gets out.

"You've been busy," says Meredith.

"Look here," he says. "I won't lie to you. I didn't pay my dues just to be the kind of guy who'd let someone with slick ways breeze into town and hurt my friends. Maybe nothing turned out the way we expected, Meredith, but you've got to be rich to worry about that."

"Chubb, right now I'm afraid I'll say something we'll both regret. Can we talk about this some other time?"

"Why bother? You can't tell me anything I don't already know. Even by myself I'm all alone."

"What a sad sad story," says Baby Toy.

"We learn the world through grief," says Chubb and walks back to his Buick.

He's about to pull out of the lot when Eddie appears next to the car. Chubb rolls down his window.

"I've got to talk to you," says Eddie. His eyes go soft and he starts talking through his nose. "Listen, I just want you to know how much this means to me." He reaches through the window to shake hands.

"Beat it," says Chubb.

Chubb has just parked at Boudreaux's that evening when he sees the Tempest—La Pistola—heading east toward the highway. Behind it the clouds are shot with hot golden spokes and he can hardly bear to look but he does. Eddie spots Chubb standing in front of Boudreaux's with a bouquet of carnations. He waves and drives over the tracks and out of town, taking his understanding with him.

MEREDITH HASN'T ASKED Chubb back to Boudreaux's since then. She'll say hello and when his sister died in Lake Charles she fed the dogs while he was gone. But it's not the same. Chubb and Baby Toy, they don't do the do anymore. She's too busy. Dating a young deputy from the sheriff's substation. It's Chubb's fatal doom, his sacrifice, what have you.

It's winter now, the Panama invasion last year's news. They've burned the cane fields and when he wakes up the windshields are skinned with frost. In the evenings he can hear those bones rattling away. Tonight he's sitting in the front room with his guitar, flogging an E minor to death and still trying to come up with a song. But he can't do them like Roy. Nobody can—the way he'll shine this gentle light down your memory so it doesn't matter whether you bring back a weekend with a rich woman in a fringed black dress or a few urgent minutes out in the parking lot with some sorry Wal-Mart checker because, however many years it's been, in the shadow of those smoky blue chords the way she laughed or cried or slipped off her shoes will still make you ache.

The dogs are under the house, tails thumping the floorboards. From the window Chubb can see over the levee and across the river to the bluffs of Natchez, rumpled like brown curtains in the moonlight. The kind of tunes he wants to write, they'd be about that guy from El Salvador—how his two little sad-eyed girls find their mama at a carnival, safe and sound, giving hot-air balloon rides, and the whole family flies off to Tierra del Fuego. Or about some musician who invites a lonely woman over for a drink. Just a drink, you understand. The dude looks out front and—damn!— there she is, coming up the sidewalk with a scared smile. Carrying a pink rose. How about that? How about that?

Darshon

When they got to Boston, Mom was all, "Girls, if we don't get it together this time we never will." It had been like six or seven months, it was already August, and they still hadn't come up for air. Darshon worked at a pet store, full-time now that summer school was over. Sage, her sister, baby-sat. Mom waitressed nights at some seafood place and took classes at the community college. She'd stopped smoking and drinking. Five, six mornings a week you'd wake up with her swearing at the alarm but she hadn't had any boyfriends since they'd left Texas and for once it felt like they really lived someplace.

Plus now they were going to the Jersey shore for a week, their first real vacation ever. A whole week with no school and no work, even if they had to spend it with a bunch of geeks. At the last minute Mom told them they were splitting the beach place with her best friend from high school. Shirley—Mom hadn't seen her in like two hundred years—was flying up from New Orleans with her family. They would all meet at the shore. "There's no point in getting bent out of shape," said Mom. Her eyes looked humongous behind her new glasses. "We just can't afford it by ourselves. Anyway you'll like Shirley. She's a riot. She and Hub teach at the same high school."

"Hub?" said Darshon. "Does he sell tires too?"

"Don't get cute." Mom brought out the 1969 Theodor Herzl Hebrew Academy yearbook and pointed to a pretty girl with straight dark hair and bangs. Under her picture it said, *Shirley Kahn: Class Secretary, Foreign Service Club, Art Club, Science Club, Film Society. I've looked at life from both sides now.* A picture or two to her right was Mom with a Mexican blouse and a froth of kinky black hair. *Bella Kipper: Great Personality.*

"What a couple of dweebs," said Sage.

THEY DROVE TO Philly and spent the night at the girls' grandparents'. The next afternoon Grandmom and Grandpop stood in the shade of the catalpa, looking all nervous, while Mom checked the oil and Sage and Darshon packed the old Impala. One fender was duct-taped to the doors and you had to climb in on the driver's side. When they were ready Darshon sat up front with Dudley. It was so muggy that Mom's hair was frizzled up like wool. Sage took her usual place in back; then she stuck her nose in the new *Elle* and sat there snapping her gum. The fender rattled like crazy when Mom pulled away from the curb. Grandmom and Grandpop waved and waved.

Mom turned down her country station. "Dad started renting this place when we were in grade school," she said, "and we came down here every year till graduation. We'd spend all day at the beach and hang out on the boardwalk at night. Shirley and I did our growing up at the shore."

"I wish we were going by ourselves," said Darshon.

"I'm warning you both right now, I'd like them to think there's been some direction to my life for the past twenty years so don't make me look like a jerk. Anyway they have PJ—that's Hub's daughter—for the summer. I think she's around your age."

"Big whoop," said Sage.

"My God," said Mom. "This place is unrecognizable."

Block after block of bars with fat tattooed guys leaning in the doorways. Mobs of sunburned people, motorcycles everywhere—the whole town looked like it needed a coat of paint. Mom parked in front of a three-story place a few blocks from the ocean. There was a long porch in front where old people sat like penguins in a row of rockers. Darshon could hear music from the pier, the screams of people on the roller coaster. The manager, an Indian man in a turban, gave Mom a key and they went through a courtyard where a chain-link fence surrounded a swimming pool and a Jacuzzi. A man wearing a T-shirt that said *Glory Daze Cable* leaned on the gate and talked to a couple of old ladies in red bathing suits. "Nastacious," said Sage.

In the apartment a fat girl with carrot-colored hair was watching TV. A bearded guy played Scrabble at the kitchen table with a sleepy-looking woman in an orange sundress. The woman jumped up and grabbed Mom and the two of them stood there rocking back and forth and bawling. Shirley was almost a head taller than Mom, with a huge shelflike butt. "My God, Bella, don't tell me you're still wearing *patchouli!*" She blew her nose, looked at Darshon and Sage, and put one hand over her heart. "And who can these young ladies be?"

"My little lumps of sunshine," said Mom, wiping her eyes.

"Mom," said Darshon and Sage at the same time.

It was about a million degrees and everybody was sweating. Hub, the guy with the beard, told Mom that some-one had stolen the air conditioner. He had a southern ac-cent. So did PJ, the fat girl. "Yuck," she said, when Dudley sniffed her Doc Martens, "don't let that fleabag touch me."

Out by the pool the manager was waving his arms at the man in the *Glory Daze Cable* shirt. "I say this is the last string," he squeaked. "Since you are unable to facilitate re-pairs in a timely manner I am no longer requiring your services."

The cable man gave him the finger. "Climb this," he said.

The manager put his hands on his hips. "Maybe I do that," he said.

THE IMPALA CHUGGED north on the parkway, pumping out smoke. The light was golden and shadows stretched across the marshes on either side of the road. Darshon sat up front with Mom and Sage. Darshon rolled down her window and the fender got even louder.

"What a dumb old car," said PJ. "We have a new Bronco."

"I'll probably trade this one in," said Mom, "as soon as I finish classes."

When she plugged in her new George Jones tape Sage groaned. "Do we have to listen to this suckacious cowboy junk, Esmeralda?"

"Don't push your luck, lady."

"How about some Bruce?" said Shirley. "Hub and I adore that rough blue-collar poetry."

"Blue collar, right," said Mom. "He's probably got a trust fund. Just like the rest of them."

"The rest of whom?" said Hub.

"See if there's a classic rock station," said Shirley.

"Let's stick with the cowboy junk," said Sage.

"Chacun à son goût," said Hub. "That's French for Each to his own taste."

A sound like ripping cloth came from the backseat. "That's sign language," said PJ, as the car filled with a sour cabbagy smell, "for Catch this and paint it green."

THE RESTAURANT WAS on a pier in Cape May and a little pink man was playing piano in the dining room. Hub marched to a table by a window. Over the horizon the sky looked like fire and blood. Sage pointed to the dock outside. "Hey, Esmeralda, isn't that one of those wrinkly Chinese dogs?"

Mom squinted out the window. "I think they're cute."

"Clue phone," said Sage, holding out an imaginary receiver. *"It's for you.* That's some old shopping bag and you're risking our lives driving around without your glasses."

"You know what? I've had it about up to here with you."

"Up to where?"

PJ let out this weird gurgling laugh.

"Why do they call you *Esmeralda?"* said Shirley.

"Because they think they're a couple of comedians."

Hub ordered lobster dinners for him and his family. "It's that fresh sea breeze," he said, patting his belly. "I can feel it working miracles."

Mom looked in her wallet. "It's not multiplying my money," she said and asked for a fish-and-chips special. Sage got a cheeseburger. Darshon ordered a Monte Cristo.

"Your sandwich," said Hub, "was originally named

after *The Count of Monte Cristo* by Alexandre Dumas, known as Dumas père—which means 'father' in French. Alexandre Dumas—1802 to 1870."

Darshon could see these funny wrinkles below his cheeks. "I know," she said.

"I'm flabbergasted," said Shirley. "A reader." Her nails were long and red and Darshon saw that Mom was hiding her hands.

"Sage writes the science column for the school paper," said Mom. "And one of Darshon's paintings took first prize at the All-City Art Festival. I know, I know—how did I manage to turn out such little citizens?"

The sisters looked at the floor.

"Bravo," said Hub, "however you managed it." He rubbed his bald spot and smiled at the girls. "We don't mean to embarrass you but it's hard to switch out of teaching mode. And it's a pleasure to meet youngsters who don't spend all their time watching tone-deaf Satan worshipers on MTV."

PJ belched—a big wet one. People turned to stare at them.

"PJ," said Hub, "what did we talk about this morning? I think we deserve an apology."

"Better out than in," said Mom.

Over the bar there was a big TV. On the screen big red letters spelled out *Desert Shield;* Darshon saw soldiers marching up sand dunes in the background. Her boss's National Guard unit had been called up and she wondered if he was one of them.

"Does anybody here smoke?" said Mom.

"Mom," said Darshon and Sage.

"Just asking." Mom sighed and stared out the window at the lights on the water.

The pink guy played "Memories" and Shirley hummed along in this quavery voice. All of a sudden she gave Mom a big smile. "Do you think we can get the girls to sing?"

"God," said Sage, "nobody sings anymore."

WHEN DARSHON GOT back from walking Dudley, *Dawn of the Dead* was on the VCR. Sage was painting Mom's toenails with green polish while Mom stretched out in the recliner. PJ sat between Shirley and Hub on the sofa, whacking her father over the head with a plastic seltzer bottle. Darshon got out her drawing stuff and started sketching the three of them.

"I have a book you would appreciate," said Hub. "Paintings by El Greco. Doménikos Theotokópoulos, 1541 to 1614."

On TV a bunch of zombies ripped a soldier in half and his insides flopped out like wet hot dogs. PJ burped again. "Excuse," she said.

"Really, doll," said Shirley, "are you positive they didn't have *Funny Girl?* This can't be healthy viewing."

"How soon we forget," said Hub. "From what you've told me, you and Bella used to watch old movies all the time."

"Give me a break," said Mom. "We're talking about Clark Gable and Barbara Stanwyck. Not this malarkey."

"Bella had a crush on Cary Grant," said Shirley.

"How can you say that?" said Mom. "You were the one who got all hot and bothered over him. I liked Ronald Colman."

"Well, Cary Grant is more attractive. Objectively."

"Objectively, his chin looks like somebody's butt."

Everybody laughed. PJ gurgled and whacked Hub extra hard with the plastic bottle.

"PJ," said Hub, "enough is enough." He turned to Mom. "You know, you come as something of a surprise. From what Shirley told me I was expecting quite the little wallflower."

"What are you talking about?" said Mom. "I had my moments. Sage—that tickles."

"He's being stupid," said Shirley. "I simply mentioned that you weren't all that active in school activities." She patted Hub's hand.

Darshon wiped her fingers on her overalls and the charcoal left shadows on the denim. She was working on those wrinkles below Hub's cheeks. The trick was not making them look like fish gills.

"Esmeralda?" said Sage. "Can I finish your nails later?"

Mom didn't say anything. Her eyes were still closed and Darshon could hear her breathing. Outside, the jacuzzi bubbled away and a woman was yelling in another language. On TV a guy in a white lab coat shoved an electric drill through a zombie's forehead.

WAY OUT OVER the ocean a red airplane was pulling a sign that said EAT AT ROCCO'S — WHITE HORSE PIKE. During the night, someone had stolen another air conditioner and there were cops all over the place so Darshon went down to the boardwalk. Three older girls in bike shorts and halter tops sailed by on skates, then looked over their shoulders at her and laughed. Darshon knew she was ugly. Plus she was disfigured forever. She peeked down her shirt at the banana-shaped scar low on her belly. She'd been sick all the way from Texas. The morning after they got to Boston she couldn't get out of bed. An ambulance came and the next thing she knew she was waking up all stitched and sore with Mom standing by the window.

She opened Hub's El Greco book and turned to *St. Martin and the Beggar.* The horse with his front leg raised just so and the mounted saint in that ruffled collar handing his coat to a naked beggar and everything behind them all twisted and spooky like the west Texas sky on a winter day. She was still staring at the painting when Dudley barked. Darshon looked up and saw that guy in the *Glory Daze Cable* T-shirt standing in front of her with a hamburger. White hair stuck out from under his Yankees cap. "What's up?" he said. "I saw you on the beach last night and I thought you was walking a rug." Sunlight flashed off his watch as he knelt and held out the hamburger to Dudley. Still growling, Dudley crept out from beneath the bench and rolled over, quivering on his back with his legs spread; then he stood on his hind legs and gulped the burger. "Your mom's looking good," said the man. "She like to dance?"

Darshon closed the book. "Whatever."

He brushed off his hands and looked at the ocean. "She got cable?"

A horn honked. Mom was double-parked across Beachfront Drive next to the Glory Daze Cable van. "I have to go," said Darshon. This guy reminded her of Mom's last few boyfriends—Elan in Israel, a drummer named Poot in Reno, Jaimie in Texas. She felt his droopy eyes on her as she crossed the street. Sage was in the backseat and the car still smelled like perfume ads.

"Mom," said Darshon, "you've got to look at this painting. It's the creepiest thing I've ever seen."

"I'm driving," said Mom, as they pulled away from the curb. "So who was that?"

"Some guy."

"Guess what?" said Sage. "PJ's mom used to teach with Shirley. You know what that means?"

"Don't be morbid," said Mom.

"Who was Saint Martin?" said Darshon.

"Some guy," said Mom, and giggled.

"Can you at least look at it? Promise you'll look as soon as we stop."

"We'll see."

"They all went to Kmart," said Sage. "Shirley has to fill a *prescription* and she needs some special *pillow.* Skanka-cious. I can hear her snoring right through the walls. PJ says Hub has to sleep with earplugs."

"Cut her a little slack," said Mom. "I'm sure we all take some getting used to."

They pulled up at the stoplight across from the life-guard station. Those girls in bike shorts skated through the crosswalk and pointed at the taped-on fender. Sage sank down in the backseat.

Darshon opened Hub's book. "Look, Mom. Look how creepy."

"Leave me *alone,* will you? These are *pictures,* Darshon. What's to be afraid of? For God's sake, life is not some . . . some book."

She'd had the same look on her face when Darshon woke up in the hospital. Darshon looked out the window so Mom couldn't see that she was blinking back tears.

"Darshon's not speaking to me," said Mom. "Just in case anyone failed to notice."

They were filing through the vacant lot behind their

apartment on their way to the beach. Hub wore khaki shorts and new Nikes. Like some giant Boy Scout he charged ahead through the cattails with a cooler and a canvas umbrella. It was so obvious that he was showing off. Mom carried a satchel of schoolbooks. She'd put on weight since she'd quit smoking, and below the blue T-shirt she wore over her bathing suit, crumbs of foam from the car's upholstery stuck to her thighs. Shirley walked next to her in a straw hat, butt flicking from side to side under her terry cloth robe.

"I'll tell you what," whispered PJ, "you could build a church on that ass."

As they were crossing Beachfront Drive the cable man drove by and wiggled his tongue. "Hey, Queenie!" he yelled. "I'm in love!"

"He likes Shirley," said Darshon. "He told me so."

"I despise men like that," said Hub. "What does the Bible say? 'For the wicked boasteth of his heart's desire—'"

"Hub," said Shirley. "Please? Remember, honey? I told you how Bella always went for the roughnecks. While I was attracted to the deep, brooding ones."

"Like who?" said Mom. "Danny Bigelmann? Bigelmann, the Marxist, whose mother paid him three hundred a month not to grow a mustache?"

"Say what you like," said Shirley, "he was smart and ambitious. I wouldn't be surprised if he were a senator by now."

PJ and Sage looked at each other and laughed. Darshon stopped on the boardwalk to take off her red high-tops, then made her way down to the beach. To the north the chalk-colored lighthouse stuck up from a puff of mist. The sand was hot. Horseshoe crabs were scattered all over like old shoes, and behind the lifeguard tower, rows of sweaty old couples shone in the sunlight. Somewhere a radio blasted "Graceland."

"Now aren't we a bevy of beauties?" said Shirley. "Just like old times, isn't it, Bella?"

"Uncanny," said Mom. The nails on her right foot were bright green.

Darshon ate a carrot stick and watched some soldiers tossing a Frisbee down by the water. "Nothing wrong with the view," said PJ. "Look at that tall one with the tattoos. You can see that big old love muscle right through his shorts."

"PJ," said Hub. "Control yourself."

Shirley shielded her eyes with one hand. "Now, girls," she said, "despite what you may have heard the phallus is neither muscle nor bone."

"Shirley," said Hub, "for crying out loud."

PJ elbowed Sage. "No shit, Miss Big-Ass," she whispered. "It's *meat.*"

Ice rustled as Hub grabbed a Rolling Rock from the cooler. "Bella?" he said. "Ready for a cold one?"

"*Mom,*" said Darshon and Sage.

"Get off my case, will you? *Mom. Mom.* You sound like a couple of goats. No thanks, Hub."

"Tell me, girls," said Shirley, "what does a young person do for fun in Boston these days?"

"All we do is work," said Sage.

"I'm glad I don't have some dumb old job," said PJ.

Shirley took off her hat. "I think it's time for a swim," she said. Darshon watched her and Mom head down to the water with that funny walk of grown-up ladies in bathing suits. She looked at her own legs, pale and blotchy with fleabites below the cut-off overalls, and imagined the cool lick of water against her skin. But she hadn't even brought her suit. She wondered if she was adopted. She was dark, after all—darker than Mom, scrawny and hairy—while Sage had Dad's reddish hair plus you could tell she would end up with Mom's figure. Maybe it was worse than being adopted. Maybe she was from another planet.

Shirley stood waist deep in the surf now. Way past her, out where the water was dark blue, Mom was swimming by herself. A wave broke over Shirley's head and she stumbled back to the shore. Pretty soon Mom came out of the water and the two women headed for the snack bar with light dripping from their skin.

"Beauty and the Beast," said PJ.

"Esmeralda's had lots of boyfriends," said Sage.

"They're both very attractive women," said Hub.

"I heard Danny Bigelmann was a great big hog," said PJ, "with a pile-driving ass."

Hub slapped at her and she ran gurgling down to the water. "I'm sorry," said Hub. "I don't know what's gotten into that girl this summer but she's about to drive me nuts." He took a swallow of beer and rubbed his bald spot. "So is your mother presently involved with someone?"

"Calling all cheeseballs," whispered Sage. She looked at Darshon and stuck her finger down her throat. Then she got up and walked to where PJ was digging in the wet sand.

Darshon could feel Mom and Shirley's footsteps through the sand. Mom stretched out on her towel with a can of root beer. Darshon felt the coolness coming off her; it was like standing in front of an open refrigerator. Mom dumped her books out of the satchel.

"Graphic design," said Hub. "From what I hear, that's where the money is."

"Yeah," said Mom. "We've been here a day and a half and I'm practically broke. At this rate I'll be able to retire when I'm a hundred and fifty."

Hub found his shorts under the beach towel and took a business card out of his wallet. "New Orleans isn't quite the backwater you may think it is. And you can't beat the cost of living. If you ever feel like making a move give us a call. I'll see what I can do."

"What do you suppose those two are up to?" said

Shirley. The soldiers and a bunch of screaming little kids had gathered around PJ and Sage. You could hear the soldiers laughing. Some old ladies in pink bathing caps were leading a couple of lifeguards toward them. Then the lifeguards started blowing their whistles and one of them yelled at Hub. "Hey, dude—you want to put a leash on your kids?"

Hub jumped up and ran down to the shore. When the soldiers moved out of his way Darshon saw that the girls had molded a man out of wet sand; sticking up between its legs was this huge dick with a beer can stuck on top of it. Hub kicked it over and dragged PJ back to where they were sitting. "Conference time," he told Mom, while he packed up the cooler.

Sage sat next to Mom and Shirley. "You two are really blowing it," said Mom. She gathered her things and followed Hub and PJ back toward the boardwalk.

"It was just a joke," said Sage.

"I'm afraid that girl has a lot of growing up to do," said Shirley.

Darshon took Hub's book out of her pack and rolled onto her stomach. She flipped through the pages and there was *St. Martin and the Beggar* again. It was like she was falling. She couldn't bring herself to touch the page so she closed her eyes. The sun was hot across her shoulders and she felt the thump of the surf through the sand. She woke up drooling on her towel. In her dream she'd been back in

Israel, waiting at the Tel Aviv bus depot with Mom and
Sage early one morning while some soldiers in dirty uni-
forms watched them and laughed.

Sage sat with her chin on her knees, talking to Shirley.
It was overcast now and the sailboats were black chips in
the sky. Except for two women walking a poodle they were
the only ones on the beach. Darshon heard thunder. She
sat up and Shirley took her by the arm. "So, sleepyhead,
I'm dying to know. That cable man—what did he really say
about me?"

"He wanted to know if you liked to dance."

"Interesting." She squeezed Darshon's arm. "And has
your mother been talking about me?"

"Not really. I mean, how come you don't ask her? She's
your friend."

"Ah," said Shirley. "Friendship. You know what friendship is, doll?" She was squeezing really hard now.

Darshon looked into her face and saw that the pupil of
one eye was bigger than the other. "That hurts," she said.

"An edifice of vapor," said Shirley, and let go.

"It's raining," said Sage.

THE STARS FADED in and out of rags of fog and all
around her Darshon could see the blue flashes of fireflies.
Dudley ran ahead, a shadow skimming the beach. Every
few minutes the beam from the lighthouse swept the sky

and the windows of the motels along Beachfront Drive would turn silver. When she and the dog cut through the empty field the smell of wet roses seemed to rise from the ground.

Red lights flashed by the tennis courts. When Darshon got closer she saw three cop cars parked around the Glory Daze Cable van; the back doors were open and inside were stacks of air conditioners. Some cops were putting handcuffs on the cable man. "Hey!" he yelled, when he saw Darshon. "Tell Queenie I want to *dictate* to her!" A car alarm whooped blocks away.

The light was on in Mom's room. A bunch of people were in the Jacuzzi and when Darshon walked past she heard Hub's voice. "'Morgan the Pirate—1635 to 1688.'"

Sage was watching TV. On the screen Darshon saw rows and rows of awful-looking couches; in front of them was this bald guy with a wet-looking mustache. He wore a blue kilt and held a set of bagpipes. On each side of him stood a couple of women in bikinis and high heels. "Hoot, mon!" said the bald guy. "Here in Trenton all the lads and lassies are beating the heat at Bigelmann's Discount Furniture—home of cool deals."

"And *Danny Boy!*" shouted the women.

"Where's PJ?" said Darshon.

"Upstairs," said Sage. "She was using Hub's electric razor to trim the fuzz off her sweatshirt. And she broke it."

THE NEXT AFTERNOON they had lunch by the pool. Hub was still all hyper because Darshon had left his stupid book outside overnight and it got soaked. "Just tell me what you were thinking," he said. "Can you enlighten me on that?" The top of his head was sunburned and he hadn't shaved.

"I didn't want it in the house," said Darshon. She liked Hub. Why was he being such a creep? She reached under the table to give Dudley some toast. "I could feel it in the dark."

Hub looked around. "Translation, please? I'm supposed to understand that she was afraid of a painting?"

"She's entitled," said Mom. "People are afraid of a lot stupider things than that."

"Fine," said Hub. "So I'm some kind of reactionary ogre." He touched his bald spot.

"Please," said Shirley. "Let's try to have a good time, OK?" She kept squeezing her hands.

"Well, someone has to walk the walk, darn it. Flagrant irresponsibility, unrelenting vulgarity—I'm supposed to just ignore these things? Come on, Shirley, that was a *library* book."

"I'm begging you," said Shirley. "This is our last day together."

"It's Zoloft time," said PJ.

Shirley's face crumpled and she started to cry. "I can't believe she said that to me."

Hub turned bright red. "PJ, you will apologize right now."

"Excuse," said PJ and took two chocolate doughnuts out of the box on her lap. She bit one in half and started to hiccup.

"God," said Sage, "nobody gets the hiccups anymore."

"PJ," said Hub, "I don't want you hogging those. Share them with your friend."

"She ain't my friend," said PJ. "She ain't nothing but a big old pile of dog squat." Dudley whined and nuzzled her feet. "Get this mutt away from me!" she yelled. "He smells like a funky shoe. How come you all don't just put him to sleep?"

"Because it would be a sin," said Darshon. "Old dogs are sacred."

"Oh, really," said Hub. His face was purple now. "And just how do you get this—this privileged information? 'Where wast thou when I laid the foundations of the earth?'"

PJ scowled. "Who said that?"

"God," said Hub.

"Sounds paranoid," said PJ, and stuffed a whole doughnut into her mouth.

IT WAS DARK when Darshon and Sage got in line for the Ferris wheel. Everyone in the Fun Zone—the girls with their clown faces, the boys with their mean eyes—looked loaded. Every time the line moved Darshon tried to

keep her butt from wiggling. She was looking at the pictures
Sage and PJ had taken in the photo booth—various poses
of them flipping off the camera—when someone tugged
her overall straps. It was Mom. "Don't step on your lower
lip, sourpuss." She sat between Darshon and Sage and the
chair went up into the night. "Everything's changed since
we were kids."

"No duh," said Sage, and leaned against her shoulder.

The beach was dark but you could see the white line of
the surf curving off into the night. Fireworks sputtered
over the ocean. Far below Darshon saw Shirley and PJ in
front of the Whack-A-Mole booth. There was Hub in his
tennis outfit, the top of his head smeared with white oint-
ment. When he pointed to himself Shirley turned away and
walked to the rail at the edge of the boardwalk. It looked
like PJ was crying. Mom brushed Darshon's hair out of her
eyes. "Look," she said, "you can't tell people *everything*."

"Whatever," said Darshon. "Shirley says friendship is
an Oedipus of vapor."

"A what?" Mom was quiet for a while. "Well, I'm sorry
I yelled at you. You get older and the years don't last anymore. You look at your friends and wonder, Who *are* these
people? But they're all you've got. I mean, there was a time
when everything was so perfect it hurt. The sky was just the
right blue and the ocean had just the right smell and I'd
think, hey, my life is a thing of beauty." She took a Kleenex
out of her bag and blew her nose. Darshon smelled her

sunscreen. "And then you know how it ends? You wake up one morning and you're looking at a roomful of boxes. I don't know. I guess I'm just tired."

"It's all right," said Darshon. She saw how it was. Your life would grow around you, all tight and shiny like the varnish on an old painting, and you wouldn't even know it. The sad aching nights would come, millions and millions of them. There was nothing you could do—you were as alone as dust. The chair was coming back down; the people on the pier were growing larger.

"What's wrong?" said Mom. "Honey? What are you thinking about?"

"Horses," said Darshon.

Eddie

Halfway across the New Bridge Eddie smelled something burning and when he looked in the rearview mirror, sure enough, the stupid car was trailing sooty fumes all the way back to Port Allen. Horns blared—just a couple at first, then an angry chorus. Before he knew it smoke had eclipsed both lanes behind him and there was nowhere to pull over. Eddie tasted bile. His ears rang. Out of the corner of his eye he could see the river below him snaking in brown curves toward a smudged horizon. He kept the Tempest at fifty-five and watched downtown Baton Rouge rise slowly before him against the sky. Any second now, he was sure, he would start crying.

The whine of the tires dropped a couple of tones as he came off the bridge. He missed the first exit; just before taking the next one he caught a glimpse of a lake, rusty cypress trees rising from brown water. The horns faded behind him as he coasted off the interstate and the next thing he knew he was cruising along a street lined with gutted stores and boarded-up houses, all of them dripping leafy vines that shone with a dim spectrum of hallucinatory greens. Weeds grew through cracks in the pavement. Opposite him concrete barriers blocked the interstate on-ramp. The lake was nowhere to be seen.

Down the block from the overpass he pulled into a dirt lot next to a bar and, with the Vise-Grip clamped to the broken-off column shift, put the car in neutral. In the lot a rangy guy in a tie-dyed tank stood talking to a woman with bleached hair and a change apron. She wiped her eyes on her sleeve as Eddie climbed out of the car. Smoke still billowed from the rear wheel wells. He swore with helpless rage as he confronted his own folly—a rickety auto with nudes ineptly airbrushed on the door panels and LA PISTOLA painted across the hood. "Damn, damn, *damn.*" He blew sweat off his lip. It had to be close to a hundred and his shorts and polo shirt, the last of his clean clothes, were soaked.

"I'm talking to you, bro." The guy in the tie-dyed shirt was ambling across the lot toward him, two stars blazing in the lenses of his sunglasses.

Eddie raised his eyebrows. "Say what?"

"I said, that's some ride."

"Indeed." Eddie felt the parking lot shake as traffic rumbled across the overpass. He cleared his throat. "I know it looks weird. But my own car—my Civic—broke down on me. What can I say? I was out in the sticks and this one was available. Obviously it's temporary."

"You're saying you got took by some country boy?" The man smiled as he knelt and poked his head under the rear bumper. His long blond hair was pulled back in a greasy braid that hung halfway down his back. He reached gingerly up behind one of the tires and dragged out a smoldering shower curtain; from its folds tumbled the singed corpse of a cat. Eddie looked away as the smell of scorched plastic and something alarmingly close to fried pork chops rose in the air. "Some country boy messing with your head too," said the man.

"Stretch?" hollered the blond woman behind him. "You got something for me or not?"

The man wiped his hands on a soiled red handkerchief and took a long look at the car. "If you're heading to New Orleans how about you take me with?"

Eddie eyed the syringes tattooed on the guy's forearms. "I don't know if that's such a great idea."

"Stretch?" yelled the woman. "My break's about over."

"Got you covered," shouted the man without turning around. "Give me ten minutes here, darling." The woman went inside and he gave Eddie a smile that might have been good-natured. "Now look here," he said, with a clownish wink, "I know you ain't the kind of man to leave a bro in a tight spot."

Eddie couldn't help laughing. "All right," he said. "No smoking in the car, though."

As they pulled out of the parking lot his passenger theatrically fanned himself with a handful of what looked like twenty-dollar bills. "They call me Stretch," he said. "The Lean Machine. The *Big* Boy. And I am one sweet-talking *fool.*"

HOW TIRED EDDIE was. Tired of driving. Tired of thinking ahead. He could smell his dirty laundry and it was as if the scent had been following him ever since he could remember, as if it were in fact the sour odor of his own life. It had been a long time since he'd been on his own. Now not only was he cut loose but the sanctuary he expected on the road kept eluding him. Time, he found, had coarsened those lives he'd passed through so long ago on his way west. Off to his left was the lake he'd seen earlier, clusters of girls with enormous bows in their hair cycling along the shore.

Stretch elbowed him. "Wishing you was a bicycle seat?"

Eddie sighed. "Excuse me?"

Stretch took off his sunglasses. It was as though behind those dirty green eyes he was shuffling cards. "Just a joke, man. Don't go all highbrow on me."

Eddie stared straight ahead. Before him the pavement trembled in the heat and to the right of the interstate he could see a billboard striped with flashing lights, which, as he drew closer, resolved into words: THE FOOL HATH SAID IN HIS HEART, THERE IS NO GOD. The skin along his arms erupted in goose pimples. He caught the next exit and pulled into a Texaco station. Willing his passenger to vanish, he kept his back turned resolutely to the car while he filled the tank. Across the road a blue panel truck was parked off the pavement. Between the truck and a hand-painted sign—SHRIMP—an old woman sat on a Styrofoam cooler beneath a beach umbrella. She waved and held up a bulging plastic sack. Eddie pretended not to notice. When the pump stopped ticking he went inside and passed Hilary's Visa to the attendant. He glanced in the overhead mirror; there was Stretch, winking at him from the magazine rack and holding up a centerfold of a naked woman in a hard hat.

"Sir?" said the clerk. "Card's been canceled."

"That's not possible."

"It's possible, all right."

"Well, look, do you think you could—" Eddie looked down into the kid's stiff smile. "Never mind."

Stretch appeared at his side. "Play it cool," he said, holding up the roll of bills. "I got you covered."

Eddie stood there as Stretch paid. Twenty-seven dollars left in his wallet. And he hadn't eaten since last night. This was unacceptable. He went to the phone booth outside and called Hilary back in California. Through the

Plexiglas he could see dark clouds boiling in from the Gulf. "Hey," he said, when she answered. "There's been some mix-up with the Visa."

"I had to make some difficult decisions."

"Couldn't they have waited till I'm on my feet? I mean, I would have paid you back."

"Listen to you. Just how stupid do you think I am? The agreement was, you could use the card for *essentials* till you got settled. I mean, my God—*massage oil?* What was going through your head?"

"Just because you're unable to tolerate imperfection—"

"You make me sick, Glamour Boy. That's what I get for hanging out with someone who dyes his hair."

The smell of ripe shrimp wafted through the booth and Eddie fought to keep from gagging. When he looked across the road the woman was again holding up a plastic bag. He shook his head no. It sounded as if Hilary was whispering to someone. "Babe?" he said. "Are you alone? I can't believe this is your idea. Aren't you going to listen to your heart?" But she'd already hung up.

Stretch was in the passenger seat, smoking a joint. "Put that out," said Eddie. "Right now. I don't feel like getting busted."

"Just a little something for my nerves," said Stretch, and held up a bottle of peach brandy. "How about a drink?"

"Forget it." Eddie started the car and pulled out of the

station. The air was thick with skunky smoke and he started coughing. "Damn it, I told you no smoking in the car. I don't *need* this."

"Edward, Edward. You got to calm down." Stretch took one last leisurely drag off the joint and dropped it into a plastic film container.

"Calm *down?* What do you tell a woman who claims you've never done an unselfish thing in your life?"

"So long."

"That's easy for you to say."

"A woman putting you out ain't no big thing."

"Nobody put me out. If I did anything wrong it was staying too long. I should have left six months ago." From the depths of his misery came a tableau that still made him wince: Hilary holding between thumb and forefinger the pair of bikini underpants she'd found under the futon. He'd always managed to invoke women's forgiveness, as a rule with the same extravagant claptrap that kindled their interest in the first place, before things got to this point. Flat denial, sulking, pleas of confusion, hot kisses up and down her back—all the usual tactics had failed. Eddie managed a wry smile as they headed up the on-ramp. "It's just that we've grown. We've developed new economies. And when I got offered a position in New Orleans I took it. What would you do? Now it sounds like our relationship has turned into a group project. Sisterhood is powerful, right? I mean, they've got it so rough these days."

"They can get nasty on you," said Stretch. "Now you take me. The other day I head over to the Quarter to score some crank, right? I make my connection and drop by the K&B to hit up my old lady for a little loan. And the girl turns me down. In front of everybody." Stretch pointed with both hands to his own chest. "Can you believe that noise?"

"Absolutely. She's trying to work and you come in loaded and try to borrow money. What do you expect?"

"Same thing you do."

"Somehow I doubt it." Eddie swung into the center lane and held it at sixty-five. Soon the used-car lots on either side of the interstate gave way to open fields strewn with trailers and ranch houses. Armadillo carcasses littered the breakdown lane, spindly legs thrust at the sky. "Look," he said, "you know what the problem is? They're never satisfied with what you're willing to give them."

"I mean. They after your personal balls and liver too. Talking to their girlfriends? Night and day. And, son, I don't have to tell you about *their* advice, do I?"

"Well, stupid me. I expect a relationship to be based on mutual respect — not this medieval possessiveness."

Stretch looked at him over the top of his sunglasses. "Remember, now, Edward, you're talking to a boy who knows a little bit about women."

Eddie slipped into the right lane to let a convoy of army vehicles creep past. "And I don't? Listen, I used to live with the perfect woman."

"Big old titties and a satellite dish?"

"Give me a break. She made me laugh. She used to sing 'Some Enchanted Evening' to her dog." Reaching under his shirt, Eddie pulled out the tarnished *I Ching* coin that hung from a silver chain around his neck. "She gave me this," he said and let out a wistful laugh. "But she died."

"Now ain't that pitiful."

Eddie's cheeks burned. "What's that supposed to mean?"

"Supposed to mean I ain't going to sit here with a straight face while you run a sorry-ass con like that on me."

"Hey, I don't care if you believe me or not." Eddie was shocked at the sound of his own voice, shrill and petulant. Could he be stoned from a mere sniff of secondhand pot smoke?

"What kind of job did you say you're moving here for?"

"The insurance field." Eddie cleared his throat. "Marketing rep, actually."

Stretch spat out the window. "I got me two rules. Never work with a partner and never tell your woman what you do for a living. You hear me?"

"And what do you do for a living?"

"Why, I'm an outlaw."

A few raindrops spattered the windshield. Eddie wondered how long the woman in Baton Rouge had waited for this moron. He kept his eyes on the road and tried not to think about food.

A HALF HOUR later they were sitting at the counter of a truck stop. It was pouring outside and every so often Eddie heard a muffled rumble of thunder. The booths behind him were jammed with overweight drugged-looking men in cowboy hats, all of them bawling at one another in Texas accents over beeping video games and the lugubrious wailing of a steel guitar on the jukebox. The waitress brought menus. "Thanks again, Stretch," said Eddie, rather sheepishly. "I appreciate this."

"Man does not live by bread alone. But he got to eat."

"Orange juice," Eddie told the waitress, "wheat toast, and a side of cottage—"

"Girl," Stretch cut in, "just bring us two short stacks, some hot links and biscuits, a couple—no, make that three—orders of cheese grits, and a big old pot of coffee."

"Wait—" said Eddie, but the woman had already hung their ticket. "Damn it, Stretch, I don't want to seem ungrateful but I've been off animal protein for a long time now."

"Did you a hell of a lot of good, didn't it?"

"I happen to think so. Fat weighs down the spirit." Behind him someone laughed and he lowered his voice. "It's slow poison. Look it up."

"I'll take your word for it, Nutrition Boy."

"It's not nutrition, it's politics. Look at that—that *flesh,*" he said, pointing to the tiers of bacon, ham, and sausage sputtering on the grill. "Nitrates. Nitrites. Sulfates. Whatever. You couldn't pay me to even put it in my mouth."

Stretch elbowed him. "That's what *she* said."

To his horror Eddie heard himself laughing. He sounded hysterical. Stretch beamed as Eddie got up and made his way past the booths to the pay phone. He nodded absently to a young woman in a UVa T-shirt who smiled and blushed. Eddie took a scrap of paper out of his wallet and dialed the New Orleans branch of Poughkeepsie Insurance Solutions. It was busy, as it had been every time he'd called.

His order was on the counter and Stretch was already mopping his own plate with a biscuit. Pancakes and sausage —Eddie had to admit it sounded pretty good. His mouth was watering. Surely after all these years one small lapse wouldn't hurt. Suddenly Eddie felt the spring of his old confidence. He was still in control. He leaned back in his seat and took a swallow of coffee. Lining the wall across from him were rows of black-and-white publicity photos: singers, wrestlers, a comedian with two blacked-out teeth. Eddie hadn't heard of any of them. "Why am I doing this?" he said. "Driving halfway across the country for some stupid job? Maybe I ought to look into the outlaw business."

"Step one," said Stretch. "You got to be feeling right." He held out his right hand. A huge white tablet lay in his palm. "Myself, I popped two this morning."

"I'd just as soon stay in my right mind, thanks."

"Edward, you make one piss-poor outlaw."

THROUGH THE RAIN a wall of trees rose from the swamps on either side of the interstate. Here and there Eddie could see soggy egrets roosting in the branches. The ringing in his ears had risen to a steady whine. His stomach was churning, his mouth filmed with the flavor of tainted pork, and when he saw a deserted truck scale he pulled over to the shoulder. Traffic hissed by, trailing plumes of muddy water. "Stretch," he said, "I'm sick as hell. You're going to have to drive." He walked around the car and collapsed in the passenger seat. "Christ," he groaned, "I knew better."

Stretch tuned the radio to a country station. Then he passed Eddie one of the white pills. "Take this," he said. "It'll fix you up till we get you to Chain Drive's."

"Who?"

"Just do it. Burn a little fat off your spirit."

By the time they got to New Orleans the rain had let up. Stretch was singing along with some nasal hymn to adultery as he caught an exit and followed the off-ramp's descending spiral past the Superdome. Then they were driving beneath a tangle of overpasses. Sunlight slashed the street ahead of them. Through a veil of nausea Eddie watched the city roll past—liquor stores, bail bondsmen, storefront churches, block after block of houses with barred windows, black men staring flatly back at him from the porches. Just past some mustard-colored projects Stretch made a right, then parked in front of a storefront whose windows were emblazoned with red letters: NEW SEVEN POWERS DRUG STORE—CANDLES—GOOD LUCK BAGS PLUS MUCH MUCH MORE. They got out and crossed the street to a two-story apartment building. Up the block some little black girls were jumping rope, chanting words Eddie couldn't understand. He followed Stretch up a flight of stairs to the balcony. His legs felt like Jell-O. Stretch knocked on some louvered shutters spray-painted with the phrase *Smell My Head,* and a man wearing only a faded pair of jeans answered the door. His bald head was cruelly sunburned.

"Chain Drive," said Stretch. "Behold the man."

The guy looked Eddie up and down. "What's this, Stretch? Your long-lost twin?"

"Edward here's going for an outlaw," said Stretch.

"I just need to lie down for a minute," said Eddie and followed Stretch into the apartment. The place was suffocatingly hot and stank of liquor and cigarette smoke and cats. Eddie felt sweat dribbling down his sides. At a table in the kitchen sat a big blond woman and a freckled boy with huge ears. The woman looked from Stretch to Eddie and Eddie saw her eyes widen. He smelled fried fish. Gurgling apologies, he tripped over an orange cat and went stumbling down the hall to the bathroom. Moments later, purged, he sat down heavily on the edge of the tub and listened to the two men talking in the front room.

"Where'd you pick up this cherry anyways? Trolling for punks?"

"Now, Chain Drive, kids coming up today, they don't understand the outlaw lifestyle. Remember, you was cherry too once."

"He looks like he could be on the *Young and the Restless,*" said the woman.

"He looks like a punk."

"Wait till you see his ride," said Stretch.

Algae-colored light filtered through the bathroom window and across the backs of Eddie's hands. Over the ringing in his ears he could hear the girls chanting in the street. *Now I like gin,* a man was saying in the next apartment. *Now I like gin.* Over and over again. Memories from the past couple of weeks bubbled through Eddie's mind—the jagged rhythm of night, day, night, dawn bleeding over the mesas and a flat tire outside Albuquerque, dying Texas towns where everybody wore a cowboy hat, strolling into a fried chicken joint near Monroe where the very locals who would foist the Tempest off on him stared as though they knew his story better than he did: Cherry.

He rinsed his face and went back to the front room. He found Stretch and Chain Drive and the blond woman bent over a mirror hatched with white powder. On the far side of the room the boy with big ears was trying to stuff the orange cat into a Quaker Oats box.

The woman directed Eddie to a pay phone at the end of the block. Wobbling a little, he made his way back down the stairs and past the girls with the jump rope. Before him the whole block was in shadow, and steam rose from the puddles. He dialed the number again and this time a man answered. "What's up?" In the background a calliope peeped away.

Eddie cleared his throat. "Is this Poughkeepsie Insurance Solutions?"

"McGibsie?"

"Poughkeepsie."

"Ain't no McGibsie here."

"Well," said Eddie, touching the coin under his shirt, "I'm supposed to speak with Maudie. Is Maudie there?" He could feel his heartbeat.

The man chortled. "Man, when Maudie go on a drunk you don't even need to *think* about talking to her."

Eddie called his brother in Massachusetts. The number had been disconnected. A spasm of panic made his knees wobble. He stood for a moment, looking at his Tempest, jingling the keys in his pocket.

The blond woman smiled as she let him back into the apartment. She wasn't bad-looking. He imagined taking her out for a drink, tossing off a few lines from one of his poems, then stopping with a rueful smile in the middle of a sentence—*God, when I look at you I smell apples and the cords of my heart shake like cello strings.* For the first time ever he wasn't sure it would work. In his despair Eddie accepted a hit off a joint. The woman offered him a glass of vodka and peppermint schnapps and he took that too. Then he had another one.

Stretch appeared in the hallway wearing a green silk shirt and bolo tie, ostrich-skin cowboy boots. "Step two," he said. "You got to be looking *good.*" He held out another cowboy shirt, black with embroidered red roses. "Here you go, Edward. Now you can stop bellyaching about your laundry."

"That's OK," said Eddie. "Thanks, though." But he ended up trying the shirt on anyway. He went to look at himself in the bathroom mirror. It wasn't a bad fit. With his two-day stubble he actually looked sort of dangerous, as long as you ignored the shorts and Birkenstocks.

When he came back Stretch was clogging in front of the stove. "They call me Stretch," he said, "but I'm tall, that's all." He stopped dancing and motioned to the mirror. "Knock yourself out."

"I better not," said Eddie. But he changed his mind. The events of the day shot up the straw and exploded against the roof of his skull and came sifting back to him in sweet spangles of pleasure. He flashed Stretch a tight grin. He stood up and began pacing back and forth in front of the TV. "Wow," he kept saying. "Check it out."

Stretch nodded to Chain Drive. "Told you," he said. "Told you Edward was good people."

"If he ain't," said Chain Drive, turning his pink wasted eyes on Eddie, "I feel sorry for him."

"Have us a *big* time," said Stretch. "I *mean.* Tear this town every way but loose. Search and destroy, you all."

"Anytime," said Eddie. "I feel great. I feel strong enough to pick up this whole house."

"Hey, Useless," said Chain Drive. "You know the word on Ted Bundy?"

"I'm not sure what you mean."

"He was Christ."

"Mister?" said the boy. "You really from California?"

"Indeed," said Eddie.

"You all must talk funny out there."

IT WAS GETTING dark as Eddie drove up Esplanade with Stretch riding shotgun, the others squeezed into the backseat. He stopped in front of a K&B and kept the engine running while Stretch went inside. Clouds of insects shrouded the bulbs of the streetlights. The faint breeze smelled of nectarines and bleach. "Well, I like this car," said the woman.

"Shit too," said Chain Drive.

Before they'd left the apartment Stretch had talked Eddie into eating two more pills. When Chain Drive saw the car he nearly went berserk, screaming loud enough to run the neighbors off their porches that they might as well drive a car painted with BUST ME in bright red letters. Eddie's ears were buzzing like mad and he could barely feel the clutch pedal. He was wrecked. And he didn't care. He was an outlaw.

An old man with an eye patch pushed a frankfurter-shaped cart up the street toward them. Along one side, yellow letters spelled out LUCKY DOGS.

Stretch came out of the drugstore, walking fast, hands at his sides. He tossed two cartons of Kools into the backseat, then opened a fresh bottle of peach brandy and drank half of it down. "Ain't it amazing," he said, "what three little words can do?"

Eddie was pulling away from the curb when a pale woman in a blue uniform came running out of the drugstore. He could see her name tag bobbing up and down.

"Stop," said Stretch. "Hold it right there."

Eddie hit the brakes. Distantly he marveled that he was able to drive at all. The woman came puffing up to the car. "Sylvester!" she hollered. "You sorry low-life thief!"

The Lucky Dog man looked over curiously. Stretch reached into the waistband of his trousers and pulled out a pistol.

"Wait a minute," said Eddie. "What's going on?"

"Step three," said Stretch. "We got us a *crime* spree." He thrust his upper body through the window. "Girl!" he yelled. "I ain't no thief—I just got me a new economy!" He fired two, three times. Across the street a ragged line of holes appeared along the side of the Lucky Dog cart. Steam hissed from the punctures.

Chain Drive was kicking the back of Eddie's seat. *"Move!"*

"That's what *she* said."

Chain Drive grabbed him around the neck. "Get funny with *me?*"

The Vise-Grip slipped from the column shift and the engine died. Stretch folded himself back into the car and shoved the muzzle under Chain Drive's chin. "Back off now. While you still can." Eddie felt the fingers relax around his throat. Stretch nodded to him. "Get it, son."

Eddie clamped the Vise-Grip back onto the stub of the column shift, yanked the car into first, and skidded away from the curb. In the rearview mirror he saw the Lucky Dog man and the woman from the K&B staring after them.

"Let me have him," begged Chain Drive. "I want his ass."

"This ain't no time to jump bad," said Stretch, tucking the pistol back into his pants. "We got to stick together now."

"Shit too," said Chain Drive.

Eddie ran a red light. His foot shook on the accelerator. He cleared his throat. "Can somebody tell me where we're going?" Chain Drive slapped him across the back of the skull. Stretch directed Eddie along the surface streets and after a mile or so of heavy traffic they picked up 90 and took it over the river. The signs said they were heading toward Morgan City. Before them the sky was cherry red. "What three words?" Eddie wanted to know. *"Smell my head?"*

Everybody laughed—Stretch, the blond woman, the kid. Even Chain Drive.

"Give it up," said Stretch.

"Give it up," said Eddie. "Give it up. Give it up."

Chain Drive whacked the back of his head again. "Quit trying to be a wise-ass, Useless." Next to him the boy was hacking at the upholstery with a steak knife.

"Hey," said Eddie, "what's he doing?"

"Overlook it," said Chain Drive.

THE BOY SNORED in the backseat as Eddie sped through the swamps, holding under his tongue the dime Stretch had given him. Black shaggy trees flickered past, and from time to time he saw the starry incandescence of fishermen's lanterns. The night was heavy with wisteria and he felt empty and buzzed and knew he could drive forever.

"If I call you my friend," Chain Drive was saying, "then you my friend. Even if you wrong. If I call you my enemy then there's going to be blood on your chest. Even if you right."

"I hear you," said Eddie.

Chain Drive clouted him across the back of the head. "Nobody's talking to you, Useless." Beside him the woman was puzzling over one of Eddie's notebooks, which she'd pulled from the stack underneath his dirty laundry.

"Here," said Stretch. "Let me see that dime, son." When Eddie passed it over he chuckled softly. "What did I tell you? Black. You done been *fixed*, son. Hoodooed. Have to get you some Van Van Oil. Florida Water. All that good trash."

"Can I see it?" said the blond woman. To the south, lightning flashed against the sky. In the rearview mirror Eddie met her eyes as she took the dime and slipped it into her mouth.

"That does it!" howled Chain Drive. "Stop this car!" He lunged across the seat.

Eddie swerved out of his lane and back again. Stretch grabbed Chain Drive's arms and, climbing halfway into the back, pinned him down in the seat. "Edward," he said over his shoulder, "you'd best do what he says."

Eddie pulled over and turned off the engine. Through a fringe of cottonwoods he could see a dead moon floating on water. A rank weedy smell hung in the air. Stretch kicked open his door and wrestled Chain Drive out of the car. "Cool it," he kept saying. "Cool it, man. It don't mean nothing."

"But he been steady snaking on my woman!"

Stretch led him behind the car, talking fast the whole time, and then Eddie could no longer make out what he was saying. He licked the inside of his mouth. He still tasted peppermint schnapps, the faint metallic tang of the dime. He could fall right through the world, here, tonight, without an echo, without a ripple. No one would ever know. He knew he should be scared to death but he wasn't.

"I like this," said the woman in the backseat. "'The more futile,'" she read haltingly, "'seemed this chase back along the trail of hearts grown cold.'" She closed the notebook. "Is it hard to write poems?"

"Harder than I thought," said Eddie. He was clenching his fists experimentally when he felt her fingers on his hair.

"It's so soft," she whispered. "Ever since I seen you I just been dying to touch it. I bet the girls used to call you Sweet Boy."

The ringing in Eddie's ears was gone. His mind filled with Bella—naked, watching fireworks from his rooftop. The vision faded, leaving the transparent afterimage of her heart-shaped bottom lingering in the dark. "I'm not what you think," he said. "I'm not anything."

Outside, the men's voices rose again. Chain Drive appeared in front of the car, stripping off his shirt. "Let's get down to it!" he shouted. He slapped his pale chest. "Get on out here, Useless. Or do I got to drag your scrawny ass out of that ride?"

Stretch stepped up to Eddie's window. "Nothing I can do for you now, Edward. You going to have to stand tall, look mean, and give it your best shot." His smile seemed almost kindly as he opened the door. "That's just politics," he said.

"This is step four?"

"You got any better ideas?"

"I don't have any ideas at all."

"There it is."

For a second Eddie thought about running for it. He felt the urge deep in his belly. They'd never find him out there in the dark. He tried to imagine himself, loaded and half drunk, floundering through the swamp in shorts and a cowboy shirt, but he couldn't. He opened the door, stepped out into the rising whine of cicadas. Palmetto bugs crackled beneath his feet, and behind him he heard the door slam.

Toby

The moment Toby took over as graphics scheduler at McLaughlin & Rotary he set Dr. Rotary himself straight Tobias-wise. He was Toby. Not Tobias, not Mr. Garfield. Toby. And when Hilda and Deirdre, the senior graphic artists, started calling him Mr. Garfield he put a stop to that pronto too. These attempts to saddle him with some weighty appellative reflected nothing more than doubts about his ability to manage, specifically to manage employees who were in some cases nearly twice his age. The problem was what Mr. McLaughlin called his schoolboy charm: the freckles, the red hair—everything, in other words, that made him look even younger than twenty-seven. But he believed then and he believes now that there are more creative ways of establishing and maintaining leadership than this tired New England reserve. Why would anyone cling to such a strategy anyway, except to camouflage a timid and conventional mind? Open the windows, for heaven's sake. It's the nineties. Let in some air. Start thinking out of the box. Isn't the important thing that team members learn to think of management as an ally? Toby's feeling is this: As long as it doesn't impact productivity, why not go for that personal touch?

Such a philosophy, of course, has its hazards. Without clearly defined boundaries some employees will inevitably go haywire. In fact Toby's baptism by fire began with an abuse of that first-name informality.

The problems began during the Gulf War. Because of the sudden mobilization of reserves, the graphics department found itself short two graphic artists, and when Dr. Rotary complained about a two-day turnaround on some presentations, Toby called an employment agency. For the rest of the week a parade of candidates ranging from merely incompetent to clinically insane filed through his office. Dopeheads. Drunks. Thieves. Ill-dressed, gangling girls—it was Deirdre, by the way (neither she nor Hilda stands more than a tidy five feet in flats), who pointed out the eerie uniformity of stature. To call these sad cases unemployable would be putting it kindly. Finally that Friday morning, after interviewing some tipsy beanpole who tried to slip his stapler into her purse and asked him to let her "hold ten dollars," he called the agency and said that for the time being M&R would just suffer along without reinforcements. A cheerful voice asked him to wait until he'd spoken to one more candidate. Bella Kipper.

Shortly after lunch Hilda ushered this recruit into his office and the air suddenly went heavy with a dark woody scent. As they shook hands Toby saw to his relief that Bella was an inch or so shorter than he—buxom, attractive in an outdated sort of way, with one of those hawklike Mediterranean faces and, despite her business attire, a hint of some former gypsyish flamboyance. When she sat across from him the light from the window disclosed spirals of gray in her rampant hair.

"Believe it or not," said Toby as he studied her résumé, "you're the first person I've ever met from Philadelphia." Seeing her weary smile, he asked what brought her to Boston.

"I heard it was a good place," she said, "to make up for lost time."

Through the window behind her Toby could see sunlight flashing on the Charles. In the silence, he held out one foot at a time, watching the play of light on his new tasseled loafers from L. L. Bean. "Lost time?"

"I have a couple of kids in high school. My skills are too good for me to be temping for ten bucks an hour with no health insurance. I'm ready for some kind of future."

"At M&R that depends on you."

The phone rang. It was Toby's grandmother, calling again from Hibernian Meadows, her nursing home. "Toby? Toby? Someone has stolen all the televisions."

"Gran, that was over ten years ago. There's a new one in the recreation room. A nice big one."

"But it's time for the *Guiding Light,* Toby. And my television is gone."

"Have you taken your medication, Gran? Please try to focus." He hung up and Bella fixed him with bruised-looking eyes. Unaccountably he found himself sweating. Did he have misgivings at that moment? Of course. But her résumé was exemplary, her references glowing. She knew Mac and Windows, she knew Excel, PowerPoint, PhotoShop, Illustrator. And she typed ninety words per minute. So, misgivings or not, Toby signed her up. Later that afternoon as he reviewed her paperwork he could still smell her perfume. Hilda told him it was patchouli.

"Attractive girl," said Dr. Rotary. "Beats looking at the same old warhorses, wouldn't you say, Toby?"

"Easy on the eyes," he replied with a wink.

At first Bella kept pretty much to herself. She would come in early (by eight, when Toby arrived, the hallways were already fragrant with her scent) and work steadily all morning, then eat lunch with Hilda and Deirdre and the copy center employees at the support staff table, hurry back to her cubicle, and leave after the others. Her billable ratio was a dazzling 75 percent. Almost immediately the turnaround time dropped to a matter of hours.

At the end of her second week on the job Dr. Rotary came to Toby's office, followed by none other than Mr. McLaughlin himself, and put a hand on his shoulder. "Now our Toby," he said, fanning him with sour fumes of corned beef hash, "our Toby has worked miracles here. Miracles."

Another coup in his campaign to be human resources manager.

That afternoon he left early and took the Red Line from Charles Street to Central Square, where in front of the Lebanese market he had his shoes buffed to a military gloss by a mustached man in a yachting cap. Toby tipped him a dollar and picked up some takeout at an Indian restaurant. Chicken Vindaloo Dinner steaming beneath one arm, he strolled up Inman toward his apartment. The days were turning cold. Over his head the wind stripped flurries of brittle leaves from the branches, and before him the brick sidewalk shone gold in the last light. Toby was a happy man. This, he thought, is life.

HE'D SCHEDULED BELLA's get-acquainted chat for the following Monday. "This is your time," he said with an expansive gesture when she stepped through the door. As soon as she'd completed a form for his files he brought her up to speed on M&R's corporate culture and core values.

He went on to tell her about Hilda's avid interest in professional wrestling, Deirdre's church choir, his own Monday night folk dancing. He drew her attention to his OED and the matted portrait of General "Chinese" Gordon hanging over his desk. "I suppose," he said, "that you could call me an Anglophile. Which, given your last name, bodes well for you."

Bella said nothing.

"You can laugh," said Toby. "That was a joke."

Another brooding silence. "Well," said Toby, "what do you see yourself doing in another five years?"

Again that weary smile. "Come on."

Toby wasn't used to being patronized this way by the rank and file and frankly he wasn't thrilled about it. But he let it go. "Remember," he said as she left the office, "the name is Toby."

Her billable ratio remained the highest in the department, but it wasn't long before she stopped coming to work early and staying late. After her first month she seemed more concerned with getting the other graphic artists fired up over nonissues like sexist language and the semantics of job descriptions than with laying the groundwork for any kind of company future. During lunch Toby could hear her across the cafeteria, raking his gender over the coals. Men were, it seemed, lazy, brutish, and deceitful; they were silent when they should be communicative, garrulous when they should be taciturn, and, worst of all, *linear*. He'd heard it before, the usual tiresome litany of a woman unable to manage her own life. Predictably, delighted laughter followed her remarks.

"She's wicked funny," the mail clerk, a pimpled giant from Southie, told him.

One morning, a week or so before the Christmas party, Toby found her in the conference room with Deirdre and Hilda, passing around a jar of mango chutney. He reminded them that Dr. Rotary limited meal activities to the cafeteria. They looked at one another and laughed.

"*Meal* activities," said Bella, sending her cronies into hysterics. "Give us a break, Tobe." She ate a spoonful of chutney. "I suppose you could call us mangophiles."

"How droll," he said, then returned to his office, where he spent a good five minutes blushing and trying to wipe the grin off his face. *Tobe.* It wasn't just that it sounded funny; it was that in Bella's enunciation of that final consonant there was something like an implied tickle under the chin. He planned to take her aside that very afternoon and, after warning her about what the M&R bylaws call "destructive criticism," casually mention that those same bylaws limited fraternization between management and staff. But by the time he composed himself she'd gone home.

The next morning her cubicle was empty.

"She's going through a period of transition," said Hilda.

Deirdre nodded vigorously. "She needs a lot of support."

Transition? Support? The prospect of these Charlestown matrons with their blue rinse jobs and dewlaps and ten-year service pins parroting such concepts was too dispiriting to think about. Toby called his therapist—he was of course out—and left a message on his machine.

When he came to work the following morning he could smell patchouli over the usual winter odors of coffee and damp wool. From Bella's cubicle came the sound of voices. Without really intending to, he slipped into the empty cubicle next to hers.

"Honey," Deirdre was saying, "you're only flesh and blood. You can't take care of your kids and work full-time and go to school on top of that."

"I don't have any choice," said Bella.

The telephone rang back in Toby's office and he pressed the flash button, transferring the call to the phone in front of him. It was his therapist. "Toby? From your message I gather that you're having to deal with some issues of—"

"I really can't dialogue at this particular point in time."

"What I'm picking up from you now is a lot of anger."

At the sound of his voice the women had stopped talking. A second later all three appeared at the cubicle entrance. "My broker," said Toby as he hung up. "I *told* him not to call me at work."

"Sure," said Deirdre. "Like we believe you, Tobe."

So, without really making a decision, he found himself living with the silly diminutive. In short he let it go.

To the Christmas party he wore charcoal wool trousers, hand-stitched braces, a pink oxford, a burgundy bow tie, and his suede saddle shoes. He swept into the lounge of the Marriott and spotted Dr. Rotary rocking on his heels near the Christmas tree at the far edge of the dance floor. The band, a phalanx of bored-looking oafs in tuxedos, was playing "White Wedding" and the mail clerk was dancing with Bella, whose idea of holiday fashion was a black dress that laced down the front and bared an astonishing expanse of olive skin.

"By God," growled Dr. Rotary when Toby came to stand beside him, "she's all woman."

Toby made his way back through the crowd to the bar. The Puerto Rican bartender looked up from the ice tray; when he saw Toby watching Bella he winked conspiratorially. Toby responded with a stern look. "A tequila fluff, señor."

"Huh?"

"Tequila and ginger ale."

"*Ginger* ale?"

"*Precisamente.*"

The bartender was still muttering under his breath and throwing bottles around when the band took a break and Bella, flushed and tousled, came over to the bar to stand between Toby and the drummer. She ordered a club soda. "Great tie, Tobe. What do you think of my vendetta outfit?"

He could scarcely avoid noticing through the laced bodice what looked like stretch marks along the pale inner curves of her breasts—not what one would envision as a particularly edifying sight, yet he suddenly found himself short of breath. "Frankly I think it's just a little bit tacky. Which is fine. As long as you don't expect to be taken seriously."

"By who?"

"Dr. Rotary, for instance."

"Tobe, what could I possibly do that would make that horny old creep take me seriously?"

"You could start by dressing professionally."

"Don't you *ever* lighten up?"

"You asked." He ordered another drink as Bella turned to the drummer .

"How about you?" she said. "Do you think I'm tacky?"

"Mama," said the drummer, "I'm on your side."

Bella asked if the band did "These Arms of Mine."

"For you we do."

Toby noticed Dr. Rotary making his unsteady way toward the bar, eyes locked on Bella, as the band returned to the stage. Bella looked at Toby over her shoulder and asked if he wanted to dance. Dr. Rotary paused, looked from Bella to Toby, and almost imperceptibly, shook his head no.

"Sure," said Toby. He finished his drink and followed her onto the floor. Bella closed her eyes and put her head on his shoulder.

"Tell me," he said, "does Dr. Rotary really—"

"Tobe," she said. "Please don't."

Maybe it was because he wasn't used to drinking, maybe it was the sheer novelty of holding her, smelling her hair, feeling her belly against him—how soft she was, how miraculously supple her every movement—but whatever the reason, he closed his eyes and when the song ended they just kept dancing. Toby looked up to find themselves alone on the floor. The support staff stood watching, Hilda and Deirdre wearing the look of blurry suspicion that comes with too many drinks. Dr. Rotary frowned at him from across the lounge. Through his own intoxication Toby felt a distant alarm at his loss of composure. "There are those," he heard himself say, "who may not find my behavior entirely appropriate. Actually."

"What are you, his dog?"

"Oh, shut up."

Bella let out a croak of laughter. "You little twerp. You're drunk, aren't you?"

She was right. As Dr. Rotary grabbed his coat, Toby followed him through the lounge and out the door in his shirtsleeves. It was snowing, the crystals sparkling in the halos of the streetlights. "Dr. Rotary," said Toby. His voice was flat in the white hush.

Steadying himself on a newspaper stand, Dr. Rotary turned to him. "Toby," he said, "if I'd been born thirty years later I'd be a young man too." Then he turned and began working his way down the sidewalk toward the waiting taxis.

Inside, four or five of the department heads, aglow with martial fervor, were leading the crowd in singing "God Bless America." Bella asked him for a ride to her apartment in Jamaica Plain.

He maneuvered his Plymouth Sundance cautiously through the drifts toward the BU Bridge.

"Christ," said Bella. "You drive like an old lady."

By the time he pulled onto the Jamaicaway the heater had kicked in, enfolding them in the cozy smells of scorched air and patchouli. Toby asked Bella if she had any hobbies.

"Yeah," she said, "I like to lie on my back and spit into the ceiling fan." She shook her head. "Hobbies. You are so weird."

He got off on Pond Street. Bella directed him to Lamartine and made him drive around the block while she scrutinized the parked cars. Finally she told him to stop in front of a gray triple-decker.

"One thing you have to understand," she said, "is that people like me pay. And people like you don't." She quickly opened the door, slipped out of the passenger seat, and picked her way across the street, her shoes squeaking on the fresh snow. He waited until a light appeared in one of the second-story windows. As he motored slowly back toward Cambridge he realized that this was the first time he'd ever driven a woman home.

MONDAY MORNING, WHILE Toby was passing out invitations to his New Year's Day brunch, she called in sick. Later that day as he was bringing a couple of parcels down to the mail clerk Mr. McLaughlin waylaid him outside the men's room. "Dr. Rotary," he said, hitching the crotch of his trousers and with watery blue eyes daring Toby to laugh, "indicated that he has some issues around Bella's attire at the Christmas party."

"Really? I thought she looked rather nice." Toby had scheduled a visioning session for the Office Beautification Committee and he was in a hurry.

"It's not just that," McLaughlin went on. "I understand that she's taking night classes."

"And that's an issue?"

"It is if she does class work on company time. Her billable ratio is suboptimal—down almost fifteen percent. Unacceptable, Toby. Unacceptable. And, darn it, when is she going to get that newsletter out on time?"

"I wasn't aware that there was a problem."

"That's your job, Toby—being aware. Awareness is one of the drivers of excellence. Dr. Rotary has put his own reputation on the line, talking you up as human resources manager. Don't let him down now."

"No, sir."

By this time the mail had already gone out and he was late for the visioning session. On his way to the conference room he spotted Hilda and Deirdre taking a coffee break in the cafeteria. He asked Hilda to run the parcels down to the post office.

She looked at Deirdre, then back at him. "Is that in my job description—*Tobe?*" The tone was far from friendly.

Both women met his eyes defiantly. He was furious but rather than have it out with Hilda he decided to wait and focus his rancor where it belonged.

As he stepped out of the elevator the next day he encountered Dr. Rotary leaving Graphics and received only a brisk nod. He found Bella in her cubicle, where he planned to give her the word, but she was weeping silently.

"I'm *tired,*" she said. "I'm so tired I could die."

Toby had never heard a voice so utterly crushed with fatigue, and without thinking, he reached out to touch her shoulder. She grabbed his hand, began to sob. Her features were screwed into a grimace that clearly showed her age and she should have looked ugly. But she didn't. She didn't. Toby stood there stroking her hair with hands that trembled like an old man's until she leaned away. "I need this job," she said and blew her nose. "I need it."

When he tried to bring up her absences she just shook her head. "Not now, Tobe. Be good."

"This is *serious*. You've used up almost a whole year's worth of sick days." It was at that moment that Toby fully realized his dilemma: How can you bawl out someone who calls you *Tobe?* So instead he invited her to his New Year's brunch, then ended up sending her home early.

When he left work it was raining. The train, jammed with frantic Christmas shoppers and smelling of cheese and stale perfume, stalled between Park and Kendall for twenty minutes of sweaty anxiety while the passengers pretended not to notice a cluster of youths in parkas and baseball caps mugging some fat boy with a neck brace. Folk dancing was a dispiriting interlude: scratchy records of Syrian village music, a crowd of myopic MIT students solemnly trying to *debka* around a chilly room odorous with garlic and wet plaster. Outside, the sidewalks were ankle deep with slush. He got off the subway at Central Square. The windows of the Lebanese market were covered with plywood over which someone had spray-painted *Go back to Irak!!!* By the time he got home his feet were soaked and he was chilled to the bone.

A hunter-green cardigan had come from J. Crew; after trying it on he stretched out on the couch (dinner had given him indigestion) and leafed through the new catalog. The female models were, as usual, grotesquely tall. By holding the pages at a certain angle to the light he could see their areolae. In disgust he tossed the catalog into the trash. He got up and paced for a while. He poured himself some chablis and put Vaughan Williams's Second Symphony on the CD player. But he grew only more restless. The next thing he knew, he was dialing Bella's number.

"Hello," she said. Toby was silent.

"If this is who I think it is," she said, after a moment, "I'm going to come over there, you old goon, and cut your balls off. At least I would if you had any."

Still he said nothing.

"Asshole," she said and hung up.

Toby wondered if he was becoming ridiculous.

NEW YEAR'S EVE he took the train into Harvard Square to pick up a prescription. He rented some videos, then window-shopped for a while on Brattle. On impulse he went into a children's store and bought a stuffed owl for Bella, something to keep on her desk. It might, he thought, cheer her up, perhaps leverage her productivity.

The next morning he dusted and vacuumed, cleaned the bathroom until it sparkled, prepared crudités and hors d'oeuvres. He wrapped Bella's gift, placed the package conspicuously on the mantel, and sat back with a glass of sherry to await his guests. He cued Brahms's Fourth Symphony and rehearsed a faraway look. "Ah," he would say when Bella arrived. "The Romantics."

Three o'clock rolled around and no one showed. Toby

divided the food into lunch-sized portions, which he wrapped and stored in the refrigerator. He plugged *Brideshead Revisited* into the VCR. When the phone rang he grabbed the receiver.

"Toby? Toby, do you have my television?"

"Gran, what did Dr. Finestone tell you?"

"He said to tell him if I experienced ringing in my ears."

"No, Gran, he told you to focus. Now, please—just use the television in the recreation room."

Around seven the bell rang and into the foyer stepped a nervous-looking Bella, followed by two girls, the younger hand in hand with a tall black boy wearing sunglasses and a leather coat. Corkscrews of blue hair dangled from under his New York Yankees cap. Bella introduced the girls as her daughters, Sage and Darshon. The boy was Earl and his handshake nearly broke Toby's fingers. Toby slipped some newspapers over Bella's present and stood by the window as she and her daughters sat together on his couch. They kept their coats on. Toby brought out a tray of smoked turkey, an assortment of crackers, a jar of caviar. The younger of the two girls made a face and whispered in Bella's ear.

"Stop that moaning," said Bella.

"It's not moaning. It's your daughter reminding you to keep your promise."

"Yo," said Earl. "Where you hiding the ashtrays, man?"

"Actually," said Toby, "this is a no-smoking zone."

"Do what?"

"He doesn't want you to smoke in here," said Bella.

"Then why he don't say so?" Earl turned back to Toby. "How old are you anyways? When you go to the liquor store, the man let you buy alcohol?"

"Of course."

Earl laughed into his fist. "What's wrong, Tobe—I'm making you nervous?"

Bella said something to her girls and they all stood up. "OK, everybody," she said, "let's go." She waited by the door, mouthing vague apologies, as her entourage filed into the hall.

Toby could hear Earl laughing as they stepped into the elevator. He washed the dishes. He poured himself another glass of sherry, put on Elgar's Cello Concerto, and sat at the window, watching the Citgo sign flicker through its changes on the far side of the Charles. When the music was over he turned out the lights and went to bed. He lay there listening to the traffic on Mass. Avenue until he fell asleep.

THE MORNING AFTER the president announced the bombing of Baghdad one of Bella's daughters called and said her mother was sick. Toby dialed her number several times from the office and each time got her answering machine. After lunch he was returning from the counter with a cup of Earl Grey when Dr. Rotary, wearing the smile of a man disclaiming a failed joke, called him over to a table crowded with consultants. He motioned Toby into the chair next to his. "I'm hearing a lot of verbiage around Bella's absenteeism."

"I'm taking care of it."

"Meaning you're covering for her?"

"Meaning she's a darned good employee. Not to mention the intellectual capital she represents. She simply happens to be going through a period of transformational change."

He shook his head. "Well, I don't mind telling you that Mr. McLaughlin has some issues around your failure to deal with this proactively. You're expected to incent the team, not simply benchmark. It doesn't look good—especially for a future human resources manager."

Mr. McLaughlin came up behind Toby, holding a tray. "Excuse me," he said. "But I believe you're in my seat."

Feeling his face grow hot, Toby rose and glanced around the cafeteria. "This tea is *scorched*," he said. "It tastes like *medicine*." His voice cracked.

"Little shit," muttered someone across the room.

"*Tobified*," said somebody behind him and everyone in the cafeteria, Dr. Rotary included, laughed.

BY THEN BELLA had used up all her sick days, and though Toby despised micromanagement, he had no other choice than to wordsmith a report and send her to a

disciplinary conference with Dr. Rotary. When she returned he asked her to walk with him along the river to
Kendall Square, ostensibly to pick up some coffee. To the
west the sky was turning pink. The Charles was frozen
solid, with serpentine ski tracks disappearing into the hard
shadows below the Longfellow Bridge. "Listen," he said, "I
can't cover for you anymore."

"Who's asking you to?"

"Let's cooperate. I'm on your side."

She laughed, her breath steaming in the cold air.
"Right."

"Bella, I'd like to offer you something beyond the
boundaries of a purely work relationship but that's just not
in the cards right now."

She looked amazed. "Hey," she said, "don't flatter yourself, buddy. I've got all sorts of plans for the future and
you're not in any of them."

"Fine," he doggedly went on, "but going forward
it would probably be a good idea if you'd start calling
me Toby."

"I'm getting cold," she said.

What could he do? He was outflanked. Intellectual
capital or not, she was a woman on the way down and he
knew it. Why participate? He had a fairly good idea what
that would get him: bounced checks, four-in-the-morning
telephone calls, public scenes—a chance to shoulder some
of the shabby luggage that her sort dragged through the

world. So he fell back on the forms. Sometimes, he realized, you have nothing else. General Gordon, for example—to some his putting on full dress uniform and stepping to the head of the stairway to await an unspeakable death might seem an act of despair. Not to Toby.

She lasted until the end of Desert Storm.

That final morning Toby dressed with more care than usual: again the burgundy bow tie—this time, though, with an argyle vest. When he came into Bella's cubicle with the termination form she glanced from the paper to him. "Tobe," she said, "you don't have a clue, do you?"

"I'm sorry. I'm afraid it's out of my hands now."

She gave him a tight smile and nodded. For a moment she stared at his five-year service pin. Then she kissed the tips of her fingers and pressed them to his cheek.

Toby took back her keys and magnetic card and escorted her from the premises. Hilda and Deirdre pretended to be deeply engrossed in their work as the two passed. Bella and Toby stood in silence for a few moments on the front landing. Even though it was sunny, the magnolias already dropping their waxy blossoms on the sidewalk, the morning was cold and she was shivering.

"I wish," said Toby, "that this could have turned out differently."

"Show me somebody who doesn't." She went down the steps and headed off toward Kendall Square, wobbling a little on her high heels.

He marched back into the office and, after explaining that Bella had left to pursue other opportunities, dropped a stack of photocopying on the desk of each graphic artist.

"Photocopying," said Deirdre, "isn't part of our job description."

"Your job description," he parried, "includes additional duties as assigned by the graphics scheduler. Section two-zero-six of Employee Ethics, moreover, requires employees to respect the administrative authority of those directing the work. Now let's clear the decks for action."

Deirdre tried to put a bold face on it. "Aye aye, Tobe."

"And the next person who calls me that goes before Dr. Rotary with a charge of insubordination. If you think I'm joking go right ahead and try me. *Comprende?*"

They didn't like it but by that time they knew better than to bandy M&R bylaws with Toby Garfield.

He spent that afternoon cleaning his office. Everyone had gone home for the day when he came upon Bella's stuffed owl in the back of his file cabinet. He'd just decided to take the thing outside and toss it into the Dumpster when the phone rang. It was Dr. Rotary.

He took the elevator to the sixth floor. The sun was going down as he stepped into Dr. Rotary's office. "Toby," he said, "you've been hiding an iron fist beneath that velvet glove." The words had clearly been rehearsed but there was, Toby felt, no mistaking their sincerity.

He made grateful noises.

Dr. Rotary peered at the stuffed animal in Toby's hand. "What the devil have you got there—a frog?"

"Just something I found in my office."

"Well, I have a granddaughter who'd love it. Do you mind?"

"Of course not." From the window Toby had just enough time to pick out his apartment and then the last light melted like butter between the buildings below. Darkness fell quickly, leaving purple lights trembling on the river. So, he reflected, Hilda had wrestling, Deirdre had church, McLaughlin had Rotary, Rotary's grandkid had Bella's stuffed owl. And what did Toby Garfield have? Not a darned thing.

But he was wrong. The next week he was promoted to human resources manager. He had, after all, proven himself. Admittedly his response to the crisis was a little slow in coming but when it finally did come it made plenty clear the peril of interpreting his laid-back style as a symptom of weakness.

Everything has run smoothly since then, and that brief skirmish, like the Gulf War itself, seems to belong to the distant past. Months afterward Hilda ran into Bella coming back from class on the subway around ten at night, half asleep over her books. She was temping again. Once as Toby stopped for gas on his way back from Hibernian Meadows he thought he saw Bella coming out of a pet store in a Bob Marley T-shirt. When he looked back she was gone.

Of course that was years ago. Since then, according to Dierdre, she moved to New Orleans. But every so often —walking through the Common, sitting in a theater— Toby will catch a whiff of patchouli and find himself tempted to call her and ask how things are working out. Her number must be listed.

Frank

Frank owned a little music store—ToneDog—and it was right before the Gulf War that Wycek called him there. *Tell me, Prez, what kind of guitar would you recommend for a two-thousand-pound man?*

Frank hadn't heard that voice in years but he knew it right away. "A large one," he said.

Wycek started laughing and went into a long coughing fit. When he recovered he wheezed that he would be at the Greyhound terminal the following afternoon.

Frank spent the next morning regaling his less-than-spellbound staff with stories about his old war buddy. When it was time for him to leave, two Honduran boys with pink hair were trying out amps over by the guitar display, blasting ill-tempered E chords loud enough to shake clouds of dust from the walls. The racket was unbearable.

Frank changed the register tape and shouted instructions to Tuyen, the new salesclerk. The kid was a freshman at Berklee College of Music—a hard bop zealot—and since Frank was leaving him in charge for the first time he felt compelled to explain once again how it works: If you treat every customer who prefers Slash to Charlie Christian like a moron you're not going to move a whole lot of gear; if you don't move a whole lot of gear you're going to be out of a job. "Look," he yelled, "just try to be diplomatic for an hour or so. That's all I'm asking."

Tuyen stared with loathing at the pink-haired boys. "Diplomatic," he mouthed.

Frank stepped out of the store into a light snow. Feedback howled behind him as he ducked across the street and caught the subway to the city.

The Greyhound terminal was packed, the floor awash with slush, strewn with sodden napkins and crushed paper cups. Unshaven men in baseball caps streamed to and from the pay phones, and over by the lockers some Central American Indian women wearing bright red tunics sat impassively in a row of molded plastic seats in front of pay TVs. Then he spotted Wycek. This was how life laid its little jokes on you. You remember a lean dark-eyed guy with a handlebar mustache, the joker who extended for two heavy tours, then came home and ran AK-47s to Colombia, the one who sends postcards every year or so from places like Lima and Khartoum. And who shows up? Some little man in a leather jacket, two puffs of curly gray hair sticking out like earmuffs from beneath his Lakers cap. Even from where he stood Frank saw the yellow tinge of Wycek's eyes. A garbled announcement blared from a loudspeaker as Wycek humped a stained daypack onto his shoulders and worked his way through the crowd toward Frank, wearing his age like a hand-painted tie. In a cloud of tobacco and sweat he came up and put an arm around Frank's shoulders. "My man," he said. "Freewheeling Franklin."

On the way back to the subway station they cut through the Public Gardens. The weather had cleared and the late sun cast pink streaks across the frozen ponds. The spines of the trees were black against the sky. Wycek lit a joint. "Suit yourself," he said when Frank demurred. "Time to go home, Prez. Time to go home. I haven't put in an appearance in a long long time." His voice rose an octave and took on a dizzy singsong lilt. "I'm thinking when I get to Baltimore I should zip over to DC and check out the Vets' Memorial. See if they turned it into the Search and Destroy Theme Park yet."

On the other side of the river they stepped at his insistence into a bar across the square from the soldiers' home and took two stools near the window. The TV behind the counter was tuned to CNN and the president was talking about spending the night in prayer with Billy Graham. "I got a bad feeling about this," said Wycek. "Try to find a skin flick on cable and every channel got nothing but camels and lifers."

"America's standing tall," said Frank.

"Means it's time to get down." Wycek signaled the bartender, a pockmarked Asian kid with shoulder-length hair. "Hey—Prez—how about a couple of double Wild Turkeys down here?"

"Ginger ale for me," said Frank.

As soon as the drinks came Wycek took off his cap and wiped his dome with a cocktail napkin. "Still buying shots from some Saigon cowboy. Now ain't that one hell of a note?" He flinched and bent over the bar. Blisters of sweat popped out on his forehead. "Hold one," he said, and wobbled off to the men's room.

The bartender fixed Frank with a nasty grin. "Don't look like your partner's doing so good, dude."

Frank stared at him till he went back to the far end of the counter. Through a clear patch in the steamed window he could see the silhouettes of tattered half-frozen figures on the benches across the street. Wycek returned, bright-eyed, flaring his nostrils. "Back in the *mode,*" he said, drumming his fists on the counter. He knocked back his drink and called for another.

It was dark when they left. Across from the Salvadoran record store down the street two tiny women were locking up Madame Dixon's Fortune-Telling Parlor. Sneakers dangled from the telephone wires, and beneath the recent bloom of yellow ribbons and red, white, and, blue bunting, every flat surface was spray-painted with the insignia of local drug lords. The two men headed up the hill toward a triple-decker set back from the street. As they came up the walk past the ice-glazed maples Frank saw his younger brother, Eddie, staring morosely down at them from the third-story kitchen window.

WHILE WYCEK SHOWERED, Frank looked over his bills, then stuffed them into the freezer. Eddie sat at the table with his hair slicked straight back, fragrant with the Uncrossing Oil he bought at Madame Dixon's. "I called in sick today," he said. Eddie stocked produce at a market around the corner from ToneDog, and the immigrants he worked with rode his ass without mercy. "I couldn't handle it," he said. "Yesterday they stole my umbrella."

"Sorry about that."

"Diversity's fine but it works both ways. Speaking of which, that girl who gives lessons at your store called. She says she'll meet you here."

Frank still couldn't get over the change in his brother. Years ago, before Frank got drafted and Eddie went off to California to become a poet, women used to stop on the sidewalk and stare after him. It wasn't just his looks. Eddie was striking all right but more than that it was a barometrically precise instinct for style. Hair. Clothes. Just watching him cross a room back then, as close as you could get to a swagger while still projecting vulnerability, Frank knew his brother was destined for the sorts of blessings he himself was forever denied. Why? Some dinginess of spirit, he supposed, perceptible only to whatever gods amused themselves with glossy folks like Eddie.

That summer Eddie had called from Louisiana. He'd been beaten cross-eyed and left for dead deep in the swamps —but as for how and why he'd ended up there and who had done it Eddie hadn't a clue. A few months later he showed up at Frank's doorstep, a pale and subdued version of the kid who'd left more than a decade before. For sure, he still had a victim's chastened air, as if at any moment he expected a slap across the back of his head. The drowsy insouciance of old was nowhere to be seen. After he moved in, Frank noticed a photo in his room that showed him on a sailboat, tanned, long-haired, one arm around a pretty, dark-haired woman, facing the camera with the old insinuating smile.

Wycek stepped out of the bathroom with a towel around his hips and went into the front room. Eddie stared at the burn scars lacing his back.

The buzzer rang and up the stairs came Ramona, stooping the way tall girls do, with her guitar in a gig bag. The Dominicans across the street had their boom box out on the fire escape. Frank's windows rattled along with the horn riffs and percolating bass. *"Merengue,"* said Ramona and wiggled her hips.

"Right," said Frank. As if he knew anything about it. The truth was, he'd pretty much stopped listening to music. "Hey, this is Wycek. The guy I was telling you about."

"Sweetheart," said Wycek, squinting up at Ramona, "me and this cat go back a long way."

"Yeah, Frank was telling me about the war."

"The war," said Wycek, nodding rapidly, as if something had been confirmed. "I'll tell you about the war. Here's all you need to know. When we came back we landed at McChord—two days out of Lang Vei and still wearing muddy jungle boots, right?"

Ramona looked toward the door. "Is this going to take long?"

"Dig this. Waiting for us on the runway are three girls in Santa Claus hats and red minidresses. Shitload of reporters. When you'd walk by, the girls would hand you a little sack of candy and say, *Merry Christmas.*"

Ramona's band, Barbies with Muscles, was playing that night in Cambridge; Frank had talked Wycek into going to hear them after dinner. Eddie decided to go and the four of them walked down the hill to a Portuguese restaurant. The place was jammed but they found a corner booth opposite the door where Frank could sit with his back to the wall. Wycek ordered a Wild Turkey, then lurched off to the men's room. Five younger guys in blazers and Santa Claus hats grabbed a table across from them and started bellowing about hospital mergers. Ramona asked Frank why Wycek called everybody Prez.

"It's a joke," he told her. "Just a joke."

On the far side of the room a chubby dark-haired man

in a pink suit raised his wineglass. "This *Eddie!*" he shouted. "I *naw-jus!*" The two women with him snapped their gum and watched Frank's table with dead eyes.

"For crying out loud," said Eddie. "It's my boss. The one day I call in sick I have to run into him." He returned the toast with one of those smiles worn by men forced to walk toy poodles. "He's the worst of all. Talking about me in Portuguese. Making everybody laugh."

Wycek came back, wiping his nose. His skull showed beneath the waxy skin. Ramona asked if he was all right.

"Head cramps," he said and tapped his fingers on the table until the water glasses shook. "Nothing but head cramps."

"The thing is," said Ramona, "you're making me nervous."

"Nervous in the service? Nervous in the time of the abomination? Nervous in the latter time of the indignation?"

"This *Eddie!*" yelled Eddie's boss. "I *naw-jus!*"

"Boss problems," Frank told Wycek.

"You got a boss," he said, "you got yourself a problem. I'll tell you what—you should try the job search number if you've done a little bit of time. Back in Detroit I was flat getting down next to it."

"Next to what?" said Eddie. "Poverty?"

"*Poverty?* I'm talking about ain't got no money. A couple of these johns even asked me to take a urine test. I mean, I spent two years in the bad bush—you know this is no shit

—and I did it *high.* And now I'm supposed to piss in a bottle so I can ring up rubbers for some silly tool in a crewcut?"

"This *Eddie.* I *naw-jus!* "

Eddie tried to make himself small. "This is getting old," he muttered.

"Sorry about that," said Wycek. "Why don't you just stroll over there and sift some sand? Take that fool down to Knuckle Junction."

"I need the job."

"In that case, Prez, keep your story to yourself because I can't use it in my business." Wycek grabbed three rolls from a basket on the table and started juggling them. "This is the type of thing that takes total concentration," he said. "You got to be centered. Got to feel the Tao."

"Wait a minute," said Eddie. "You think I don't know what this world is like? You think I don't know it's just waiting to trash me? Shit," he said, looking from Wycek to Frank. "*Shit.* I don't believe you two even *have* a story."

One of the men at the next table said something and the others laughed unpleasantly.

Wycek tossed the rolls back into the basket and smiled at Frank. "How about it—do we have a story?"

Before he could answer, the TV in the lounge started blaring "America the Beautiful." All around them people rose from their seats with exultant smiles and began to sing. Eddie started to get up too but Wycek grabbed his arm. "Sit," he said.

One of the men at the next table peeled off his blazer. "I suggest you stand up," he said.

"I suggest you put your little jacket back on," said Wycek. "Before you catch cold."

Frank couldn't hear the music anymore and he was feeling better than he had in years. The man's eyes changed. "Hey," he said, with a fake grin. "I'll see you later."

"Pack a lunch," said Wycek.

Frank heard the music end and the room came back into focus as people reclaimed their seats. "I don't think they're going to serve us," said Eddie.

"Do tell," said Wycek.

By the time they walked to the subway station Wycek seemed to have wilted. He wobbled across the sidewalk to the curb and sat down heavily with his head in his hands. "I don't think I can hack going to a club," he said. "I'll just head on back to Franklin's crib by myself."

Frank looked at Ramona. "You go ahead," he said. "I'll catch you next time you guys play."

"In that case," said Eddie, "maybe I'll tag along after all."

He and Ramona went down the stairs to the station and Frank watched until the red pompon on top of Ramona's ski cap disappeared. When he looked down Wycek raised his eyebrows. "Didn't mean to blow your scene."

"What scene?"

Wycek heaved himself to his feet. "Franklin no smoka the dopa. Drinks ginger ale. That's your secret—the straight life? That's how you got next to that sweet young beanpole?"

"She gives lessons at the store. Heavy metal theory, two-handed tapping, that sort of thing."

"I hear you talking," said Wycek. "And I hear what you're saying."

"It's not like that."

"It's always like that."

The beauty parlor across from the market where Eddie worked was filled with Latinos sporting Clark Gable mustaches. Wycek shoved his face against the window. "We're *trouble!* " he yelled. "We're *bad* trouble!" The men stared back impassively. "Go on—ask us if we're trouble."

"Why should they?" said Frank. "We'd lie."

By the time they made it up the hill Wycek was staggering, soaked with sweat. Frank barely managed to get him up the stairs.

"I keep looking at that picture of Eddie and that chick," he said while Frank fixed him a bed on the couch. "How does a cat like that end up with a two-thousand-yard stare?"

"The chickens coming home to roost, probably. Bounced checks. Borrowed cars that ended up in the city yard. A lot of other guys' girlfriends who all of a sudden wanted to explore their feelings for him."

"So how did he lose that smile?"

"Head cramps," said Frank.

FRANK NEVER SLEPT well. He didn't like the dark. Way back in his mind the shutters would open and he'd start thinking of all the faces he'd never see again. It was as if the dead came to his door, covered with red dust. He'd hear them gathering on the porch—tired ashen boys with short haircuts and old men's eyes.

He was lying with the lights on, trying to figure out how to make the rent, the car payment, payroll taxes, when his mother and older sister, Patti, called from Providence. "How's Eddie?" asked his mom. In the background Tennessee Ernie Ford was singing "Old Rugged Cross."

"Hanging in there." Frank could hear the chop of small-arms fire from down the hill.

"Such a well-spoken boy," she said. "How could anyone do something like that to him?"

"We called," said Patti, "to let you know we've been talking to Gina."

"She's remarried," Frank's mother went on when he didn't say anything. "To a wonderful man."

"Yes," said Frank. "She would be."

"Listen to him," said Patti. "Right away, that attitude. Just because she's getting on with her life."

"Oh, and I'm not?"

"They'd like kids of their own," said his mother. "Their own family. And Gina's husband wants to adopt little Ruthie. They'll pay for everything. All you have to do is sign some papers."

"I'll think about it."

"Ask yourself what's best for Ruthie. This way she'd have the same last name as her sisters and brothers."

"Can we talk about something else?"

"The great entrepreneur wants to talk about something else," said Patti.

"I'll never understand any of this," said his mother and started to cry. "Oh," she sobbed, "what happened to our family? Why can't we be *normal?*"

Later as Frank lay listening to Wycek snore in the front room he thought about a black-and-white snapshot his father took when Frank was about five. Eddie sat on his lap and they faced the camera with gap-toothed grins. The photo hung in the hallway the whole time the boys were growing up. When their father stared at it Frank used to imagine that he was thinking something like this: Here is what we fought for; here is what Bastogne was all about. But after he got back from Vietnam—before Pop got arrested for stealing TVs and vanished from their lives— Frank would catch him glancing every so often from that picture to him with the expression of a man who keeps adding two and two and coming up with zip.

RAMONA DIDN'T HAVE any more lessons for the day so it was easy for Frank to talk her into coming with him to the aquarium. They caught an inbound train. While they clattered through the dark Frank tried to explain Wycek.

"Once," he said, "I thought he was the only truly righteous man I'd ever met. I mean, this is the guy who told me how it works: Sometimes you ride it like you find it. Or you die."

"That doesn't sound like much of a favor."

"I was new. No one said he had to tell me anything."

The train lurched and threw Ramona against him in a welter of bony angles. She blushed and moved away.

That evening he got home and found Wycek and Eddie listening to a Marvin Gaye tape. They'd already gone through a six-pack of Rolling Rock. Wycek was juggling potatoes. Eddie sprawled on the couch, plunking away on Frank's bass, which he'd found in the closet where Frank kept old pictures and clothes—things he didn't need anymore. Halfway through "Mercy Mercy Me" Wycek tossed the potatoes to Eddie. "Come on," he said, bobbing his head like a turkey. "Show me what you got, Prez."

When Eddie just sat there, Wycek looked at Frank and the next thing he knew the two of them were shuffling around the floor in a clumsy Temps imitation, snapping their fingers, and lip-synching to "What's Happening Brother." Back in the mode, grooving, just like down in the bunker. Eddie stayed put, flipping the potatoes from hand to hand. The song ended. Wycek collapsed in a chair, gray-faced and coughing, and squinted up at Frank. "Eddie and me are going over to Somerville to hear Barbies with Muscles. What do you say?"

"I say Ramona and I see enough of each other at work."

"She is pretty young," said Eddie.

"Did I say I wanted to marry her?"

"I forgot," said Wycek. "You just want to guess her weight."

"I'll give you some advice," said Eddie. He dropped a potato and bent to pick it up. "You only get one shot at true love."

"What's this?" said Frank. "The poetic perspective?"

"One shot," said Eddie. "If you blow that you've got to adjust your expectations a little. For convenience. And for a user-friendly relationship you want somebody young."

"Me," said Wycek, "I go for a mature babe. See, if she's using a walker she can't outrun me."

"You want somebody good-looking," Eddie went on, "and not too smart." Suddenly he was bright red and his eyes glistened. "And you absolutely, absolutely stay away from the ones you can't forget."

Wycek rose with some difficulty and slapped him on the back. "Edward," he said, as he pulled on his jacket, "I believe you got a story your ownself."

The buzzer rang and he and Eddie went trampling down the stairs. Ramona's laugh rang out in the stairwell. *"Pendejo,"* she said. Frank waited for her by the door. A moment later he heard footsteps on the stairs and someone knocked. He yanked open the door. There stood two young black guys in porkpie hats, looking him up and down with stony contempt. "Yo," said one of them. "Where's Wycek?"

"Word," said the other. "Where's the man?"

"The man," said Frank, "been gone longer than you could ever imagine."

THE BOMBING OF Baghdad had been going on for a couple of days when Frank came home and found Wycek and Eddie glued to the TV. A roomful of reporters in Tel Aviv, voices cracking with panic, were putting on gas masks. On the coffee table was a mirror heaped with coke. Wycek asked if Frank wanted a taste.

"Listen to me," said Frank. "I've made a conscious decision not to live like this. Don't bring this scene into my house. I don't want to be around it." He looked at Eddie, who sat with three lemons in his lap, smiling sheepishly at the floor. "And you—I thought you knew better."

"What did I do?"

"What did you do. Look at you. Sitting here in the dark, watching the tube like a couple of junkies."

Wycek laughed silently. "Prez, you phenomenon my mind."

"How can you even stand to watch this anyway?"

"It's history," said Eddie and made a half-assed attempt to juggle the lemons.

"History? *History?* You know what history is? History is alibis. These people are going to die right in front of you."

"There's a lot of that going around," said Wycek. "Anyway it's just another trip on the planet. In the latter time of the indignation."

Frank went to the kitchen, poured a glass of water, and drank it down. Through the window he saw the moon hanging over the Prudential Building. A few dim stars. This, it suddenly seemed to him, was how it would end: a bunch of terrified people in a sealed room, trying to figure out how to put on their gas masks and wondering if there was anybody out there watching.

"Four out of five doctors," said Wycek, "recommend morphine to their patients with head cramps."

Frank opened the freezer and stared at the stacks of bills bearded with frost. "Have you eaten anything, Wycek?"

He didn't answer.

"Wycek," said Eddie a few minutes later. "He wants to know if you're hungry."

The TV droned on. When Frank heard the lemons thumping on the floor he turned and saw Wycek's head silhouetted against the screen. Eddie stepped gingerly into the kitchen. "Hey," he said. "You better come in here."

FRANK PUT A ticket on his Visa, left Ramona and Tuyen in charge of the store, and flew to Baltimore. It was a cold bright day. Wycek's three brothers met Frank at the airport. In a Chevy wagon that smelled of tobacco and Right Guard they drove past miles and miles of sooty red-brick row homes to a cemetery. Frank was the only friend who showed up for the funeral. Wycek's mother wore a hat with a veil; after the service she stumbled back to the car with the flag under her arm, her husband a couple of steps behind her. The brothers and Frank stood for a while under the bare trees, breathing out clouds of steam. There was some stiff, vaguely accusatory talk about how Sheldon had never stayed in touch. Frank tried to show by his expression that he wasn't responsible but everyone was clearly relieved when he caught a bus to the Amtrak station.

He bought a ticket to Washington. Despite the cold the Mall was swarming with tourists, most of them waving little American flags. By the time he got to the Memorial with its T-shirt booths and paunchy sobbing vets in camouflage fatigues and boonie hats he was ready to bag it but since he was there he searched the Wall for a couple of medics from the company. He found them at the far tip of one black marble wing, ran his fingers across their names. And didn't feel a thing.

On the flight back he closed his eyes and thought about Ramona, her plump lower lip and crooked nose in the aquarium's blue light. He took a cab home from the airport, dropped off his bags, and walked to the store in a freezing rain. Broken umbrellas jutted from the trash cans, loose ribs and ripped nylon flapping in the wind. Tattered fliers for Barbies with Muscles clung disconsolately to the telephone poles. When he arrived at ToneDog the windows were steamed over and a kid with a blond perm was mangling Paganini Caprices on a sunburst Strat. Eddie sat on a stool next to the counter in hysterics. "I walked out," he bawled. "I told my boss to screw himself. I'll end up on the street."

"Get on the phone," said Frank. "Call him."

"I'll *die*."

"Eddie, it's simple. Call the guy and tell him you're sorry."

"It's too late."

"Do it now."

While Eddie dialed the market Frank unplugged the kid with the Strat and told him to beat it. Then he stepped into the break room and turned on the lights. Tuyen and Ramona sprang off the couch. Frank looked at them for a moment, then closed the door and went to sit behind the counter. Eddie was gone. In the parking lot across the street some kids in parkas were ripping the windshield wipers off a red Plymouth Sundance. Ramona, pink-cheeked and disheveled, came out to the showroom. "The thing is," she said, "we were just talking." A horn beeped outside.

"You lock up," said Frank. "You and Tuyen. I'm going to the aquarium."

It was dark when he got to the subway station. He caught an inbound train and sat across from a couple of girls carrying Tello's bags and an old man in a pipe-fitters jacket. Good-looking and not too smart—who else would ever take men seriously? Somewhere past Maverick Station he looked up. The pipe fitter was gone and staring back at him from the window was his own reflection, this guy he confronted with varying surprise every morning in his bathroom mirror. The one who knows how it works.

IT SNOWED AGAIN on Monday and he closed up early. On the way home he stopped by the market. Eddie, wearing a new cotton turtleneck under his green apron, was juggling mangoes for Ramona and her bass player, a burly young woman with pierced eyebrows. Eddie dropped one of the mangoes. "Don't panic," he drawled, "it's organic." When he saw Frank he motioned to the back door. The women whispered to each other as the brothers went out to the parking lot.

"It's all straightened out," said Eddie. "And I appreciate your advice."

"It wasn't that big a deal."

"Indeed? Well, it was for me." He brushed snow off his shoulders. "As you know, Prez, I used to be somebody else."

And Frank wanted to waste him. He wanted to empty a clip in his face, watch it dissolve into a pink mist. "Don't call me that," he said and walked away. Back home he drank two glasses of water and stepped into the bathroom to wash his face. Eddie's bottle of Uncrossing Oil was no longer on the stand next to the sink; in its place was a fresh bar of olive oil soap. Frank drew the blinds and crawled into bed.

The Dominicans' boom box woke him up. He went to the kitchen window. It was still snowing but on the other side of the river the sky was dark blue, the Prudential Building flashing in the sunlight. He wrestled open the window, and smells of cilantro and onions blew into the kitchen. A snowplow went clanking past. The bent old women from Madame Dixon's came up the hill, long skirts crusted with snow. When they saw Frank at the window they stopped, as if they were waiting for something.

And he found himself thinking about a night long ago, in Vietnam, when he and Wycek slipped into a village to buy some weed. They crept back out in the moonlight, stoned silly, through a cemetery cratered by air strikes. Something crunched beneath their boots. They grabbed each other's hands, like little kids. And at the same instant they both shouted.

Bones!

Stretch

Behold the Lean Machine. The Big Boy. Truth be told, Stretch has been known to get a little wild. Trouble clamors in his very blood and won't be denied. But his sentence—six months, minus time served, chopping elderberry alongside every paved road in Orleans Parish—is behind him now. And the morning after his kickout finds him in the Ninth Ward, heading for Chain Drive's place, hoping his old partner will be in a reasonable mood. Reasonable enough, anyway, to put the past behind him and give up a few Percosets. As it happens, Stretch is beset by nerves. It's late summer, a nervous season for the Big Boy.

He's been pounding on Chain Drive's door for nearly five minutes, the only white face in miles, when a woman in a Malcolm X T-shirt steps out of the New Seven Powers Drug Store across the street. "You looking for the bald dude," she says, opening up a big red umbrella against the sun, "you ain't looking for nobody at all."

When Stretch asks where he is she shakes her head indignantly and goes back inside. Stretch catches a bus in front of the plasma center, transfers at Canal, and plunges into the Quarter. By noon he's managed to hustle a couple of grams of stepped-on crank to some offshore workers in Jackson Square. At the A&P he buys a Milky Way and a bottle of peach brandy. It chaps him that his partner's booked. Fortunately, Chain Drive's sister, Blondelle, works at Mystic Orbit, a fortune-telling joint on Royal.

He's half a block away when a blue van with script painted across the back door whips past on Toulouse. Stretch sees a brindled sheepdog bolt from the sidewalk toward the van. It gallops with a brute purpose that suggests a personal grievance. Everything slows down. A family in identical T-shirts and green visors points to the oncoming van. Their faces are stamped with disbelief. The driver hits his brakes. Everything speeds up again and the family scatters as the van heaves onto the sidewalk. It plows through some trash cans and screeches to a stop. Five or six stiff-looking black men in suits climb out, shouting at one another in French. With the speed of desire a crowd gathers. A woman in a white blouse pushes through the tourists in front of Mystic Orbit. "Dudley!" she screams.

When Stretch gets there she's kneeling on the pavement. Blood spatters her sleeves. Beside her the dog lies there in the lumpy way of all dead creatures and Stretch peels off his cowboy shirt and covers him up. The woman grabs his arm. "My God," she says, "it can't be like this. Tell me it's not like this."

Her curly hair is streaked with gray and she's squeezing his arm, so close he can smell patchouli. "No," he hears himself say. "It's not like this."

The cops are coming and there's nothing he can do so he steps into Mystic Orbit. Incense is burning and upstairs someone is listening to ZZ Top. Blondelle sits at a table with a tarot deck in front of her, the ring in her nose catching the light through the window. She sweeps up the cards and shuffles them but not before Stretch gets a good look at what's on top: the Fool. "Well, well," she says. "Look what they let out on the street. I thought we'd seen the last of your sorry ass."

"That makes two of us." He'd sworn he wouldn't come back after the Mardi Gras Zulu Parade back in '91— some fool high-stepping behind a brass band, had his little boy wrapped up in tinfoil and cardboard to look like a missile. The fool carried a sign that said SADDAM HUSSEIN THIS SCUDS FOR YOU! Up and down both sides of Canal everyone clapped and a mood came down on Stretch. He split that very afternoon. But a couple of years on the road convinced him that it was the same everywhere. And here he was, back in the Quarter.

He moves to the window and sees the woman still

kneeling next to her dog while the cops talk to the black men. He turns back to Blondelle. "What did you tell that poor girl?"

"Told her to leave that dog outside."

"You call that good business?"

"I call it I'm tired of everybody coming around here looking for they lives to work out different. Looking for Disneyland. What do you want anyways, Stretch?"

"Something for my nerves."

She shakes her head like what can you do and goes upstairs. Even with the incense Stretch can still smell patchouli. A few minutes later Blondelle comes back down with one of the bikers who own the place, a sorry wasted dude with a mouse-colored beard. "Things a little dry now," he whispers. "Having to dip into my own personal stash." He hands Stretch an ancient can whose faded label reads *Asthma-Dor.* "Just take what you can pick up on the tip of a blade," he says. "And not no more." Stretch hands him a bill and he goes upstairs. The music gets louder. Stretch catches Blondelle looking at his wallet, that picture of his younger brother, Hallett, at the missionary school in El Chorrillo, standing behind a bunch of solemn dark-haired kids in white shirts and blue shorts. Blondelle gives him a nasty smile.

"You're so slick," he says, "how about you tell my fortune?"

"That's wrote all over your face."

"Does it say I'll get next to that little pigeon who just left here?"

"Say you best save your charm for my brother."

What it is, he's never gotten around to paying Chain Drive for the truckload of cowboy shirts they boosted before Stretch left town. "He moved, girl. Where he is?"

She lights a cigarette. "Over at the Hummingbird Motel. One thing—don't let him know I was the one told you."

Stretch hits her with a little air guitar. "Blondelle, you got to trust the Lean Machine." He holds up the can of Asthma-Dor. "You figure this will fix up my nerves?"

She blows smoke from her nose. "Nerves be the least of your worries."

STRETCH RENTS HIMSELF a room at the Capri and the next morning he breezes back over to the Quarter to make his rounds. Rumbling air conditioners drip rusty water on the sidewalks. It's so hot the air's turned a fishbowl green. Break time finds him on St. Ann, kicking back on a cement stoop with a bottle of peach brandy. His nerves are getting worse. The next thing he knows the shutter behind him flies open and whacks him on the head. And there in the doorway stands the pigeon, holding a box full of kitchen supplies. Her hair is pulled back in a thick braid.

"Come on, Chief," she says. "You've got to give me a little room here." She picks her way down the steps past him and loads the box into the trunk of a brick-red Saturn with *'Round Midnight Graphics* painted on the door. The backseat is already stuffed with clothes and more boxes. On her way back she stops at the foot of the stoop and lifts the braid off her neck. "That was you yesterday, wasn't it?"

"I mean."

"Sorry about your shirt."

"Sorry about your old buddy."

"Well, as a dog my old buddy was fairly worthless. But he made a terrific witness. Every time I'd turn around there he was, snuffling along behind me like I knew where I was going. And all the dumb little rituals—buying his food, filling his bowl, taking him to the vet. Oh, what am I going to do without him?"

She's about to lose it so Stretch looks her up and down, kind of sly, and holds up the bottle. "How about a taste?"

"It's a little early for me," she says. Turns away for a second to bank a sad smile off the sidewalk. She likes his style. *Hot* dog—a righteous woman's laugh in the corner pocket.

"Looks like you're fixing to leave us," he says.

"I'm moving into my own house," she says, and Stretch notices a pale crease on her lower lip where a long time ago somebody must have busted her a good one. "*My* house," she says. "I mean, can you feature what that feels like?"

"No," he says. "Not hardly."

"Well," she says, after a minute, "take care of yourself." She goes into the apartment.

And Stretch sees himself floating in those eyes like a dead leaf in God's still waters. He's been Slain in the Spirit. On the corner of Iberville and Burgundy two motorcycle cops watch him breeze past. "There goes a twenty-four-carat shitbird," says one. Stretch doesn't mind. He's got a good buzz on now. The last woman he had, this is back when his little brother was alive, she worked at the K&B and couldn't relate to his lifestyle. All hamburgers and cigarettes, she said. But who's to say a man can't turn it around?

THE NEXT MORNING Stretch cruises down Royal past Mystic Orbit. It's quiet, with only a few spooked-looking tourists on the streets. Lying in the shade in front of The Five of Clubs is Colonel, Turley's old basset hound. The dog heaves himself up off the cement and follows Stretch inside. George Jones is on the box. In a booth by the back door some sailors are half asleep. Turley puts down his paper and tugs his yellow Hawaiian shirt over his gut. "Stretch," he says. At first he's not about to give up any drinks but Stretch jives him about his nerves and the time of year till he finally pours a draft. "That dumb shit calls himself Chain Drive was in last night," he says. "Hollering all about you got something belongs to him."

"The Lean Machine got something for everybody."

"Jesus, Stretch, this here's your life. Look at yourself."

"Look at your ownself."

Then they're both staring at the picture over the register: their little brother Hallett after his first year at Bible college, right before he went to Panama. He's on the dock at the family camp, got old Colonel up on his hind legs and they're dancing. "Damn," says Turley. "He was really something, wasn't he?"

"I mean." All of a sudden Stretch is having a hard time talking. Maybe a month after the Panama invasion he and Turley picked up Hallett at the airport, sad-eyed, his skin mottled with the pink of healing burns, looking about three sizes too small for his suit. He was quiet till they got to St. John Parish, but a mile or two off the interstate he spotted the yellow ribbons painted on the oaks alongside River Road. "Let me out," he said. "Right here."

"Now, look," said Turley, "you got pretty near the whole town waiting on you."

"Let them wait," said Hallett. He got out and started walking back down River Road. Between the shoulders his suit was dark with sweat.

"Well," said Turley, "what do we tell people?"

"We tell them our little brother been qualified."

Dead too many years now, Hallett still lies in Stretch's memory like sunshine on broken glass.

Turley flips old Colonel a pickled egg and snaps his paper. "Anything else I can get for you?"

"How about a job?"

"I got enough troubles without you on the payroll again."

"Turley, I won't beg you. Like the song says, I been born again. There's a change in me. It's time to scope out the straight life."

Turley looks out toward the street where some old boy pushes a Lucky Dog cart through a slick of sunshine. "Well," he says, "I know somebody looking for a fry cook over at the lake shore."

Pigeon, Stretch is thinking, as Turley writes down the particulars, you got yourself a *boy*. Turley hands him the napkin. "Don't make me ugly," he says.

Time to make his rounds. Stretch picks up a couple of Milky Ways and a coffee at the Circle K. He cuts over to Conti and heads toward the levee. Across from the old courthouse, cooks and taxi drivers step from the shade to give him high fives. *What's up, Stretch?* Gold teeth flashing, everybody having a good old time. Truth be told, he's starting to feel pretty mellow his ownself. A job coming up, spending loot to flash for You-Know-Who. Dancing in the Spirit.

Then who should come strutting up Decatur but Chain Drive, bald head flashing in the sun. "Hey," he says. "Where's my shirts?"

Stretch isn't crazy about his attitude but he jives him a little anyway. "Behold the man," he says. "Behind the beat and back on the street. All that good trash."

"I asked you something, Stretch."

He's seen what Chain Drive can do. A few years ago—this was way out in the country by Morgan City—Stretch watched him beat a California boy into bad health. He'd be lying if he said it wasn't an ugly thing to see and God knows he'd forget it if he could. Is the Lean Machine packing? You know he is. And there was a time when he would have drawn down on Chain Drive's ass but he decides that lifestyle's behind him now—the sift-downs, the stabbing and slabbing. So they scoot back down Decatur to the French Market. Cold air licks them through the doorways of the clubs. Past the fruit stalls, Luther from the Desire Projects has a booth where he sells hats and alligator heads. It was Luther that Stretch used to sell those cowboy shirts to, fifty dollars a pop, before he did his time. If Luther were a car he'd be a Lincoln.

They decide that Luther will run them out to the lake shore. Stretch can sign up for the job and on the way back they'll drop by Acadian Mini-Storage in Metairie where he stashed the rest of those shirts. "Gentlemen," he says, "you all can split what's left. I'm putting this lifestyle behind me."

Luther starts folding T-shirts. "Thought you was a man of leisure, Stretch. Thought you here for the *reason,* you understand what I'm saying? How come you going for some raggedy-ass fry-cook job like this here? Planning to sell steaks on the side?"

"Why, I'm in love, son."

"I'll tell you what," says Luther. "That's a shame."

As soon as Chain Drive leaves, Stretch picks up a half-pint of peach brandy and walks back toward St. Ann. The Quarter steams with smells of crawfish boil, liquor, cologne. That blue van drives by and this time he sees what's painted on the back door. *II Tim. 4:2 Prech La Parole.* Scripture. Zack Broussard, whose daddy, the Honorable Troy C. Broussard, sent Stretch up for those cowboy shirts, cruises past in a black Cherokee. In the passenger seat sits the pigeon. The sight gives Stretch a bad minute or two. He passes Mystic Orbit again. Inside Blondelle turns away, pretending she doesn't see him.

Evening falls like a wet shirt as he heads back to his room. Blondelle, Chain Drive, Luther—they buy it raw, this redneck riff, laughing at him (behind his back, no doubt about that) while he's miles ahead of anyplace they'll ever be. *Miles* ahead. Cut him some slack. He doesn't expect ever to touch this pigeon. He just wants her to understand. That's all.

NEXT MORNING CHAIN Drive and Luther roust Stretch at the Capri, where he's still sacked out after what he can't deny was one hell of a night. He'd ended up tangling with the night clerk's brother-in-law, a laid-off welder from Houma. He's got a black eye, a pavement burn over one ear, and his shirt's torn to rags. "Gentlemen," he says, "you got to help me out here. I'm feeling wrung out and strung out and I can't go for no job interview looking like this."

Luther opens the trunk of his Seville and unpacks a leopard-skin T-shirt and a cowboy hat. Stretch feels a little more, a little more *presentable*—that's the word—but there's still no two ways about it, his nerves are shot. And as soon as he climbs into the backseat he helps himself to a taste of Asthma-Dor. They drive out Canal. The air is thick with the smell of rain and over the rooftops the sky is lathered with bruised-looking clouds. Stretch takes out his wallet and studies that photo of his little brother. There's an old strip of paper from a fortune cookie; faded red letters read *Your dearest wish will come true.*

As soon as Hallett got back from Panama he quit Bible College. Stretch was tending bar at The Five of Clubs that summer. After work he'd hear Hallett walking out to the porch then back into the house, over and over. Stretch was working the midnight to six shift when Hallett called. "Sylvester," he said. "I'm sorry. But something just went out of me down there." For all Stretch knew those were his last words.

Now Stretch, he'd seen an army chaplain shoot a woman dead in Lang Vei. He'd run security for the Mustang Ranch way out in Nevada, tended bar for Turley, begged on the street, and done a little time. That's right. But the whole time, he hung onto his religion. Maybe he never sat in church Sunday, listening to some preacher put down a bunch of sorry jive, but he said his little prayer every day—yes, he did—and there was a place in his heart where all things, *all* things, were holy. He was raised by the Word and he flat lived by the Word. Still you can never tell what it is will throw you. For Hallett it was whatever happened to him down in Panama. For Stretch it was picking out his little brother in the city morgue. Because something went out of him too.

"Ground zero," says Luther. There's the lake. They pull up in front of a white clapboard seafood place with a green shingled roof. The clouds are dark now and Stretch feels thunder along his backbone. Things are starting to look funny. Those trees along Lakeshore Drive where his little brother went for the gun, they've gone all ropy, as if they're fixing to pull up their roots and do the Funky Chicken. And now over on the sidewalk two mailboxes are dancing. Off toward the horizon the lake boils into the clouds.

"Stretch?" says Luther. "You sure you up for this?"

"Gots to," he says, though, truth be told, he's Drunk in the Spirit and having trouble just standing up. Lightning stains the world blue. He wobbles across the lot and steps through the screen door. In the kitchen a cook is cleaning shrimp. The walls melt away and all around them stand black-haired kids, hundreds, thousands of them. They're burning. The whole time they watch Stretch with empty eyes.

The cook takes one look at him and shakes his head. "Help me, Jesus," he says. "What the hell you supposed to be, man?"

"An outlaw," says Stretch.

HE'S CRAWLING THROUGH the puddles like a bug, trying to make it back to the car. Then he's lying on the blacktop, rain falling on his face. Luther studies the Asthma-Dor can. "Stretch, this here is belladonna. How much you take?"

When he answers, the words come frothing out in a language he's never heard before. Speaking in tongues.

"Will it hurt him?" Chain Drive wants to know.

"Kill his ass, he took enough."

Chain Drive pulls back his fist and nails Stretch in the chops. "Sucker!" he yells. "You best not die before I get my shirts!"

Don't ask how but Stretch is up and rubbering along Bayou St. John like Plastic Man. Behind him the children of hell call his name. It's raining frogs, the ground beneath his feet erupting in nasty bubbles. The night sags down on him, an inky bladder. He wallows past Old Spanish Fort, blue moonlight burning on the water. Angels. He hears a choir of angels and turns down a side street toward a lit-up storefront. Music spills from inside. That blue van is parked out front, scripture dripping down the door panels like a drunk woman's makeup. When Stretch pushes through the storefront door the singing stops. A million black faces turn to stare at him but he's looking past them, past the preacher in his blue suit, to a painting of a woman big as the moon who sparkles like all the fireworks in the world. She's watching him with the saddest eyes he's ever seen. Looking for that place in his heart. Who wouldn't hide?

He finds himself in St. Louis Cemetery, crawling across the pavement by Marie Laveau's tomb. Little crosses scratched with brick on the sides. Over the tops of the statues he sees traffic flash by on I-10. He turns over on his back and closes his eyes. He's trying to say his little prayer when somebody laughs.

And there's Hallett, sitting on the old girl's tomb, blazing like glory. "What it is," he says. His eyes are empty.

"Hallett," says Stretch. "Hallett, you got to be my witness. I'm saying my little prayer."

"Now, Sylvester," says Hallett, still laughing. "Who would listen to a prayer from a place like this?"

STRETCH WAKES UP ugly and looks around for his shoes. They're gone. So is his wallet. An orange sun steams in a white sky and snails drip down the sides of the tombs. It's like the song in that old cowboy movie—everything's falling on his head, only he's not talking about raindrops. He makes his way out of the cemetery and limps fourteen blocks up Tulane to the Capri. They've locked him out. Down

Tulane again to Lee Circle. At the Hummingbird, Blondelle answers the door and starts ragging on him about those cowboy shirts. He asks about a shower, comes close to pleading, but she won't let him in. So it's back to the Quarter to make his rounds. He's far from looking his best as he passes those two motorcycle cops. "Here comes the shitbird," says one.

"Yeah," says the other. "Barefooting."

He feels their mean little eyes. Young eyes.

Over in Irish Channel he scrounges up half a catfish po'boy and some muscle relaxers for his nerves. By the time his blistered feet push him up St. Ann the shadows are getting long and there's the pigeon coming down her steps with a pile of books in what must be her work outfit: blue jacket, white blouse, a black skirt sticking to her legs. And those legs run all the way down to her shoes. Zack Broussard waits for her in his Cherokee. When the pigeon sees Stretch she smiles. "Hey, Chief. I was hoping I'd run into you. I washed out that shirt the best I could."

"You hang onto it, darling. I got a million of them."

Zack Broussard gets out and stands there with his crewcut and red suspenders. "About time you're moving," he tells the pigeon. He gives Stretch a look that says, *You're shit on my shoes.* "Seems like every time I come down here there's more trash on the street."

Stretch knows he should throw down on him. But what good would it do?

He makes his way to Jackson Square and picks out a bench. Lying on his back, he watches the night come dripping like blue tears through the trees. Yes, there's been a change in him. But even if she understood—tops, all he could expect would be a visit sooner or later from Zack Broussard or some other suit come around to give him the word. As he lies there with his thoughts rattling and cracking together like wet rocks, he throws together a picture of the pigeon's eyes when she smiles at him. Suddenly he understands the difference between love and true love. It's the difference between running barefoot because you're hot and running barefoot because you've got no shoes. He starts to prophesy.

Step one. He's got to look his best. Behold: turquoise bolo tie, black silk shirt, ostrich-skin boots.

Step two. He's got to be feeling right. First stop, Nutrition City. Coffee, cheese grits, and a couple of Milky Ways. Pop two Percosets and chase them with some peach brandy, just for the taste. Next thing you know he'll be cruising up Magazine toward Lee Circle.

He sees himself at the Hummingbird, curtains drawn, Chain Drive's head shining under the light. There's a heap of crystal on the table and Blondelle's lighting up doobies. Does Stretch whiff some crank? You know he does. Bip-bip-bip, like unzipping the top of his skull. Having him a big time. Then two more Percosets, just for luck, and he's smoking back down Magazine. Out in the parking lot Blondelle turns into fire. "Stretch, darling," she'll holler. "You are one grandstanding *fool!*"

"Yes," he'll say as he turns down Dauphine. "I have been known to get a little wild."

Can't nothing hang him up now. He looks up St. Ann. Sure enough the pigeon's out front next to the black Cherokee. And there's Zack Broussard, talking his trash. Stretch can't hold himself back. He sees himself flat *moving* over those bricks. Old Zack spots him, knows he's packing, loses his smile pronto. Time for Stretch to make his play. He draws down but does he cap Zack Broussard's ass? Not hardly. No, he just stands there like a dead pine, holding out the piece and waiting for the sirens.

Say it's all over. Say the Man's got him down, cuffed, ripped up bad. Say the pigeon kneels on the sidewalk and looks down at him with those big sad coffee-colored eyes.

Why then it's time for Step three. "Baby," he'll say. "I did it for your precious love."

Eddie Agonistes

No one ever figured out why Eddie's father stole all the TVs from Hibernian Meadows, the nursing home where he'd worked ten years as an orderly. When the state troopers found the van and its illicit cargo parked on the interstate median he was passed out cold behind the wheel with an empty pint of cherry vodka. There was talk, mostly from the in-laws, about another woman but there always is. Why speculate? Men do stupid irrevocable things all the time and their families just keep taking care of business.

"My life was choking me," Eddie's father pled in his defense. The judge, unmoved, sentenced him to five years at Deer Island Prison. Eddie, who'd sat in frightened silence while his father had drunkenly crowed his approval of the Kent State deaths, was far from heartbroken. "You're the man of the house now," said Pop just before the bailiff took him back to prison. "Try to act like one."

Eddie moved with his mother and his two sisters into a cold-water flat over Fat Tony's sub shop on Shirley Ave. Frank, a year back from Vietnam, was living in Chelsea, playing bass with a band called the Moondogs. As it happened, the band's manager knew a recently widowed photographer across the harbor in Nahant who was looking for a gardener—the perfect job, it was decided, for Eddie.

The first morning he was waiting in front of Fat Tony's when his brother and the drummer, returning from a gig in Maine, pulled up in a rusted Econoline van reeking of pot smoke and Jade East cologne. The fog was lifting. Over the rooftops, Eddie could see the Cyclone roller coaster at Revere Beach. They drove around the harbor, stopping at the foot of a driveway that curved up a hill and vanished into some willows. "You can still back out," said Frank. "The band's going places and we can always keep an enterprising young stud like you busy."

Eddie shrugged. "I better not. Now that you moved out I'm the man of the house."

"Yeah," said Frank. "Lucky you." He popped a can of Budweiser and slugged Eddie's shoulder. "Am I right or am I right?"

"The moving finger writes," said Eddie. Playing to an imagined audience of Italian girls in Revere High jackets, he strode up into the damp shadows. He could hear a dog's

crazed barking growing louder. Presently a blue house appeared through a fringe of willows. A realtor's sign stood
next to the mailbox. Below, past the grassy terraces and gray-
green humps of the willows, lay the harbor, blue and wrin-
kled. A tanned barefoot lady with a blond shag answered the
door in shorts and a work shirt. A howling collie tried to
force its way past her. Inside the house a TV was tuned to the
Watergate hearings. "Aren't you bright and early," she said.
"I'm Gudren."

"Does your dog bite?"

"Anubis? Not really. You're pretty tall for, what, fifteen?"

"Sixteen."

"Indeed." She seemed to think it was funny. "Well, I'm
moving to Taos—that's in New Mexico—as soon as this
place sells, and in the meantime I just need it spruced up.
Do you think you can help me do that?"

"I guess."

Eddie started mowing the bottom terrace. The day was
hot and by the time he'd worked his way up to the backyard he'd stripped to his cutoff jeans and sneaks. He turned
off the mower and heard Gudren through the screen door,
laughing on the phone. Certain that she was talking about
him, Eddie was trying to get closer when Anubis exploded
through the door in a snarling blur and snapped at his ankle. To call it a bite would be stretching it—the skin wasn't
even broken—but dogs terrified him and as he sat trem-

bling at the picnic table he was close to hysterics. "I was just going to ask for some water," he said.

"I suspect you'll live," said Gudren and touched his leg. "Look at you. The sun on your skin. Like an angel by Raphael. The painter?"

The following Monday he looked up around noon and found her watching him through the kitchen window. She held up a tomato and beckoned him inside. The TV was off. Piano music played on the stereo and the house smelled of incense. On one wall hung a painting of a woman robed like the stained-glass saints at St. Teresa's. "I picked that up in Haiti," said Gudren, following Eddie's eyes. "Our Lady of Perpetual Help—their patron saint?—which, God knows, is appropriate."

"I'm not big on religion," said Eddie, affecting a brooding expression that he fancied made him look like Al Pacino. "Not after the stuff I've seen." Over avocado sandwiches he went on to tell her about his father. "He killed a couple of guys," he said with a tone of weary resignation.

She laughed. "You're quite the little bullshit artist, aren't you?"

"It's *true*," he said hotly. "If it's not I'll put my hand right under that lawn mower out there."

"Why don't you let your hair grow out?"

"I've been thinking about it."

As the summer progressed, Gudren's house gave up

its secrets. Utility bills addressed to Rebecca Goldfarb. A tube of ash blond Nice 'n Easy. A prescription for Librium. A copy of *Fear of Flying* next to her bed. A photo of Gudren herself, younger and thinner, in front of Cambridge City Hall with a skinny lieutenant in paratrooper boots and a blue infantry braid, both of them squinting into the sun.

In July she had a show at a Back Bay gallery. The Moondogs played. Ashleigh, Gudren's ten-year-old niece from Cambridge, traipsed around in the kind of thrift-store outfits that rich kids wore, filming the event with a Super-8 movie camera. Huge black-and-white pictures lined the walls—bathtub virgins, Italian weddings, hulking IRA exiles at the St. Patrick's Day parade. A blushing Eddie wound through the reception with a tray of drinks while a tall long-haired guy read a couple of poems. Everybody clapped. A pale woman wearing a long skirt and cowboy boots went on and on about the writing life, the nobility of giving so generously of oneself.

"Natürlich," said the poet.

"Are you German?" asked Eddie.

Everyone stopped talking to stare at the kid with the bow tie and crisp white shirt. "Am I *German?*" said the poet and the other guests howled with laughter. He clapped Eddie on the back. "You know what, kid? You're almost hip."

Eddie paid his last visit to Deer Island Prison. Over a woman's steady hopeless weeping, babies howled and a couple carried on an ear-splitting argument in Portuguese. Every minute or so a swart resonant voice would bawl, "Can I please have something for the *pain?*" The visiting area sounded like a zoo.

Pop had grown a mustache and his resemblance to Burt Reynolds was too close for coincidence. "Get a haircut," was the first thing he said. "You look like a punk."

"Some people like it."

"Don't lip off to me, Numb-Nuts. You're my flesh and blood. And I love you, you little shit. I'm not ashamed of it. Where's your brother?"

"He's got a gig," said Eddie, though in fact Frank had flat-out refused to come.

"He's got no respect, is what he's got. Not for nobody or nothing."

"Please, Sully," said Eddie's mother, "tell the boy to start going to Mass again."

"Listen to your mother. You hear what I'm telling you, Numb-Nuts? Say, yes, sir."

"So long," Eddie said and went out to the parking lot.

Gudren sold the house in August. On the last day, she gave Eddie a copy of *Letters to a Young Poet.* She touched his hair, which by now curled over his ears. "I know it sounds stupid," she said, "but I think of you as my child of light." Her voice echoed in the bare kitchen. "Will you think about me?"

"All the time," he said carefully. "You're a goddess of loveliness."

When she put her arms around him he felt her heart slamming through her shirt. One moment he was looking over her shoulder at the Haitian painting, the next they were down on the floor, banging against the empty cupboards as they tore at each other's clothes. She squeezed her eyes shut and turned toward the light and he saw for the first time that although she wasn't old she was old enough to worry about it. And suddenly whatever kept him up nights, listening to the sounds of breaking bottles and traffic as the Fat Tony's sign threw purple ripples across his bedroom ceiling, whatever led him to imagine laying down his life for her (he had a vague notion of prostrating himself in front of some implacable machine, a tank maybe) as he studied *The Rubáiyát of Omar Khayyám* and scrawled *The Goddess of Loveliness* over and over again in his notebook—suddenly that was gone.

Afterward they waited by the mailbox for the cab to take her to Logan Airport. Anubis growled in his carrier. "I don't feel so great about this," said Gudren.

"Well," said Eddie, who was mentally checking his watch.

"You can go if you want."

"It's OK," he said. But he was relieved when the cab came and she kissed him good-bye. He could hear the ascending shrieks of kids on the Cyclone across the harbor. There was no way, no way he wanted to go back there—

back to his sour angry family, the dark streets, back to the prison-bound guys on the corners with their leather coats and gold chains, back to the toothless old men in scally caps—and as Gudren's cab coasted down the driveway he realized that he didn't have to.

IN THE SPRING his brother got married, then his oldest sister, Patti; when she and her husband bought a triple-decker in Providence and moved Eddie's mother into the bottom floor he quit school. He hustled Ashleigh's parents, big-time realtors, into turning him on to a rent-controlled apartment in Cambridge. He sold his records —T-Rex, Chicago, Neil Young—and bought Satie's *Gymnopédies*. He found a job at a vegetarian restaurant in Central Square. On his nights off he'd prowl the coffee shops, a lanky kid with long chestnut hair, a stack of notebooks, and a dog-eared Rilke anthology. Soon he was dating. Brilliant women, talented women, women so breathtaking that their very anger was a sacrament—they all succumbed and not one lasted more than a month. For the next few years it was common to see one of Eddie's weeping discards follow him out of a café as he strode ahead, wrapped in this theatrical air of injury. "It's not like I signed a contract," he would say later with a look of sly innocence. "And it wouldn't be fair to commit to anyone who you know isn't going to work out in the long run. I mean, what if the right person came along?"

And then one winter the pipes burst, filling the basement of his apartment with tar-colored ice. Eddie was already three months behind with the rent. It was time to go.

A YEAR LATER he dropped in at Gudren's place, a Spanish-style house outside Taos with a red-tiled roof and adobe walls splashed with bougainvillea. Gudren, her hair short and dark now, came to the door in a white cotton dress. "Hello," she said with a flat look. In the living room she sat across the glass coffee table from him. Artfully displayed on the tabletop was a copy of her book, *Ghettos of the Divine*. "You're about the last person I ever expected to see again," she said after a long awkward silence. "I thought you were living in Wisconsin. With some lady mechanic, Ashleigh told me."

"Blacksmith."

"Blacksmith, mechanic, whatever. It doesn't sound like you've been starved for company."

"Well, maybe the time was right to come see you."

"In other words you had to leave in a hurry."

"Give me a break. Didn't you tell me I was always welcome?"

"I don't know. Did I?" She lit a cigarette. "So what went wrong in Minnesota?"

"Wisconsin." He shrugged. "People and their clumsy passions. You try to set ground rules and the next thing you know they're desperate for the one thing you're not willing to give up for anybody." He sipped his iced tea and shook away the image of a strapping blond woman with soot-streaked cheeks, wounded eyes beneath the bill of her welding helmet. "Anyway I couldn't hack the Midwest anymore. Can you imagine our pioneer ancestors having to see their genetic batter all watered down and baked into these pale yeasty loaves? They'd shit bricks. Or maybe just laugh."

In the backyard Anubis let out a long ululating howl. Gudren crossed her legs and exhaled a plume of smoke. *"Genetic batter?"* she said with a grudging smile. "You just threw that in spontaneously?"

He laughed. "You should see them lumbering from Sees Candy to Radio Shack to Toys'R'Us. And the accents — those clenched perky whines. I mean, what do they want? What are they looking for?"

"More to the point, what are you looking for?"

Through her bedroom door he could see that painting of Our Lady of Perpetual Help. "Beauty," he said.

"As long as you didn't come here to be sexual."

He tossed his hair and gave her a look of lofty disdain. "That's pretty insulting."

Her eyes softened and she reached across the coffee table to touch his hand. "I'm sorry. I'm just not sure who I'm talking to. After all, you're grown up now, aren't you? It's kind of hard to get my head around that." Gudren put some Satie on the turntable and they sat without saying much as the room grew dark. Her agent and his wife—a bald guy, a woman with white bangs—came over for dinner. Gudren blabbed at excruciating length about Ashleigh and her thesis film, and by the time her guests left, she'd put away two bottles of Zinfandel. Despite her as-long-as-you-didn't-come-here-to-be-sexual declaration Eddie was relieved when she put him up on a foam pad near the darkroom. Then around midnight as he padded to the bathroom she called to him and he couldn't think of a graceful way out. Perhaps, he told himself, in some future hour of need someone would do the same for him. But he hadn't counted on her apologetic nakedness in the milky light, her pleading eyes. And beneath the scents of piñon incense and candle wax—was that the faint liverish odor of age? He did the best he could. It was only afterward when she snuggled up to him in a gruesome parody of affection that a chill spread from his core to his fingertips. He lay there stiffly, staring through the skylight at the icy stars. What was he doing here, so far from home, with this woman he hardly knew?

"How long can you stay?" she whispered.

"I'm kind of in a hurry to get to California. I've got to get serious about my writing."

"It's a hard path. And it won't be any easier there."

"Who wants to read poetry by the gardener, right?"

She rose on one elbow. "Don't be silly. What I'm saying—"

"You're saying guys like me should be hod carriers. Forget it. I won't lead a mediocre life. I'm not going to be like my brother and I damn sure won't be like my dad. Everybody acts like there's all the time in the world. But there's not."

"Do you have enough money?"

"Well," he said after a moment's silence, "I wouldn't want you to think that's why I'm here."

He awakened in the dark to the sound of clogged desperate weeping and saw light under the bathroom door. After a while Gudren returned and sat heavily on the edge of the bed. "You don't understand," she said, though he'd given no sign that he was awake. "There are some things you never get over. No matter how you build your life up again you know that behind it all there's something terribly wrong."

With a bored sweep of his hand Eddie pointed to the skylight, the tapestries, the framed photographs, the Haitian painting. "Are you kidding? With all this? What could be wrong?"

Gudren blew her nose. "Maybe California's the place for you after all."

AND FOR A long time it was. In 1978 Eddie—now twenty-one and going by the more intriguing Raphael— started waiting tables at an Indian restaurant in a college town nestled among the tawny hills of California's central coast, an enclave of spiritual seekers with smiling sun-tanned faces and names like Storm Shadow, Jara-Maya, and Nameless One. Scientologists, Buddhists, Unarians, Wiccans, Cabalists. People who swore by levitation and the regeneration of amputated limbs through meditation. He won the blessing of an English professor at the community college, a fading beauty who vowed that Eddie was doing "some really interesting stuff," and he secured a local reputation as a poet. It was as if the town had been waiting for him.

Yet about a year later he ended up falling for a vexed-looking woman of twenty-eight with billows of kinky black hair and two little girls. She drank too much, smoked, listened to country music. Unsuitable in every way. But once she turned her scornful gaze on Eddie it was all over. Everything about her knocked him out, her troubled eyes and chapped heels, the way she took off her earrings. And after a frantic courtship Bella moved in with him, left the girls with their father.

At first it was as if life had invited him to a wonderful picnic. Her moodiness and intemperance seemed charming, the sorts of inconsequential flaws that pointed up her essential perfection. Eddie knew happiness at the pitch of terror. As the months passed, though, as she blew more and more of their meager income on cocaine and quaaludes, as she began vanishing for days at a time with her lowlife friends, he began to feel more trapped than charmed. And when she was arrested for drunk driving after wrecking their car he found himself on the verge of panic.

The Saturday after her accident, while her daughters were visiting, she went to a chiropractor for what she suspected was whiplash. It was a mercilessly hot day, the sun cutting shadows so dark as to throw back to the retina a flash of electric blue. Eddie took the girls to a park downtown and bought them ice cream cones. He sat beside Darshon, on a bench facing the swing set. Over their heads oak boughs listlessly stirred the scent of scorching grass. Sage dumped her cone into a trash can. "Dad says dairy is junk food," she said, holding Eddie's gaze defiantly.

"Suit yourself."

Sage came to stand in front of him, then took his hand and tentatively pressed her fingertips into his wrist. "How come you have a TV?" Her nails dug into his flesh. "Dad says that only dopes have TVs."

"Indeed."

"Raphael?" said Darshon. "Do you like Mom more than Dad does?"

"It's not—*stop* that, Sage—it's not like that when you grow up."

"What's it like then?"

"It's hard to explain." Darshon stared up at him expectantly, her eyes concerned, unnervingly so, as if she were somehow encouraging him to articulate some deed, some wound, some story that would put him in a noble light. And despite the smear of strawberry ice cream on her chin Eddie couldn't shake the notion that he was talking to someone wiser than he'd ever be. "Different," was all he could come up with.

Bella returned from her appointment and the four of them drove out to Vern's place in Los Osos. "Sage," she said, "why do you keep *staring* at me like that?"

"I want to see how you do it."

"Do what?"

"Dad says you're going to put all Raphael's money up your nose."

That evening after dropping the girls off, Bella and Eddie stopped at Morro Bay to watch the sunset. They were sitting on a slab of driftwood, facing the ocean, when Bella burst into tears. "I'm falling apart," she sobbed. "If I don't get adjustments twice a week I'll be bedridden by the time I'm forty. I'll look like a pretzel. How am I supposed to afford two treatments a week?"

"Relax," said Eddie, a little irritably. "The guy's a quack. A hustler."

"I hope so." Bella put her head on his shoulder. The scent of patchouli rose from her hair where the fading light spun red wires. It was dark when they walked back to the car. She took his arm. "I guess I'm feeling a little fragile," she said. "I just wish the girls could stay over more often."

"Remorse doesn't become you," said Eddie.

"*Remorse?* Give me a break. Wouldn't it be great to feel more like a family?"

"That might be taking things a little too fast."

She dropped his arm. "What's that supposed to mean?"

"It means—" He tossed his hair impatiently. "Hey, I don't have to explain myself to you."

"No, but I have to explain myself to Sage and Darshon. What am I supposed to say when they ask when I'm coming home? Come on, do you want a future with me or not? Because if you do the girls have to be part of it."

"You know what? I don't really get off on ultimatums."

"Up your poop chute." Holding her shoes, Bella walked into the surf and stood with her skirt hiked up around her waist, facing out to sea.

Fog was drifting in, thick with the odor of vile boneless things, and as Eddie watched the pale breakers churn out of the dark, he brought back the view from his bedroom window in Revere: rooftops capped with grimy snow, rats scooting across the telephone lines. He remembered mornings so cold the dishwashing detergent his sisters used for shampoo froze in its plastic bottle, the rattling pinball machine downstairs in the sub shop. He had it made here. Why throw everything away for this exasperating woman? After all, what guarantee did he have that this was the real thing? They'd been together—what—a little over a year? Maybe it was simply some kind of emotional flu.

So he hardened his heart. There were scenes of

course, ugly ones, and not long after the 1980 election she and the girls left town. *We stumble into knavery,* he wrote the evening they left. Then he put his notebooks aside and moved in with Hilary.

THE SUMMER THAT Iraq invaded Kuwait, Eddie headed east with the promise of a job as a sales rep for an insurance agency in Louisiana. He spent the first night in Needles. The next morning he took his Civic to a car wash and found a buckled copy of *The Duino Elegies* in the back-seat. His inscription was on the flyleaf: *To Bella, with dizzy admiration—Raphael.* Stuck midway through the book was a yellowed three-by-five card with a shopping list in her handwriting: *Dog food. Tampons. Warm socks for Raphael.* Suddenly it was if he couldn't remember those ten years with Hilary—no winters, no springs, just this end-less sun-dappled summer afternoon during which he'd learned nothing and lost what he'd waited for all his life. He thought of Bella weeping in his driveway with all her boxes and it came to him how badly he'd wronged her.

Along the way he called a few people who'd known her. Each had a different story. She was in Israel. She was in Vermont. She was in Reno. Finally, just as he was getting ready to bag the whole thing and visit Meredith in Louisiana, he got an actual address in west Texas.

On a baking afternoon he found the Hi-Way Inn, south of Marfa. Rocks popped under his tires as he turned into the parking lot. Out front three men in Budweiser caps were sprawled around an old Dodge, drinking Lone Star and watching somebody in cowboy boots change the oil. They responded to Eddie's wave with loud belches.

A big guy with a chest-length beard met Eddie in front of the office. His eyes were glazed and he smelled of tequila. "Hey," he shouted when Eddie asked about Bella, "somebody's looking for our favorite Jewish mother."

"Went to eat and the hogs got her," yelled the man under the Dodge.

The bearded man smiled as if something had been confirmed. " Call me Jaimie," he said. "Homegirl and those spooky kids cleared out of here six months ago. But she'll come crawling back. About the time she realizes she walked out on a good thing." He handed Eddie a business card: *Doctor R. Kane Wisdom—Comedy for Health.* "Say, hoss, can you tell me the difference between a yuppie and a sack of pig shit?"

Eddie looked up from the card. "Not really."

"I didn't think so. No offense." Jaimie stroked his beard. "Hey, ever notice the way girls go crazy over animals? Take my girlfriend—please. No, seriously, she keeps a goat in our bedroom. Stink?" He shuddered. "I'd open the window but I don't want to let all my chickens out." He frowned. "That was a joke. You can laugh. Unless you're one of these Marx brothers fans."

"Not really," said Eddie.

"God bless you. Because I'll tell you what, the Jew is incapable of real comedy." He held up one hand. "I know, I know—you're going to say, What about Jackie Mason, Henny Youngman, Shecky Green? Well, they don't know who I am and I don't know who they are. All right, they can come close but in the final analysis they always blow it. I'm talking about how they have to goose up the punch line with some kind of wink, you understand what I'm saying?"

"Well," said Eddie, "I haven't thought that much about it. Listen, if Bella does come back can you tell her Raphael stopped by?"

Jaimie chuckled into his beard. "Fat chance, hoss."

As Eddie drove away he could hardly swallow. Had he truly driven Bella into the arms of this meathead? Before him, through the blistered plane of the desert, between patches of scrubby trees bent by the wind into stunted sculptures of brute endurance, the road melted into a sky-colored puddle.

IT WASN'T THAT he didn't try to remember what happened on what he came to think of as the last day. He recalled the transmission going out across the river from Natchez, trading his Civic for a junked Tempest, forcing down a breakfast of grits and hard-cooked eggs at a diner, stepping outside to find a couple of mongrels rutting in the shade of the Tempest, a man in overalls shouting from the cab of a pickup, *Say, man, do something about your dogs.*

He remembered unlocking the door, a blast of scorched air that almost dropped him to his knees, the upholstery burning his thighs as he slid behind the wheel. After that there was only a dream: a train, an ancient fire-breathing dinosaur, chuffing off toward a bloodred sky. Flames seethed between the ties. Eddie wanted to catch that train more than he'd ever wanted anything in his life. But it inexorably outdistanced his rubber-legged pursuit and left him in a hot void tolling with anxious voices.

He awakened in a room dappled with greenish light. Looking down at him was a doctor in surgical scrubs. "Son," he said as he took Eddie's pulse, "do you know where you are?"

Eddie's jaw was wired shut so he just shook his head. Through his left eye the world swam behind a pink haze of pain. His stomach turned with each thump of his pulse.

"You gave us some anxious moments, boy. It was touch and go there for a while."

It turned out that Eddie was in a New Orleans hospital with a ruptured spleen and a shattered jaw. A couple of men dipping for crawfish had found him sunk up to his waist in a roadside ditch and driven him to the hospital.

He'd been there three days when a slender black man with gray hair showed up during visiting hours. "I'm Cecil," he said. "James's cousin. When you didn't show up at the office he said to call the hospitals. What it is, ain't no more Poughkeepsie Solutions in Louisiana. Ain't no Poughkeepsie

Solutions nowhere. James, he broke. Now I know you don't need no more bad news but you may as well get it all at once. You out of a job." He winced and looked away from Eddie. "Man, someone didn't like you much."

Eddie tapped his nose.

His headaches started, brutal sieges of pain, small deaths; in their aftermath his vision was blurred, objects haloed with blue. Three times a day he would sip chocolate Ensure, drawing the nasty stuff with painful slowness through a straw jammed between his upper incisor and canine. In the afternoons he would watch daylight wash across the linoleum and leak back out the windows. When *Jeopardy* came on the TV he would shuffle up and down the corridors, linked to his IV rack, probing the empty socket in his past, and every so often—when palmetto bugs would snap off the windows or someone would come in from outside, bringing the smell of wisteria—the outline of a memory would flicker in that void but as soon as he tried to bring it into focus it would melt away like old film stalled on a projector, leaving only a singed crater.

"What you going to do?" Cecil asked the day before Eddie's discharge.

Take bus to Boston, he wrote in the notebook he kept beside his bed.

"Look at you," said Cecil. "You got any clothes? No? You got any money? Then what you going to do? You weak as a kitten. You wouldn't make it out the parish." The next morning Cecil and his son, Carlton, a small boy wearing thick glasses and baggy shorts, brought Eddie a bundle of clothes and drove him in an ancient Chevy pickup to Tubbs Junction, a town on River Road. Carlton sat between them, rubbing one skinned knee with a spit-dampened finger and staring solemnly ahead as Eddie laboriously slurped down the pineapple milkshake Cecil had bought him. Eddie glanced in the side mirror and saw his shorn stitched head. He groaned.

The cab smelled of tobacco and coconut oil, and in the deep green fields on either side of the road cotton bloomed like popcorn. They pulled onto the lawn in front of a brick house with a satellite dish. On the porch stood Cecil's Aunt Bertha, a plump regal woman who, Cecil told him, owned an herbal supply store—The New Seven Powers Botanica —in New Orleans. "This Eddie," said Cecil. "He staying till his mouth open up."

Aunt Bertha greeted him courteously enough but even pasted on pain meds he didn't miss the exasperated look she shot Cecil. Eddie stayed in a tiny trailer behind the daylily garden. Cecil ran an extension cord from the kitchen to the trailer and Eddie turned on the fan and slept. When he awakened the shadows were long and the sappy fragrance of mown grass rose in the air. He lay there, toying with the *I Ching* coin. Through one window he saw Carlton's head silhouetted against the blue glow of a computer monitor. He could hear voices from the kitchen.

Why you doing all of this for that boy?

How I'm supposed to walk away? He dumb as a box of rocks and James send him out here with no job. If I don't do right by him what he going to do?

Eddie spent the first few days in the trailer with the blinds drawn, besieged by headaches, studying the family's routine. Six nights a week Cecil worked at his nightclub, Club Chill, on the edge of town. Carlton stayed late at school every day with the Computer Club. On Sunday Cecil invited Eddie to services at the Victory Trumpet Tabernacle but he demurred and saw relief in Aunt Bertha's eyes. He watched them—men in blue suits, women with veils and odd-looking hats, girls in white dresses, Carlton in a suit and bow tie—walk through the heat ripples past Dixie Video, the Piggly Wiggly, and Comeaux's 1-Stop, in front of which a rusted sign advertised BOILED CRAW FISH. Later as Eddie sat on the steps of the trailer, writing a letter of supplication to his brother, he heard, over the lush chording of a piano, the congregation's soaring voices.

The day his jaws were unwired Cecil took him fishing. Eddie sat on the dock, nodding in and out of a Percoset haze. He could hear the murmur of Cecil and Carlton's voices, the reverberant thump of their boat hull against the tea-colored waters of the lake. His thoughts drifted back to that night on the beach with Bella, her indolent hip-tossing walk. Why did everything afterward—the whole decade in fact—seem so insubstantial? He'd acquired and shed women, and back east his father had gotten out of prison and Frank had ended up in detox. But other than that the years were a blur of strident pageantry—assassinations, squalid little wars, red cars, loud movies, bad music. Somebody else's memories. But whose?

It was evening, the cypress trees spiked against a red sky, when Cecil and Carlton docked and dumped a soaking gunnysack heaving with catfish on the warm planks. Eddie watched them cleaning the day's catch, thumbing offal into the water. "I'll never have a family," he said. "I'll never have what you have."

Cecil laughed incredulously. "How you know what we have?"

When they got home a check had arrived from Eddie's brother, enough for a one-way bus ticket to Boston. Eddie decided to leave in the morning. That night he ate supper with the family. Over the window fan's rusty whine he could hear the shriek of cicadas.

"Daddy," said Carlton, "does Eddie know where Uncle James is?"

"No, baby. Nobody know."

"Mmm-*hmmm*," said Aunt Bertha. "James come back from Vietnam and decide to spend his life chasing the almighty dollar. Forget all about the Almighty. Let that be a lesson to you, baby."

"If I teached Eddie here how to use the computer he could get him a *good* job."

"Yes," said Cecil. "That's right. Only you too late now."

"I need something to put these table scraps in," said Aunt Bertha. "Take them over for Ludella's chickens. Now who going to bring me a croker sack?"

Eddie jumped up and went into the kitchen. A moment later he returned with a plastic trash bag. "Is this what you're looking for?"

Carlton, Cecil, Aunt Bertha—the whole family roared with laughter. "Boy," said Aunt Bertha, wiping her eyes, "you a *nut.*"

The last morning dawned hot. Dew soaked the grass and silvered the pickup's windshield. Aunt Bertha packed Eddie a box lunch and scolded Cecil for trying to leave with a can of malt liquor. "That look so bad," she said and insisted that he put it in a paper sack.

At the bus stop Eddie, feeling a little sheepish in his borrowed silk shirt, low-cut loafers, and ribbed socks, shook hands with Cecil. "I guess this is it," he said.

Cecil handed him a small red flannel pouch. "Don't open that up," he said. "*Damn.* Aunt Bertha *made* that for you. Made it up and fixed it with uncrossing oil. Maybe you don't believe in hands, mojos, tobies—all that. Maybe I don't. But it look like you could use some good luck."

"Listen," said Eddie, "if a woman comes around looking for Raphael can you let her know where I am?"

"Raphael?" Cecil took a sip of malt liquor. "That ain't none of your name."

CHEEKS SUNKEN, HIS hair streaked with gray, Eddie moved in with his brother, who ran a music store just across the Tobin Bridge from Boston. He unpacked his souvenirs: a photograph of him and Bella on a sailboat and the red flannel bag from Aunt Bertha. He found a job stocking produce at a Brazilian grocery. That fall at his mother's wake in Providence he broke down in front of his stone-faced sisters and was utterly unable to compose himself.

On the way back Frank took him to the aquarium. "Watch these guys awhile," he said, pointing to some huge fish with undershot jaws drifting glumly past the window. "Does it look like they're worried about anything?"

"It's kind of hard to tell," said Eddie. "I don't understand what's happening to me. I just can't seem to get it together. It's like my spirit has developed a stoop. My dreams have gone bad. I'm getting maybe three or four hours of sleep a night." He shrugged. "That's all."

Frank slugged his shoulder. "Come on, young stud. Everybody's got to start over once in a while. And it's not like you're old. Give it some time. You can still make something of yourself. Am I right or am I right?"

"I guess."

One evening on his way out of a Star Market with a Halloween pumpkin Eddie bumped into Ashleigh. She'd grown into a spindly woman with huge pale lips and was busy cranking out short films with titles like *Love Squat* and *Menstrual Pliers*. "Gudren asked about you," she said. "She's got another book coming out—pictures of Haitian religious art? Isn't that awesome?"

"Some people would call it appropriation."

Two vertical anger lines creased Ashleigh's forehead. "Well, some people are obviously never going to get it."

"Did anyone ever tell you that you have cheekbones like Winona Ryder's?"

"Not lately." Red blotches spread from her ears to her neck.

"I'm staying with my brother," he said. "Give me a call." He turned and bore his pumpkin across the parking lot into the darkness. A couple of months later he accompanied Ashleigh and her entourage, an insufferable bunch draped in black, to an open-mike poetry reading in Central Square where the bouncer checked everyone's ID except his. "Hey," said Eddie, trying to make a joke out of it. "Don't you want to see my license?"

"Got you covered," was the reply.

Once, Eddie wouldn't have given a woman like Ashleigh —plain, abrasive, dubiously talented—the time of day. Now, though, he didn't have the luxury of waiting for someone suitable, and the year after the Gulf War—once Frank had recovered from Wycek's death—he moved into her studio, one of her family's many properties in Boston. It was a drafty loft not far from South Station, overlooking the muted red bricks and tarnished copper trim of the Hickox

Academy of Dance, and, beyond that, the harbor. It was far from a love match but all relationships were trade-offs, he reasoned, and what he got in exchange for his shopworn cachet was two rent-free years and enough relative prosperity to make a down payment on an Escort with fifty thousand miles on it.

ON THE WAY back from a résumé workshop one winter afternoon he thought he saw Ashleigh step out of an outbound train on the opposite platform of Charles Street Station, arm in arm with a man. All Eddie could see of the guy was his glossy ponytail. By the time he reached the turnstile the couple was halfway across the pedestrian overpass, borne with the bundled-up crowds down the iron stairs and along the sidewalk toward the Public Garden. "I thought I saw you," he said, that evening. "At Charles Street."

Ashleigh fixed him with a look of withering scorn. "I was doing postproduction all day. Sorry to disappoint you."

By the time they took the train to New York for the premiere of *Dipstick* they were speaking in terse monosyllables. A bunch of Ashleigh's friends met them in the East Village. It was raining and an acrid smell of wet ashes clung to the streets. Ashleigh went off to call Gudren, whose publisher was putting her up at the Chelsea.

Gudren met them at a Polish place on Avenue A. Her hair was frosted and she wore a red gaucho hat that tied under the chin. Eddie had been wondering what she would make of seeing the child of light looking, of all things, out of place but to his alarm her gaze seemed to hint at some remaining intimacy. He sat between her and a young Hispanic guy with a ponytail—a Cuban performance artist named Pablo.

"My niece, the celebrity," said Gudren and pointed to a three-line notice in *The New Yorker* that mentioned *Dipstick*'s premier at some theater on Fourteenth Street. She raved on and on about the film, in whose final fifteen minutes a young man beats an elderly woman to a pulp with a poker, then sets himself on fire. "It's hip," she said, "it's indisputably *now*. And what I find most astonishing is its curious tenderness. I feel that its vision somehow reifies the restless spirit of our age."

"It's not exactly *Fanny and Alexander*," said Eddie.

"Excuse me?" said Pablo. He turned to the others, hands upheld in stagy bafflement. "*Fanny and Alexander?* Isn't that one of those movies about people with clean hair?"

Throughout the remainder of the meal Eddie could feel Ashleigh's friends asking each other questions with their eyes. While everyone was ordering coffee Gudren took his arm. "You'll let me know," she whispered, with an inquisitorial arch of her eyebrows, "if there's anything I can do, won't you?"

Eddie told the others he was going to call the theater and check the show times. He left by the back exit and took a cab to Penn Station. The train clattered and groaned through Connecticut. Outside, past his harrowed reflection, long shadows stretched across frozen marshes tufted with yellow grass. Eddie closed his eyes and pressed his forehead to the glass.

The next day it snowed. From the window he looked down at the dance school across the street. Tiny girls with woolen caps and sagging black leotards skipped from the foyer to waiting cars. When it grew dark he turned on the radio but his favorite station was choked with static; only Bach's B Minor Mass came in clearly, and after a moment or two of those gloomy chords he turned it off. He made a peanut butter sandwich. In Ashleigh's study he found a videocassette marked *Old Super-8 Stuff: Gudren Reception.* Eddie plugged it into the VCR and there he was, a wide-eyed kid with mussed hair, holding a tray of drinks. On-screen, the kid's mouth moved: *Are you German?* Suddenly everything was mercilessly clear—the lies, the stupid ambitions, the utter absurdity of his life. How had it come to this?

He awakened the following morning with a sore throat. His joints felt clogged with sand and in the brittle winter light that angled through the windows his skin looked old. By the time he managed to drag himself out of bed and call in sick he was so dizzy that he could barely stand. He fell in the bathroom and smashed his head on the sink. With the *I Ching* coin glittering against his chest he sat shivering on the icy tiles, stanching the blood with wads of toilet paper.

He spent the week in bed. His fever finally broke on the following Monday. He was sitting by the window in sweatpants and a stained robe, watching the windows of the dance school, when Ashleigh returned from New York, flushed with jubilation. "Thanks for your support," she said. "Bailing out on me like that. I shouldn't even speak to you. But it's your loss. We got to hang out at the Chelsea. And you know who was at the premier?"

"I give up. Orson Welles?"

"Werner Herzog's nephew, asshole. And he said *Dipstick* put a human face on postmodernism. Can you believe how awesome that is? Do I rock or what?"

"Where did Pablo stay?"

"Let me breathe!" she shouted. "Stop smothering me!"

Eddie felt one of his headaches coming on. "I don't think I deserve that," he said.

"You don't think this, you don't think that. Look, dude, this—whatever it is—just isn't going anywhere. I mean, I don't really even know you. Do you have any idea what it's like, trying to think while you practice that bogus juggling? You've got banana stains all over the floor. All my friends hide their fruit whenever we come over."

"Who's calling who bogus?"

Ashleigh looked away with an exasperated laugh. "If I were you," she said, slipping what looked like her diaphragm case into her bag, "I'd find someplace else to live."

"Natürlich."

She gave him a week. Eddie went back to the market, only to find that through no fault of his own he'd lost his job. It was the economy, his supervisor explained. Taxes, the stock market, whatever. He promised to get in touch if things changed. Employees in green aprons walked briskly past with stiff smiles, avoiding Eddie's eyes.

Ashleigh was in New York the day he moved back in with his brother. He split the butter pecan ice cream in her freezer with his niece, Ruthie, who was spending the weekend with Frank and had come along to help carry boxes. On their way out Eddie took a felt-tip pen and wrote *the worst are full of passionate intensity* on the bathroom mirror. Ruthie kept staring at the phrase and rubbing her chin.

"Something wrong?" said Eddie.

"Kind of negative, isn't it?"

It was a bad time to be out of work. The Massachusetts Miracle of the eighties was nothing but a fond memory. A temp agency placed him as an administrative assistant. On a sweltering morning Eddie borrowed a tweed sport coat from his brother and took the subway to the offices of McLaughlin & Rotary, a Cambridge consulting firm. He had a huge cold sore on his upper lip. By the time he arrived he'd sweated through his clothes. The human resources manager, a short guy with fiery red hair, took in with ill-concealed distaste Eddie's rumpled tie and sodden sport coat. "I've cleared the decks for action," he said. "I

don't mind telling you that we needed you onboard yesterday. So it's key that you get up to speed pronto."

As it happened, Eddie had greatly exaggerated his
computer literacy. Young nattily dressed consultants kept
dropping work off at his desk, darting him concerned looks
as the stacks of paper mounted, and after a couple of hours
spent trying to print out a spreadsheet he overheard the
human resources manager on the phone. "I'm afraid," said
the little creep, "that Edward doesn't appear to be very in-
terested. Going forward, we need team players."

He drove out to Revere, where Fat Tony's was now a
Cambodian video store and the Cyclone had long since
burned to the ground. He talked to one cousin about a construction gig, to another about a job at his auto parts store,
but they just shrugged and looked uncomfortable. Eddie
scraped through the next year on temporary assignments
—clerking at Logan's duty-free shop, working the grave-
yard shift at a doughnut bakery in Chelsea—but he wasn't
making it. He blew off a couple of insurance premiums. Before he knew it he was months behind on the car payments.
Imagining he saw repo men everywhere, he began parking
his Escort in a friend's garage.

On his thirty-seventh birthday he got a letter from
Gudren. She was meeting Ashleigh and Pablo in Rome and
needed someone to house-sit her place in Taos for the
summer. All Eddie had to do was get there. He lay awake
that night, thinking over the proposal. To an unemployed

high school teacher, occupational therapist, or hydrogeologist, he knew, the offer might be worth, at best, a moment's wishful thinking. But to take her up on it—would that be folly, running, losing? He awoke the next morning to the sound of thunder. Outside his window gusts of rain lashed the maples. Frank was at work and Eddie sat at the kitchen table, drinking coffee and leafing through a week-old issue of the *Village Voice*. In the Arts section was a review of an opening in Soho. The artist's name was Darshon Kipper.

> Working out of a ramshackle motel in west Texas, on
> the periphery of the art world's attention, this fiercely
> independent artist creates unnervingly primitive large-
> scale nightscapes where Georgia O'Keeffe meets Dubuffet
> and Soutine. Make no mistake — these creations pack a
> wallop, but at the end of the day one can't help asking if
> anything, really, has been revealed.

Looking at her picture—the spray of freckles across the bridge of her long nose, the skeptical eyes—he remembered with slow-dawning exultation the first time he'd felt Bella's heartbeat. Surely Darshon would know where she was. He would stop in Texas on his way to Gudren's. No way was the house-sitting gig a loser's move. It was destiny.

EDDIE LEFT ONE muggy morning in the spring of 1994. The fishy smell of the harbor cloaked the city as he crossed the BU Bridge and glanced at the Charles curving off into the haze. He settled into the rhythm of the drive, shifting his butt from time to time as the interstate flowed under the tires. He made Roanoke the first night. The next afternoon found him speeding across the flatlands of Alabama. A couple of hours west of Birmingham the sun set and Eddie rolled down his window and breathed in the night's flavor, like mildewed peaches. He spent the night in Hattiesburg. There were slivers of glass in his bed, mushrooms sprouting in a brown ring around the ceiling light, and as he fell asleep he heard rats scuttling behind the TV. He awakened in the dark, certain that Bella had called his name.

In the morning he rose and drove on into the amniotic haze of Louisiana. As Eddie gave himself over to memories, he was suddenly moved to the quick by something in Cecil and Bertha's lives, their gruff gentleness, the soft blur of their voices, that he was forced to call beauty. Without giving it much thought he turned off the interstate and drove south to Tubbs Junction. The sign in front of Comeaux's 1-Stop now read OILED RAW FISH. When Eddie parked in front of Club Chill four or five youths in baggy shorts and backward baseball caps were standing in the shade near the entrance. With a shock Eddie realized that one was Carlton. "Hey," he said, "I should have taken you up on those lessons. If I'd been a little computer-savvy I'd still be in Boston."

"Yeah," said Carlton. His supercilious smile revealed a

gold tooth. "Well, I ain't into that no more. I got me a little thing, you know."

The other boys guffawed and slapped one another's palms. Eddie stepped through the door into a fog of sweat, smoke, and cologne. Everyone—the guys at the pool table, the men at the bar, the old men playing dominoes— stopped talking and turned to face him. Cecil came in from the back, humping a case of beer. "What's up?" he said with a tight smile, and Eddie realized that the man didn't recognize him.

"It's me," he said. "Eddie."

"Well, all right now." Cecil began rinsing glasses beneath a shelf where pickled pigs' feet stirred like lab specimens in gallon jars of cloudy vinegar. Eddie was trying to think of a graceful exit when a huge man in purple sweats and a shower cap grabbed his hand and wouldn't let go. "Hey, white boy, you know po-lice beat black men?"

"Leave him be," said Cecil.

"Can't I ask him a question?"

"He qualified," said Cecil. "Now leave him be." He looked at Eddie. "Maybe this ain't the best time, you know?"

Carlton and his friends were gone when Eddie got back into his car. He headed for the interstate. Before him the road tunneled through a coiled mass of trees. The clouds thickened around Lake Charles; to the south, lightning laced the sky. It was dark by the time he crossed the Sabine River and an hour or so past Houston he drove into a thunderstorm. His head was killing him. Sheets of rain lashed the windshield. The wind whipped snaky patterns across the flooded pavement. In the flashes of lightning he saw spectral arches of the interstate still under construction, jumbled concrete barriers. He was rolling down his window to read a jumble of conflicting detour signs when air brakes squealed behind him. Headlights flared in the rearview mirror. Eddie yanked the wheel to the right, lurched off the pavement. Two semis blared angrily past, then plummeted into the storm.

Once he stopped shaking he got back onto the road and searched the channels for music. He tried not to move his head. Other than a show hawking cassettes of Aunt Grace—a dead evangelist broadcasting, so went the claim, from Glory—he could find only strident Mexican stations that faded in and out. Finally he gave up and sang old Neil Young tunes to the slap of the windshield wipers. His headache was worse, hot tendrils of pain creeping around his eye sockets, and after driving for an hour or so without seeing a single sign he pulled off the road and slept in the backseat.

Eddie awoke to a fine cloudless morning. His headache was gone. The desert breathed a thin piney odor and it was already hot. Even with the sun still low in the east he could feel each photon, sharp as a needle, against his skin. He stood on his tiptoes and stretched. His neck popped, the beads of sound falling without an echo into the vast baking silence. When he started the car the wiper blades shuddered on the dry windshield. Pricked on by the transformation of the landscape, he sped west through the dusty towns, passing pale green border-patrol vehicles every few miles. Next to the sagging billboards lay dead cows, plucked-looking vultures perched on the rumpled hides. The longer he thought about it the more outlandish seemed the notion that he could explain anything to anybody, much less Bella. Still she'd *liked* him. It was worth a shot.

LATE SUNLIGHT WAS flowing like red syrup across the desert when he pulled into the parking lot of the Hi-Way Inn. The place had been painted since his last visit and a swing set straddled a patch of grass in the center of the parking lot. The woman in the office directed him to a unit opposite. A rusted Chevelle was parked in front. Bella's daughter came to the door in paint-stained overalls, charcoal smeared along one cheek. Eddie's back hurt and his brain still throbbed with road fatigue and he knew he was staring but he couldn't help it. "I read about you in the paper," he said. "I used to know your mom."

"She's not here," she said. "She lives in New Orleans. Hey, I know you. You're Raphael, aren't you?"

"Not anymore."

Inside, a spattered tarp covered the floor and the room smelled of oil paint and patchouli. Above a narrow, monastic-looking bed a print of El Greco's *St. Martin and the Beggar* was tacked to the plaster. When she bent to move some milk crates from a chair the braid fell away from her neck and he could see the dark silky hairs along her spine. Eddie heard the wind rising as he glanced over her collages —stark earth-toned things bristling with barbed wire and bones, feathers and religious medallions. Huge canvases were stacked along the walls and on an easel rested a painting of what looked like dark-skinned children with flaming hair.

Eddie rubbed his eyes. "I can't go any farther tonight. Is there somewhere we can get dinner?"

"There's a Mexican place. It's not fancy."

Back in his room he showered and sang "Cowgirl in the Sand" in a wobbly tenor. It was dark when he returned to Darshon's cabin. She'd washed her hair, which hung in black tangled ropes on either side of her head, dripping water on her denim jacket. Eddie's back still hurt and it took strict concentration not to limp as he matched his pace to hers. On their way through town they passed an abandoned Sinclair station, its rusted antique pumps capped with murky glass bulbs, then a boarded-up Greyhound depot painted with faded invitations to the diner inside. At a restaurant called Gilda's they ordered *chiles rellenos*. A chalkboard behind the bar advertised *menudo*. A long table in the middle of the room was jammed with young Mexican couples who had clearly been at it for a while—Eddie counted fifteen empty beer pitchers. A couple of the women kept glancing at him and whispering.

"The famous Raphael," said Darshon. You know how in old movies the parents were always threatening their kids with reform school? Well, that was you. Reform school. *Keep it up, lady, and you'll end up with somebody like Raphael!*"

"Look, when a woman loves you she thinks you're terrific; when you love her back you tend to believe her. And I didn't." He was quiet for a moment. "I mean I couldn't."

Darshon looked amused. "Hey, you didn't ruin her life. I mean, don't flatter yourself. She's doing great. She has her own graphic design business. She's buying a house. And she's not mad, if that's what's got you worried. Whenever she talks about you she laughs. I think you should call her. Or at least write."

"We'll see," he said.

"Yeah." Her fingers trembled as she took a long drag of her cigarette and stubbed it out in the ashtray. "It's probably time to go." She slipped on her jacket and Eddie followed her out. They walked back to the motel in silence. Every so often their hands brushed. A truck loomed behind them and their shadows multiplied, wove, and canted on the pavement. They stopped in front of her room to shake hands. When she looked up at him the moonlight shone in her eyes and stenciled her denim jacket with harlequin diamonds, and suddenly his heart was pounding and he had this insane urge to tell her his stories, dust off a few urban sutras, juggle for her.

"You know," she whispered, "I've never seen anyone look so lost."

He released her hand as carefully as if it were spun from glass. Off in the dark a door banged in the wind. It had turned cold. "I'm sorry," he said. He couldn't stop shivering. "But it's a long way from where life finds you to where it drops you off."

AROUND NOON THE following day he pulled off the highway at a tiny cemetery. The graves were adorned with paper flowers, ringed with bits of colored glass. Next to the car, he knelt and begged grace from the God of his childhood, an apparition hastily cobbled from what he could recall of weekly religious instruction back in grade school, the stifled terror of air-raid drills, dusty age-smoked portraits of Lincoln, *The Rubáiyát of Omar Khayyám*.

"Help me," he whispered. "Help me, help me."

That evening Eddie stood at the window of his ratty motel room on the outskirts of El Paso, looking south. He felt like a deserter from some forgotten war, still wearing the rags of his antiquated uniform. In the parking lot a radio blasted the sobbing accordions of a Mexican station and across the driveway big rigs idled by the diesel pumps at a FINA station. Beyond lay the desert, low rolling hills stubbled with squat piñon pines. Mexico. Eddie felt insects crawling between his bones.

Around three in the morning he was awakened by a couple arguing outside his door. "Darling," said a drunken man's voice with a panhandle twang, "what can I tell you? I'm flat busy. I got to sort my boots."

"How?" said the woman. "Right from left?"

Eddie stared into the roiling darkness and brought up, as if reflected in the curve of a windshield, the image of a naked woman rising from dark waters, irradiated with the hues of stained glass. And Eddie understood that whatever befell him from now on, her blessing would follow like piano music from an open window. He turned on the bedside lamp, opened the blank notebook he'd bought in Boston, and wrote *Until we cough out our lives like cobwebs.*

Bella

After sitting cross-legged around the fire for what seemed like hours with a bunch of women wearing expressions of rapt piety, Bella was aching for the ceremony to end. Then her illustrator, Camille, a rangy blond woman in a denim halter top, started chanting. "White Buffalo Calf-Woman," she intoned, "for the earth we pray. For our community we pray. And for our friend Bella—make the reunion with her daughters a joyous one. Restore us all, White Buffalo Calf-Woman."

"Comfort us," echoed the others, *"heal us, exalt us."*

A tall white-haired woman tossed wood on the fire. Her shadow wobbled against the canvas as she ladled water over a bucket of hot rocks. Billows of steam filled the tent, and the chant dissolved into a chorus of explosive coughing. Bella crawled outside and stood barefoot on the wet grass, gulping in the night air. Inside the tent, hesitant sopranos rose in "Shall We Gather at the River." Her knees were killing her and she felt like a sausage in the tank suit Camille had lent her. Despite busting her butt since five that morning on a theater program for the 1995 Deep South Writers Caucus, she was running late. Around six she'd discovered that the cover-art file was corrupt and after a frantic grocery run she'd raced over to the west bank to pick up a duplicate. As it happened, Camille was hosting a women's sweat lodge. *Follow us,* read the flyer she pressed upon Bella, *into deep caves of inner wisdom! Open your heart to the magik of the Wikkan nation!*

She went into the house to change. When she came back outside, women were spilling from the tent, fanning themselves, sneezing, filling the air with blurred laughter. Camille wiped the hair from her face as she strode over to Bella. "Intense, no? Now aren't you glad I talked you into staying? *For our community we pray.*"

"Like a fool I feel."

"Cynic." A trembling dachshund slunk out of the shadows and Camille snapped her fingers. "*Ici,* Yemoja." The dog's nails clicked on the pavement as it followed the two women down the driveway. "I don't know if it's worth mentioning," said Camille, "but I wasn't sure what a grackle looks like so I drew a crow."

"But the play's called *The Grackles.*"

"Hey, a blackbird is a blackbird. Incidentally, you're welcome to stick around for the Talking Stick Council."

Bella unlocked her Saturn wagon. "I better not," she said. "Darshon is going to show up at the house any minute. Plus Sage and the new boyfriend are flying in from Boston at nine-thirty. Do you think I'll be late?"

Camille looked at her watch. "*Big* time."

BELLA FELT HER hair springing into sticky curls as she sped back across the bridge. Past the glaze of the river below, lights spattered the dark sprawl of New Orleans, where people with all the time in the world were drinking Sazeracs, reading cookbooks, watering their plants.

Even with light traffic it took her a half hour to get to the airport. Sage was waiting in Baggage Claim next to a tall short-haired boy wearing wire-rimmed glasses. Bella's heart pounded as she made her way through the crowd. "Hey," she said, "how did you get so tan?"

Sage stood up to give her a dry little kiss. "We've been waiting over an hour, Esmeralda."

"I had to—don't give me that look, lady—I had to pick up some stuff at my illustrator's place."

"The least you could do was be here."

"Todd Rosenblum," said the boy, holding out his hand. "I've really been looking forward to meeting you, Mrs. Kipper."

"Call me Bella, OK?" They loaded the car and headed back toward the city. "How did you two meet?" she asked.

"We were study partners in economics," said Todd. "She's quite gifted, math-wise."

"She gets that from her father." Bella coasted off 90 onto St. Charles. She waited for a streetcar packed with tourists to clatter past, then cut through the unlit side streets to her block and parked behind a dilapidated Chevelle with a flat tire.

Darshon sat smoking on the porch in a speckled western shirt, cutoff jeans, and cowboy boots. Bella unpacked the groceries and followed Todd and Sage up the buckled walk. She brushed the dark tangled hair away from Darshon's forehead, just to see the freckles. "Have you been waiting long?"

"Compared to what?" Darshon stood up, stretched, and pointed to the Chevelle. "Talk about a major trauma. The fuel pump went out in San Antonio and I got a flat in Baton Rouge. You smell like a forest fire."

"You drove here from Baton Rouge with a flat tire?"

"I'm not stupid, Mom. I called a tow truck."

"You had yourself towed eighty miles?"

"Well, I wasn't about to leave your present in the car."

Propped against one of the porch pillars was a huge canvas to which a stuffed iguana was lashed with barbed wire. Gingerly Bella touched the lizard. Beneath it the canvas was layered with paint, feathers, Catholic religious medallions, and overlapping spirals of Hebrew calligraphy. "Magisterial," she said.

"Looks like a Mandlebrot Set," said Todd, "by Georgia O'Keeffe."

"Darsh could have gotten a scholarship to Parsons," said Sage. "Or Pratt. Or RISD. Instead she's holed up in some motel in the middle of nowhere."

"You'd be surprised who shows up there," said Darshon.

"I doubt it," said Bella, though in fact she worried about Darshon and whatever creepy vision she served all alone in the west Texas desert. When she unlocked the door the house exhaled a cool breath of fresh paint and mildew. "Can you believe it's taken me a year to get this thing in good enough shape for the housewarming?"

"Kind of gothic," said Todd.

Sage placed a package on the kitchen table. "You deserve it."

"A Dustbuster," said Bella. "How appropriate." In the next house the drapes were open, and her neighbor, a slender lawyer of about Bella's age wearing nothing but a set of headphones, was dancing by herself next to an ironing board. "I have a surprise for you," she said as she put away the groceries. "I've got us all tickets for a play tomorrow night." The girls groaned in unison. "Don't be so narrow-minded, you two. We've never had the chance to do that sort of thing and I think it'll be nice."

"Sage and I aren't really into plays and movies," said Todd. "All that nudity and violence."

"Oh, boy," said Bella. Darshon was helping her hang the collage in the front room when the phone rang; for a hot instant she was sure it was Zack.

"Doll?" said a woman with an unmistakable Philly accent.

"Shirley."

"Don't sound so excited. Have the young ladies arrived?"

"Yes, indeed." Bella watched Darshon light a cigarette. In spite of their outfits—Darshon with her cowpoke gear, Sage in her prissy sleeveless blouse and plaid shorts—the resemblance was stronger than ever, the same noses, the same tubular lips.

"I can't wait to see them," Shirley was saying. "Hub and I are dying to meet the little freshman's new beau."

"Nice guy. Still a little shaky from detox."

"Go on. Listen, doll, we were wondering if you need anything else for your party."

"According to Camille there's no such thing as too much corn bread."

When she got off the phone Sage was poking the yellowed spider plants. "Don't you ever water these things? Plus, I can't believe you're still hanging out with Shirley and Hub. What a couple of cheeseballs."

"Look, Shirley's all I've got left of my childhood."

"Where do we sleep?" said Darshon.

"You get the couch. I've set Sage and Todd up in the spare room."

Todd put his arm around Sage's waist. "We'd prefer separate rooms," he said. "We're not into premarital intimacy."

"Sleep in the kitchen for all I care. Hey," she said, as Sage started dragging her suitcases down the hall, "thanks for the Dustbuster."

Sage turned around with a smile of pure joy. "Todd helped pick it out," she said.

IT WAS AFTER three when Bella finished the program. Too wound up for sleep, she decided to pay her bills. The theater program was her biggest contract yet and as she worked her way through the checks—house payment, car payment, carpentry bills, plumbing bills, loans, six maxed-out credit cards—she thought back to how she'd gotten it. Camille's cousin, Zack Broussard, had won an NEA grant for *Fuss and Feathers,* a play about a widowed general who believes his wife has been reincarnated as a turkey, then has doubts. Shortly after Mardi Gras the playwright threw a party at Tipitina's to celebrate. Camille thought he was a pompous little shit and hadn't planned to attend, but she ended up bringing Bella; Zack, she explained sourly, was dying to meet her and wouldn't stop nattering about it. To Bella's surprise he turned out to be a shrewd-looking guy in his late twenties with a goatee, a nice jaw, and that touching gravity you sometimes saw in young doctors. He hung out most of the evening at their table, laughing at Bella's stories. "Priceless," he kept saying.

Tipitina's was jammed with sweating Broussards from every bayou and canebrake between Shreveport and Morgan City, a noisy red-faced bunch raring to trample anything that stood between them and a good time. Bella was dancing with Zack's father, Judge Troy Broussard, to "Reconsider Me" when an old woman in a neck brace (one of the Thibodaux Broussards, Camille told her later) got up and performed a drunken shimmy in front of the bandstand, then sat down and sucked her thumb. The entire club, from the waitresses to the priests at the bar, suddenly became a study in indifference until Zack crossed the floor, pulled the woman upright, and waltzed her to a table. It was a sweet and gallant move and by the time he offered Bella the contract for *The Grackles* program she could hear a voice deep within her whispering something like *Better not.*

Bella stamped the envelopes and rubbed her eyes. There were nine dollars left in her account. She made her way on stiffened legs to the kitchen for a glass of milk. She could hear the TV in the spare room. Darshon snored, still fully dressed, on the front-room couch. Bella stuffed a ragged pillow under her head and she muttered something in her sleep. Once when Darshon was around twelve (where had they been then—Akron? Texas? California?) Bella had snooped through her journal and still remembered the loopy handwriting—*Once upon a time there was a lonely princess. The only name on her mailbox was Time. They put her in a big box and dumped fruit on her. Apples, pears, bananas. Oh when will someone come along and take all this love I have to give?*

Todd stood before the open refrigerator, spooning peach ice cream from the carton into his mouth. In the wedge of yellow light his toes were long and crooked. "You probably think I'm some dumb zealot," he said. "But I'm not. I'm in love, Mrs. Kipper."

"I'm not a Mrs. And I really wish you'd call me Bella." On the way to her room her footsteps sounded plodding, heavy-heeled, and as she climbed into bed it occurred to her that even in the dark no one would mistake her for a young woman. She thought about her neighbor, the distressingly girlish breasts. Over the whisper of the air conditioner she could hear the band from the Cuban bar down at the corner. Why had she let things get out of hand with Zack? It wasn't the first time she'd asked herself. She'd been so cautious since the party at Tip's. Just phone calls, a few dinners. Strictly business. Then a couple of Sundays ago she'd accompanied him to a cast party—a bunch of young actors with pierced eyebrows and absurd haircuts —and ended up at his place afterward. The promise of a foot rub was involved. It was his apartment, furnished with little more than books, a frameless futon, and a bunch of posters for bands she'd never heard of, that set off her Bad Idea alarm—not that it did any good. She felt herself blush in the dark. She couldn't plead drunkenness because she hadn't had a drink in five years and bad idea or not it had been glorious. There was still a scab about the size of a quarter at the base of her spine where she'd rubbed the skin off against the floor. But she hadn't seen Zack since. Bella stared at the banana plant silhouetted against her window until the alarm went off.

IT HAD TO be at least a hundred when she drove back from the service bureau with the printed programs. The pavement rippled in the heat. Blocks ahead, the cemetery that bordered on her backyard dissolved into molten greens. She turned left at the Cuban bar and there was her house. In the daytime it did look sort of gothic, a purple affair with blue shutters, bricks showing through gaps in the plaster. Then she spotted Zack's Cherokee parked behind Darshon's junk-heap. Glancing in the rearview mirror, she saw herself, a stoutish woman in a sweat-soaked Bob Marley T-shirt. Her eyes were pink with fatigue and her hair had fused into a woolly gray mat.

Inside, Darshon lay on the couch, smoking and staring at the ceiling fan. Tiny white feathers sprinkled her hair. In the kitchen Sage vacuumed the cabinet tops with the Dustbuster and Zack stood at the window, watching Todd pour charcoal briquettes into the rickety backyard barbecue. "Hey, Bella," said Zack. "Where have you been, girl? Listen, I have to get those programs to the museum by three-thirty. And I hate like hell to say this but it looks like attending your housewarming is out of the question. I thought we could have lunch instead." On the way to the door he stopped in front of the collage. "Your daughter's a serious talent," he said. "I was just telling her about targeting niche markets. With work like this and the right strategy I'll bet she could pick up a nice little piece of change."

"I don't know," said Darshon. "It sounds kind of boring."

"Not to be nosy," said Bella, "but have you taken those boots off yet?"

Darshon cast a thoughtful look at her feet. "I think so. The night before last."

"However distasteful you find it," said Zack, "networking is a core competency of a successful artist. And let's face it, you're not likely to land a Guggenheim in west Texas."

"She's had a show in New York and a write-up in the *Village Voice*," said Bella. "I don't think that's too shabby."

When she stepped outside, the air smelled of fried fish. Across the street a couple of little black girls wrestled on the grass, their ecstatic squeals muted in the thick heat. She could hear Zack talking to Darshon. "Here's another issue for you to consider—shipping."

"THE PROGRAMS ARE exquisite," said Zack.

"Thanks a bunch," said Bella.

Thick clouds were rolling in from the gulf as they drove down Webster. Ahead stretched blocks of liquor stores, discount clothing shops, check-cashing joints. Clusters of wilted shoppers waited at bus stops in poses of resigned misery. "Hey," said Zack. "Admittedly I should have given you more to work with than something I scribbled on a napkin. It was bad planning, pure and simple, on my part. I'll tell you what, though—once people see them you'll have more work than you can handle. I guarantee that."

"Why didn't you call?"

"Frankly, I didn't think it was that big—why are you looking at me like that?"

"Just wondering what goes on in your mind."

He flushed. "None of your business."

"None of my *business?*"

He sighed. "OK, I'm sorry. I know I should have called. The long and short of it is, this writers caucus is running me ragged. Not to mention my play. I'm telling you the God-honest truth here, Bella. I'm a little freaked out about *The Grackles* opening tonight. A bad review at this point is exactly the sort of thing that can screw up a career in the arts." Zack parked in front of Christophe's, a Creole restaurant across from the levee at the end of St. Charles. "This place has a wonderful élan," he said. "Is that the right word?"

"Oui, oui. Camille says it to her dog."

They sat at a window booth. The dining room was dark and woody, here and there a circle of pale faces caught in panels of amber light. A tape played Louis Armstrong singing "Wonderful World." An older black man in a gold lamé jacket materialized out of the shadows with a couple of upholstered menus. "A pleasure to see you, Mr. Broussard. How's your daddy?"

"Real good, Antoine. Real good. I'll tell him you asked after him." When the wine arrived, Zack pinched the cork, sniffed it with the air of a jeweler preparing to cut the Hope Diamond, and poured himself a glass. "This is the new Beaujolais my colleagues are raving about."

"All my friends are frantic too." Bella looked out the window. The sky had turned dark gray. Across the street a young woman in an Indian print top was climbing the grassy slope of the levee with a six-pack.

Their food came and Zack started picking all the onions out of his spinach salad. "As I was saying, the arts— painting, drama, whatever—are pretty much like any other business. If you don't have a product, if you don't have some kind of consistent media presence, you're not going to sustain a customer base. You can't afford any gaps." At the sound of a woman's raucous laughter he looked up. "Shit, oh dear," he sighed.

Bella turned to see Camille coming out of the bar, followed by the tall white-haired woman from the sweat lodge. "As I live and breathe," said Camille, "it's the Colonel Sanders of the theater."

"How droll," said Zack, and grudgingly scooted over to let them into the booth.

"This is Paula," said Camille. She held up a slim paperback—*Thimbles and Propinquity: Poems 1985–1990*—with the woman's photo on the back cover. "She's coming to the housewarming."

"Howdy," said Bella. "Zack here was about to tell me how he can't afford any gaps in his life."

"Jesus Lord God," said Camille. "I've got ten years where all I remember is afternoons in some Chinese restaurant, drinking Mai Tais."

"Mai Tais," said Zack, flipping open a notebook. "That's good—do you mind if I use it?"

Paula picked up one of the programs. "These are really nice. What a gorgeous crow."

"Actually," said Zack, putting away his notebook, "it's a grackle."

Paula flipped through the program. "Do you think I could learn how to do this?"

"Probably," said Bella, "but you already have a career."

"What I've got is a nonrenewable one-year appointment at Delgado Community College."

"You need a grant," said Camille. She closed her eyes and pressed a palm to her forehead. "I see it. An epic poem. A man. A penis. A large bird."

A thousand lines crinkled the corners of Paula's eyes. "'How can those terrified vague feathers,'" she said, "'push the trousered glory from its loosening drumsticks?'"

Bella was still laughing when the women left.

"Excuse me," said Zack. "But why was that so funny? And that Paula—what a sad case."

"I like her," said Bella.

"Some sixties relic who thinks she's a prima donna." Zack patted his lips with a napkin. "A whole generation that got handed charmed lives."

"Oh, and this includes me, right? Like it was a breeze working full-time and getting my degree with two kids? And driving down here from Boston with nothing but my clothes? Floating my equipment with credit cards and hustling more work than I could handle—"

"It's cool that you're in touch with your rage, Bella, but people can hear you."

"Seven-day weeks, eighteen-hour days, living on rice and beans? That's your idea of a charmed life? Not that long ago the girls and I were sleeping in the car, buddy."

Zack closed his eyes, as if collecting his strength for the ordeal, a not entirely unpleasant one, before him. "Look, I know how hard you worked to turn your life around. You've cut out the sauce, you've cut out—all the other stuff. I respect that more than you realize. But the thing is—don't make faces, I'm serious—now's the time when you should be enjoying all the things you've worked for.

244

The winds have shifted. Do you hear what I'm saying? Maybe it's time to trim your sails."

"Where is this ship heading, Commodore?"

Zack poked the stack of limp onions with his fork. "Well, the long and short of it is that I really don't think this is such a great idea."

"You don't think *what* is such a great idea?"

"Things happened pretty fast. With us, I mean."

"I didn't hear you complaining."

"You know as well as I that you came on pretty strong."

His voice hadn't yet risen to a whine but Bella could hear it coming. "This is pathetic," she said. "I'll walk back."

Zack signaled for the check, then glanced uneasily over at the next table, where some fat men in red suspenders watched them and whispered among themselves. "Have it your way. Does that mean you're not attending tonight? I'd understand if you didn't. Under the circumstances, I mean."

"I wouldn't miss it for the world, Cheeseball."

WHEN SHE GOT home raindrops were spattering stars on the dusty windows. Camille and Paula sat on the couch, watching *I Love Lucy* with the girls. Bella's shoulders prickled with hair trimmings. She felt cool air on her scalp as she stood in the front room doorway with the humbled air of someone who's trusted her looks to a Super

Cuts stylist with a pierced tongue. Sage turned from the TV
and her eyes widened with shock. "Oh, Mom. Why did you
do that to yourself?"

"Easy to take care of," said Darshon.

"Wild," said Camille. "Très chic."

"It's cute," said Paula. "Kind of a Gertrude Stein look."
She reached into a Winn-Dixie shopping bag on the coffee
table and took out a plastic container filled with balls the
color of horse droppings. "Herbal Refreshment Time. Space
balls, anyone?"

The phone rang in Bella's office. Her heart jumped but
it was her parents calling from Philly. "Bella? Is everything
all right?"

"Sure, Mom. Why not?"

In the next room Camille was yelling at the TV. "Wise
up, honey! Form a women's support group!"

"I hear someone shouting."

"I'm having a housewarming party." Bella blew the
dust off a photo on her desk—the girls in a wheat field
south of Jerusalem. Sage wore a pale blue dress and held
her arms out like a scarecrow's, cedar-colored hair lifting in
the breeze; next to her Darshon, in a grubby T-shirt, stood
grinning with her eyes shut. "High spirits, that's all."

"Babe?" said Bella's father. "Your mother's worried
about you down there. Shirley tells us you've befriended a
lot of weird individuals."

"Dangerous beatniks." Bella went to the window. Outside, the rain beat down on shrubbery spiked with lurid blossoms, and Hub and Shirley were coming up the walk, hunched under an umbrella with a case of Rolling Rock and a couple of baking pans. Hub's dome was totally bald and the remaining hair was pulled back in a ponytail. Bella's mother started crying. "I just wish you'd get *settled.*"

"How much more settled can I be? The girls are great. I've got my own business. I've got a house."

"Become a lesbian separatist!" shouted Camille. "Build a society that values women's labor!"

"I just don't know what happened," Bella's mother was saying. "I keep thinking of you and Shirley in those little ruffled bathing suits at the shore. One summer you were going to be a detective and she was going to be a lawyer, remember?"

"And one summer I was going to be Carole King and she was going to be Joni Mitchell."

"But you had such *potential,* honey."

"Right. I could have been Elvis." When she'd gotten her mother laughing Bella said good-bye and went into the kitchen, where Shirley, Hub, and Camille peered out the window. In the backyard Paula and Darshon stood up to their ankles in muddy water on either side of the barbecue while Todd poked at the chicken wings with a coat hanger. Past the backyard fence Bella could see rain splashing off the pale tombs. The barbecue tipped over and Todd hopped away from the coals.

"Doll," said Shirley, "is that Sage's young man?"

Camille came in from the front room and poked her in the ribs. "He's a tasty little thing, isn't he, darling?"

"Frankly," said Shirley, with a frosty smile, "I was wondering if he was all there."

The others came in from the backyard, soaked and smelling of smoke, with plates of wet chicken wings. They stamped their bare feet on the mat. Todd popped a space ball into his mouth and gave Bella a long curious look. "You know," he said, "I think it's very attractive—Bella."

THE STUFFED IGUANA glared down at a roomful of people balancing glasses and paper plates, and every few minutes the doorbell rang, announcing the arrival of another guest with a tray of corn bread. Some women from the powwow were there and so were a few of the neighbors and some folks from the women's shelter where Bella volunteered on weekends. Rain lashed the windows as *Songs of the White Buffalo Clan: Volume I,* a present from Camille, thundered from the speakers. Bella nibbled another of Paula's confections; it tasted of honey and peanut butter, overlaid with a musty tang of something like alfalfa.

"This tape?" said Shirley. "It reminds me of one of those old Hamm's beer commercials."

Hub tapped his beer bottle with a fork and, with the vaguely cowed look of a man who's spent fifteen years teaching high school, held up a dog-eared paperback. "I know you all have a play to attend," he said with a Tennessee drawl. "But while we're together I think it would be nice if we reflected for a moment on why we're here. And I can best do that by sharing with you a poem, one that's always struck me as having been written for Bella."

"Did Paula write it?" said Todd.

"Rainer Maria Rilke, 1875 to 1926." Hub opened the book and cleared his throat.

"What I don't understand," said Shirley, "is why anyone would want to see a play by someone who has sex with chickens."

"He didn't *do* it," said Bella. "He just wrote about it. And anyway it was a turkey."

"I see. For a minute there I was worried."

Camille let out a shriek of laughter and turned from the stereo. "Bless your heart," she said. "What's your totem animal, darling?"

"I'm not sure I have one," said Shirley.

Hub cleared his throat again. "'Evening.'"

"If the brother depend on the other," said a black man in a yachting cap, "he won't get no further."

"That's contrary to fact," said Paula.

"Anybody want more corn bread?" said Todd.

"'Evening,'" said Hub, again, and *Songs of the White Buffalo Clan: Volume II* roared from the speakers. "All right. Forget it. Just forget it."

Bella saw tears of outrage behind Hub's glasses and in

the light rippling through the windows he and Shirley were suddenly transformed from the friends she remembered into a fussy little man and a frightened-looking woman with the crushed roses of age in her cheeks. Bella touched Hub's wrist. "It's OK," she said. "It's enough that you're all here. All the pieces."

"Shouldn't we be getting ready?" said Darshon.

"What for?" said Todd.

"For the Freddy," said Bella. "Has anyone seen my keys?"

"Todd ate them," said Camille. "He thought they were space balls."

"What's the Freddy?" said Todd.

"I believe," said Hub stiffly, "that it used to be a dance."

The windows flashed white. The lights flickered and died as thunder rattled the walls. The air conditioner gurgled into silence. The guests went trampling out to the porch. Bella could hear palmetto bugs snapping off the window screens as she groped through the chest of drawers for a flashlight. Yemoja snapped at her heels and she booted the dog across the floor.

"Ici," called Camille, from the porch. *"Ici, Yemoja."*

Bella heard someone whispering. She looked behind her and saw Paula silhouetted against the pale blue rectangle of the window. Before Darshon's collage she stood with her hands on her hips, apparently talking to the iguana:

But here there is no light,
Save what from heaven is with the breezes blown
Through verdurous glooms and winding mossy ways.

THE RAIN HAD stopped but the night was steamy and even with the air-conditioning on full blast the windows kept fogging up. Bella dropped off Paula outside a bookstore on Canal. "Thanks for the out-of-body experience," said Paula and made her way a little unsteadily between the sidewalk tables, carrying the empty shopping bag.

"I can't believe we finished all the space balls," said Camille. "There was over an ounce of pot in those things."

Bella plugged in a George Jones cassette and headed for the museum. The wet pavement reflected a rippling wash of colored lights.

"What's this play about?" said Darshon.

"Your hair's full of feathers," said Sage. "Here—sit *still*, will you?"

"I don't know," said Bella. "Zack kept the rehearsals a big secret."

"Boy meets chicken," said Camille. "Boy loses chicken."

Over the museum entrance hung a soggy banner that read THE 1995 DEEP SOUTH WRITERS CAUCUS PRESENTS THE GRACKLES BY ZACHARY P. BROUSSARD. As they pulled into a space the crossed headlight beams glazed the water of Bayou St. John.

"I am not of this earth," Todd said and vomited in the parking lot.

"You're all nuts," said Sage, then buried her face in her hands and laughed till she wept.

Inside, Zack, wearing jeans and a black sport coat over a white T-shirt, was talking earnestly with his father. When Judge Broussard spotted Bella and her entourage he waved them over and brandished a program. "Which of you," he said, looking angrily from Bella to Camille, "had the effrontery to represent this—this low scavenger—as a grackle?"

"Crow, grackle," said Bella. "Whatever."

"Inexcusable," said Judge Broussard. "Monstrous."

"Great haircut," said Zack as his father stalked away. "Is it some political thing?"

"Yeah, a state of the union message." Bella followed the girls into the theater and sat between Todd and Camille. She felt as if she were underwater. The walls were pulsing. How many space balls had she eaten? Over a sea of heads she saw a bearded guy in a rumpled suit step to the lectern. The man pressed his fingertips together. "It's been suggested," he said in a reedy voice, "that human relationships represent our final frontier."

"Next," whispered Camille, "we move on to poultry."

"It's been further suggested," the man went on, "that not race, not class, not gender, but intergenerational conflict may be the force that, like a stick of dynamite in a rotten apple, will rip this nation asunder. Combine these two issues —the loss of human relationships as we know them, and intergenerational strife—and what do you have?"

"Pabst Blue Ribbon," said Camille.

Todd clenched the armrests of his seat. His face was gleaming with sweat, waxen beneath the tan. "Why didn't that Hub guy get to read his *poem?*" He sounded on the verge of tears.

"*Stop* it," Sage whispered and went into a fit of silent laughter.

"For so long," the bearded man droned on, "we've been invested in pain. We've valorized it. What do we really want, though? We want comfort. We want intellectual companionship. We want spirituality."

"All those things," said Camille, "that you can't get from a barnyard animal."

"*Shhh,*" said someone behind them.

"In any event," the man was saying, "we're privileged tonight to share a darkly comic meditation on this provocative issue by one of the South's most gifted young playwrights. Comic, yes, but in many ways a profound work. An important work. A work of courage and pathos and beauty. Ladies and gentlemen, I give you *The Grackles.*"

The curtain rose on a stage empty except for two video monitors, a mannequin, and a couple of actors whom Bella remembered from Zack's party: a girl in a tie-dyed tank top, a long skirt, a gray wig; a long-haired boy in slacks and a white shirt with no collar. The actors' faces appeared on the monitors. They looked about ten years old.

"Tell me again, Bathsheba," said the boy, "how you saw God at a Grateful Dead concert." His trembling voice echoed through the theater.

Feedback howled from the speakers. A blue-haired actress in a leotard stumbled onto the stage and pirouetted clumsily around the mannequin. Bella was trying to remember all her phone numbers for the past ten years when she saw the girls shooting her worried glances.

"Is it such a mystery," the boy on stage was shouting, "that I aspire to greater heights than to be simply another one of your doomed relationships? Like that ex-priest in Akron? Or the vitamin salesman in California who asked you to take a flyswatter to his ass? Or the Israeli soldier who got busted trying to smuggle a truckload of combat boots—all left—across the Jordanian border? Or the stand-up comic in Texas?"

The audience tittered. Everything went white before Bella's eyes and for a long moment her mind was a drumming void.

"I'm young," the boy went on. "I need to spread my wings and fly. You and your silly generation—playing cowboys and Indians, playing revolutionaries. Small wonder indeed that in this hideous aching absence your life seems not an adventure but a series of pathetic disasters. Well, you had your chance and this is my time. The long and short of it is, I have to find out for myself."

"But what, really," whined the girl on stage, "is there to find out?"

The sound system played what sounded like squawking crows and the boy pointed to the ceiling. "Those grackles —can they tell the difference between the righteous and the wicked? Or simply between things that move and things that don't?"

Bella rose and shoved her way to the aisle, barking *Excuse me* every couple of feet. Onstage the girl in the leotard was flogging the mannequin with a bullwhip.

A THICK FOG had rolled in. As Bella crossed the parking lot she saw herself pasting a rock through Zack's windshield. But why bother? She picked her way over ragged chunks of concrete strewn with condoms and splintered syringes to the bank of Bayou St. John and sat on a slab of wet concrete. The still water breathed a gritty brown scent. Through her skirt she could feel the pebbled surface. Her temples pounded and her knees ached from last night's powwow.

Todd came stumbling out of the fog and collapsed beside her. "Sage and Darshon are looking all over for you. I couldn't breathe anymore. I thought I was going to die. And all those people acting like that play was for real. Was it supposed to be about you? How could anybody be so cruel?"

Bella started weeping, ugly, racking sobs. She couldn't stop. "Am I crazy? Why did I bring the girls to this stupid play? Just to show them my life's been some big joke?" Cicadas shrilled in the trees, and off in the fog Bella could hear her daughters calling her. "Oh, God," she wailed, "my heart is breaking to pieces."

"Bella," said Todd, so softly, "can I touch your hair?"

She didn't say anything. One by one she was counting every face she would see from her deathbed, and after a moment she felt Todd's fingers on the top of her head, moving in circles.

The Kippers

Bella hadn't taken a vacation since starting the graphic design business four grueling years ago. She couldn't afford to. But Sage was getting married. And to see at least one daughter settled and happy—she would have walked all the way to Massachusetts for that. Anyway summers were slow enough that she felt reasonably comfortable letting Camille run things while she was gone. In her heart she wasn't crazy about weddings but this one was supposed to be fairly informal. Though Sage had decreed lavender silk dresses for the other women, Bella, as mother of the bride, had only to wear "something that matched." She ended up charging a deep purple dress, flowing and a bit low-cut, and a coach-class ticket to Boston. Fortunately both daughters lived in the same state now. Six months ago Darshon, whose paintings, collages, and sculptures finally brought in a modest income (five figures for a good year), had moved from Texas to a loft near the harbor. Sage had been a consultant in Cambridge since she'd gotten her undergraduate degree.

Fortified with a half-dozen packages of Sno Balls Bella flew out of New Orleans in early July. It was a hot insufferably muggy day in New England when she arrived. Darshon was nowhere to be seen. Bella waited at the curb for a half hour, then called her from a pay phone. "Oh, wow," said Darshon. "I thought you were getting in this evening."

Bella caught a cab. After five years in blowsy New Orleans she suddenly felt sentimental about Boston; it was here that she'd turned her life around, and as the cab came out of the tunnel and the improbable skyline rose before her, she missed the place as one might the frosty and unbending magnanimity of a distant aunt. The cab got off the expressway near the financial district, bumped over the Fort Point Channel Bridge, and pulled up opposite the Hickox Academy of Dance. Bella dragged her luggage to the entrance of a former warehouse, a three-story brick building whose walls bore the ghostly outlines of a Coca-Cola advertisement. When Darshon buzzed her in she stepped into an ancient freight elevator still imbued with a faint odor of mildew and peaches. The lift whined its way upward. Through the mesh-covered window Bella could see the floor joists creep by. She took the remaining Sno Ball from her purse, scooped the melted frosting from the plastic, and popped it into her mouth. She was still licking her fingers when the elevator stopped with a jerk.

Darshon pulled open the door. Paint spattered her dark tousled hair and the paintbrush in her left hand dripped gesso on her scuffed cowboy boots. "Sorry about the screwup." The loft reeked of solvent and paint. Despite the single window fan it was stiflingly hot. Bella looked around at the confusion of welding gear, canvases, paints, and brushes. Two beanbag chairs faced a tiny television. On the inside of the front door huge letters written with a magic marker spelled out KEYS!!!

"Home sweet home," said Bella.

"A little spartan, I guess."

"Spartan? It's uninhabitable, honey. Where am I supposed to sleep?"

"I borrowed a sleeping bag from Strykor downstairs."

"My aching butt." Bella put down her bags and did a brisk pirouette. "What do you think of the new professional *moi?*"

Darshon stared appraisingly at Bella's styled short gray hair and black jumper. "I don't know, Esmeralda. A little matronly. Are those J. Crew sandals?"

"Give me a break." Bella sat at the kitchen table beneath a tattered print of El Greco's *St. Martin and the Beggar.* She kicked off her sandals and rubbed her feet, then nodded toward a canvas propped against one of the pillars that divided the loft. It was huge—like most of her daughter's pieces—exploding with hot pastels. "New?"

"It's an albatross," said Darshon.

Bella pointed to a gleaming smudge of yellow. "Is that its beak?"

"I mean it's not working out. And be careful—it's wet." Darshon lit a cigarette. "Are you hungry? I could fix you a snack." She opened a closet door, disclosing two sacks of potatoes and a gallon jug of balsamic vinegar. "I guess I'm out of anchovies. Menu-wise, things are a little monochromatic." From the apartment below came the monotonous thud of a drum kit. "That's Strykor," said Darshon. "The drummer for Barbies with Muscles."

VERN WAS FLYING in from New Mexico and the prospect of seeing him at the prenuptial dinner made Bella a little uneasy. Over the years his spiritual zealotry (he was a Buddhist) had evolved into an eccentric prudery, manifested in his infrequent letters as apologies for words or phrases that for the life of her she could not conceive of as remotely untoward. *Please excuse my language,* he would write, speaking of the house he and his wife, Luanne, were building, *but we'll be glad to see the last shipment of cinder blocks.*

That evening Bella and Darshon took a cab to a restaurant in the North End. Sage and Todd waved to them from a long table. There was Shirley and her stepdaughter, PJ, a graceful auburn-haired young woman who rose to greet them with a light Georgia drawl. Opposite them, squeezed between Todd's parents and other assorted Rosenblums, sat a woman with unnaturally dark hair and too much turquoise jewelry, and beside her a portly bald man with a white beard. Both, despite their tans, were clearly jet-lagged and nervous. The man half-rose from his seat. "Bella," he said.

"My God—Vern?"

"This is Luanne," he said, nodding toward the woman beside him.

"You'll have to excuse Mr. Sleepyhead," said Luanne, making a show of patting Vern's oxford into shape. "He's been working practically around the clock lately. The new Shaker-style gliders are selling like crazy. And the volume?" She fanned herself with the wine list. "You wouldn't believe it since we opened the factory outlet."

Sage shoved a copy of *Information Week* into her purse. "Retail means detail," she said, slapping Darshon's hand away from the antipasto platter. "Leave some for us, will you?"

"The artichoke hearts are tastacious," said her sister.

"Try the mussels," said Mr. Rosenblum. "Charlotte and I came here when we were courting." He patted his wife's hand and she blushed.

"You're looking awesome, Mrs. Kipper," said Todd.

"Fat and sassy," said Bella.

"Fat?" said Todd's mother. "If I had your figure I'd be the envy of Arlington."

"The outfit's a little Junior League," said Darshon.

"Traditional never goes out of style," said Luanne. "I simply can't believe how much you girls have grown since your last visit."

Bella felt Vern's eyes on her as she asked for a club soda, and she realized with a rush of guilt that he'd never gotten over her. They'd just ordered entrées when a nasal beep prompted Sage to take a cell phone out of her purse. She listened a moment, then grimaced and put her hand over the receiver. "Sorry," she said, "but I have to take this." She spoke urgently into the receiver. "You can always tell them that you're tone-deaf." With a sad smile she hung up. "Poor guy," she said. "It's his first assignment and some Japanese clients are forcing him to sing at a karaoke bar."

"Not everybody thinks singing is this big humiliation," said Darshon.

"I'm just glad it's not me, that's all."

"You're saying you wouldn't sing even if you got drunk?"

Sage sighed. "I suppose I would."

"So you *do* sing when you get drunk."

"Not really."

"But you just said you would."

"Leave me *alone*, Darsh. Stop driving me nuts." She turned to Todd. "When we were kids she used to wake me up in the middle of the night to ask me how many jars of mayonnaise I could eat before I hurled."

"How many?" said Todd.

On her way to the women's room Bella passed through the bar where three wolfish-looking guys with leathery tans and Key West T-shirts stood drinking beer. "Hey, Hot Stuff," said one. Bella pretended not to hear.

When she returned to the table Vern and Luanne were deep in conversation with one of Todd's uncles. Sage was still sniping at Darshon. "You look like a sheepdog with that hair hanging in your face. Paint all over you." She flung up her hands. "I'm serious, Darsh. I need you to meet me half-way on this. I had the dress made for you. I got you the shoes. I've made allowances for your—stop *kicking* me, Todd—I've made allowances for your temperament and all but I don't want my wedding screwed up. And what are you going to do about your nails?"

Darshon glanced at her paint-stained fingers and shrugged. "I'll try to think of something."

"Mom," said Sage, "*talk* to her."

"Can we drop it?" said Bella. "On the way over here we were trying to figure out where we were when Dudley bit the state trooper. Darshon says Texas. I thought it was Akron."

"This was in Israel?" said Todd.

Sage shook her head. "Get a clue, Todd. And anyway it was Reno."

"I wasn't around then," said Vern with a wry smile.

"Dudley?" said Luanne. "This is a friend of yours?"

"Our dog," said Sage. "He died in New Orleans. Mom still keeps his bowl by the back door."

"Cuteness," said Mrs. Rosenblum.

Their waiter brought Bella a double scotch on the rocks. "I didn't order this," she said.

"Compliments of the gentlemen," said the waiter. He pointed to the three men at the bar. The one who'd spoken to her raised his beer in a toast.

"Send it back," said Bella.

The men at the bar shot her accusing stares, as if she were a defector. "Who do you think you're fooling, Hot Stuff?" yelled the guy who'd toasted her. "You ain't no cherry."

"Ignore him," said Mr. Rosenblum.

"That's right, hon," said his wife. "In the old days they wouldn't have let that element past the front door."

After dinner Bella, her daughters, and Todd walked Vern and Luanne back toward the Government Center subway station. Bella was still reeling from her first sight of Vern that evening. The contrast between the lean carpenter she remembered, steady and earnest and smelling of wood shavings, and the portly codger ambling in front of her—how was she supposed to accommodate that? Had they really planned a life together? When they came out from beneath the interstate a convertible rumbled by with "Only the Lonely" on the radio. "Oh," said Bella. "Listen!" She took a step backward, found her right foot wedged between two curbstones and lost her balance. She fell heavily. Something popped in her ankle like a snapped clutch cable. The world vanished in a white blossom of pain. When she opened her eyes she was on the sidewalk with a ring of faces staring down at her. Todd and Vern looked on dumbly as Luanne and the girls tried to help her to her feet. "Forget it," she said as the pain settled into a relentless stomach-turning pulse. "I think I broke it."

"I was afraid you were having a heart attack," said Vern.

Bella glared at him. Some doughy girls with scrunchies around their wrists and T-shirts that said *Class of 2000* averted their eyes as they went chattering past. Bella flushed with shame at the realization that they thought she was drunk.

Sage pulled out her cell phone. "I'm calling an ambulance," she said.

"She may be going into shock," said Luanne.

Todd held out his hand. "How many fingers?"

THE EMERGENCY CLINIC smelled of floor wax and rubbing alcohol. "When I woke up on the sidewalk," Bella was telling Vern, "I didn't know where I was. For a second I was nine years old and my cousin Beth had just walloped me across the jaw with a baseball bat during a softball game. I couldn't figure out who all these grown-ups were staring down at me." She waited in a wheelchair next to a stack of last year's *Popular Mechanics.* Her new jumper was ripped and stained with tar. She'd lost one of her sandals (from J. Crew, as Darshon had surmised). The air-conditioning didn't seem to be working and she could smell herself. The staff plodded up and down the corridors in sweat-darkened smocks, dark circles under their eyes.

Sage whispered into her cell phone. "Note to self— hospital mergers."

Nearby a plump red-faced doctor lectured a white-haired old guy with a black eye and a bloody nose. A discolored bandage was taped over one ear. "I'm sick of stitching you up," the doctor was saying. "Don't you think you're a little *mature* to be getting in street brawls, Mr. Hoffa?"

"Not liable," said the old man.

"Not *liable?* What is that supposed to mean?"

Bella watched the doctor turn to a tall guy with a gray ponytail and a polo shirt.

"Am I missing something here? Is your father speaking in some kind of code?" Again the doctor faced the injured man. "I'll tell you what—if you end up getting killed the only one who's going to be *liable* is you. Are we communicating?"

The old man listened with a smile of friendly interest. "Say," he said, "you're a fat-assed little prick, ain't you?"

"Come on, Pop," said his son. When he turned Bella

saw the words *Video Nirvana* silk-screened across the back of his polo shirt.

"*Come on, Pop, come on, Pop.* Who asked you, Numb-Nuts? You little chickenshit."

The doctor shook his head and glanced at his clipboard. "Bella Kipper?"

"Excuse me?" said the guy with the ponytail.

"What now?" said the doctor.

But the guy was looking down at Bella. "You're Bella Kipper?"

Bella met his gaze and her surroundings flattened into a blurred mural. The girls made big eyes at each other. Vern looked as if he'd been punched in the stomach. "Oh, shit," said Bella.

"BUST YOUR LEG, honey?" asked the enormous black woman whose cab they took from the hospital.

"Just a bad sprain."

"That's a shame. And you must be here for the Fourth and everything."

"My daughter's getting married."

"Now that's what I like to hear. You see I'm from the old school. I believe in the family. True love? That's mature love. There's already too many lonely people in the world, you understand what I'm saying? Not enough family. It's like everybody looking out a different set of windows, seeing different things, trying to make sense of it all. You talk all you want—when you got confusion you got trouble."

"Can we go any faster? It really hurts to sit like this."

"That's what I tell my son-in-law. We need to know where we going. Then we need to *get* there. A child needs a guiding hand. Now when I'm talking about a family I'm talking about—God *damn,*" she shouted as some boys on bicycles flickered past. She pounded the horn and veered to avoid them. "*Old* school," she said meditatively as she pulled up in front of Darshon's place.

Bella and Darshon rode the elevator in silence. She could hear Strykor drumming.

"The injured party gets the bed," said Darshon.

Bella lay in the dark with her splinted ankle propped on a bag of frozen peas, pondering the eerie solicitude of the hospital staff who, she'd been unnerved to realize, thought of her as an Older Woman. The drumming paused. Through the open window she could hear a man's voice from downstairs. *I'm too fast for mortals. I'm faster and smarter than an atomic bomb.* A woman's voice responded with wheezes and coughs and a whinny of drugged laughter, which modulated into the rhythmic creak of bedsprings and this went on for about fifteen minutes. Then the drumming started again.

"Mercy," said Bella, groping the nightstand for her stash of Sno Balls. "How long is this going to go on?"

"It depends. Till Barbies with Muscles has another gig, probably. Hey, I can hear the plastic wrapper. You don't have to sneak those stupid things, you know. And *I'm* supposed to be the weird one. Is Dad paying for Sage's wedding?"

Bella took a bite of one of the Sno Balls. "Essentially. Along with your braces and your school clothes and God knows what else over the years. He's a pretty sweet man, Darshon."

"Yeah, but back in California you left him for that guy in the emergency room, right?"

"Do we have to talk about that?"

"It's up to you."

"What can I say? At the time it didn't seem like I had any choice. I guess I just didn't know what I wanted." She had, though. She'd wanted a pretty little thing whose smile lit her up like overhearing a conversation about how wonderful she was. And she remembered wondering—while everything, everything, everything folded—why she should so suddenly find out not only what it meant to fall for somebody but just how far there was to fall. "What difference does it make?"

Darshon rose on one elbow to light a cigarette. In the match flare Bella saw her blurry smile. "What if I told you that he came looking for you?"

"Who? He did? When?"

"Years ago, in Texas. He was on his way to Mexico. Some kind of romantic outlaw fantasy."

"I can't believe you didn't tell me."

"You were busy with housewarming and all. I figured it could wait."

"He probably wanted to borrow money. Did he try to touch you?"

"Esmeralda, go to sleep."

BELLA WAS AWAKENED, bruised and sore, by church bells striking the quarter hour. A note taped to the refrigerator said that Darshon had gone grocery shopping. Bella made coffee, then called Shirley at her hotel. "Oh, doll," said Shirley, "I heard what happened. Of all the luck. Are you going to need a wheelchair? No—that's right, PJ told Sage you're on crutches. Isn't it hard to believe that our little Sage is getting married? And of course I'm over-joyed for her. But, doll, being alone is *horrible*. I hate it." She'd been widowed for a year now, her husband, Hub, murdered as he napped at a roadside rest stop outside of Atlanta. "PJ's been wonderful," she went on, clearly fight-ing back sobs. "But I miss Hub. I miss him as much as I did when he was first gone. There's *nothing* good about getting old. *Nothing.*"

Bella hung up and finished her coffee. It was already hot and the T-shirt she'd slept in clung to her skin. She re-membered going outside to look at the moon last Passover and marveling that being alone on such a night didn't *seem* all that strange. The doorbell rang. It was Darshon. She'd forgotten her keys. Bella buzzed her in and watched her unpack two sacks of onions and a dozen cans of anchovies. "Are you expecting an embargo on comfort food?"

Darshon held up a family pack of Sno Balls. "Just for you."

When she'd put away the groceries she showed Bella the piece she'd done for Sage and Todd's wedding present. It was a small charcoal sketch, and looking closer, Bella was astonished to recognize the view from the bedroom window of their apartment building in Dimona—a drab development town in the northern Negev. In Darshon's drawing you could see some bedouin tents in the distance, a couple of camels, some junked cars.

Bella had taken the girls to Israel before they'd even started school. She'd expected something out of one of the films they'd shown at Theodor Herzl Hebrew Academy— smiling workers scything wheat fields that rolled gloriously toward a horizon piled with clouds, all to the accompaniment of a swelling offscreen *"Hatikvah."* They found themselves on a run-down kibbutz near Beersheba in the middle of winter. It was cold. It rained. Winds rank with smells of orange pulp, kerosene, and poultry blew across a beaten landscape whose very bones showed through. Each night they sat in anxious isolation at their table in the dining hall, where once a month arthritic old pioneers would stand and warble the *"Internationale"* in cracked voices. All around them kibbutzniks carried on petty feuds while teenage boys, flushed with dark vanity and too many *Rocky* movies, snarled at their girlfriends in Arabic-inflected Hebrew. Sage and Darshon cried themselves to sleep. It took a catastrophic affair with an alcoholic Israeli soldier and the better part of a year in a miserable apartment to establish that the whole thing was a Bad Idea.

"Did this take you long?"

Darshon shrugged. "Yeah."

"I don't know how you do it. I used to think that was the most depressing view in the world. But now all of a sudden it's not."

The telephone rang and after three rings the answering machine kicked in. "Bella?" said a man's voice. "This is Eddie. From the clinic last night."

"Why me?" groaned Bella. "How did *he* get this number?"

"Please call me," the message went on, "at Video Nirvana, OK? One of us is always there." He left the number and hung up.

"One of who?" said Bella.

They made a brief shopping expedition to replace Bella's sandals and jumper. Later, she browbeat Darshon into modeling the dress she would wear to the wedding. Late sunlight glazed the dusty windows, and the shadows of the pillars striped the floor with long shadows as Darshon stood in the lavender shift and satin pumps. "I feel like a dork," she said.

Bella brushed the hair out of her daughter's eyes. "You look adorable. Stay there for a second, honey, while I get the camera."

She was rooting through her bags when she heard wood splintering, then a crash that echoed through the loft. She turned to see her daughter performing what looked like a frantic backstroke on the painting she'd called an albatross. Darshon sat up and the dress peeled from the canvas with a sticky sound. "I tripped over the stupid sleeping bag," she said as she got to her feet. "How bad is it?"

"It looks like it was tie-dyed by an ape. I have a really bad feeling about this, honey. Should we try a dry cleaner?"

"Forget it. It's too late."

While Darshon got ready for work Bella called Camille back in New Orleans. "The good news," said her friend, "is we got the fire put out. The bad news is we had to put it out with the printers."

"Hee-larious," said Bella. "How droll."

"Are you having a great time?"

"Terrific, if you like breaking your ankle."

"Ouchie-wouchie. Now I've got to ask one more time before I ship Sage and Todd's wedding present. You're sure that's what they want—a file cabinet?"

"That's what they told me."

Darshon came out of the bathroom in a rumpled blue blazer with *M&R Security* embroidered on the breast pocket. "Look at this," said Bella, pointing to the purple flesh bulging between the pads of her pressure splint. "I feel like a character out of some weird German novel." Darshon's snicker inspired her to go on. "A big moose named Luba. With TB and a clubfoot. Hey, do you really need this job? I mean, couldn't you teach or something?"

"I like it. It's quiet. I wander around the offices and look into the windows of the other buildings."

"What do you see?"

"All sorts of stuff."

"You mean people are still there at night? What are they doing?"

Darshon frowned. "Oh, you know. Fooling around."

"Really? Tell all."

Darshon shot her a disdainful look. "I don't *watch* them. Did anyone ever tell you that you have a one-track mind?"

"It's possible. The question is, How did I raise two such little prudes?"

Darshon held up a plastic bag. "I'll take care of this dress tonight. One of my buddies at the hotel next door can run it through the washing machine."

That evening Eddie called again and this time Bella answered. "Why do you keep pestering me?"

"Well, I was wondering if maybe we could get together."

"Please don't call anymore," she said and hung up.

THE THROB OF Strykor's drums awakened Bella from a dream in which she was trapped with a bunch of dark-haired schoolchildren in a burning classroom. She couldn't shake the feeling that she'd died in her sleep, and when she rose and hopped on one leg to the window she didn't make a sound. It was still hot. She looked down on Fort Point Channel, where minnows of light chased one another beneath the bridge. She remembered a night when she'd taken Darshon and Sage skinny-dipping in the Sea of Galilee, little fish nibbling their feet, the lights of Jordan flickering to the east. She closed her eyes and saw the three of them, pale lilies floating in dark waters that rippled on forever.

Around one in the morning she buzzed in Darshon, who'd forgotten her keys again. Bella met her at the elevator door, holding a half-gallon carton of coffee ice cream.

"Why are you eating now, Mom?"

"To prove I'm alive. How did the dress turn out?"

Darshon smacked her forehead. "Oh, wow. I left it in the hotel laundry. I'll have to grab it on the way to the wedding. Come on, let's get some air."

They took the elevator to the roof and Darshon set her mother up on a pile of pillows facing the harbor. Across the channel, beads of lights outlined the financial district. The wind ruffled Bella's damp dress. "This is great," she said. "What a view."

Darshon lit a cigarette. "Do you think you'll call Video Nirvana?"

"What's the point? The whole thing was a disaster. And after all, the guy dumped *me*. It's a stupid idea."

"That doesn't seem to stop anybody. I don't have one friend whose folks are still together. But they never stop trying."

"I didn't give you two an easy time, did I?"

Darshon shook her head impatiently. "Don't start asking me if you're a bad mother again."

The wind died and Bella could hear Strykor pounding relentlessly away at his drums. "What is that *smell?* It's like being downwind from a shrimp cannery."

"Probably the harbor."

Bella lay back and stared at the stars. "Do you remember back in Israel when you dreamed you saw a finger writing your name across the moon?"

"I never said it was a dream. You did."

"I just wondered if that's something you ever thought you should talk to somebody about. A professional, I mean."

"Why? Do you think so?"

Bella sighed. "No. Not really. Does it still happen?"

"Not as intense. When I was driving up here from Texas a voice said, *You'll live to see a day when the rocks speak.*"

After a long silence Bella said, "About what?"

BELLA JERKED AWAKE and found herself under a maple in the Rosenblums' backyard next to Shirley, Vern, and Luanne, her foot propped on a folding chair. A bolt of pain skewered her leg, right through the meds. Shirley leaned over and touched her arm. "Doll? Isn't Rabbi Margolis distinguished-looking?"

"Stunning." Bella watched the *chupa* holders—PJ, Darshon, Todd's brother, and one of his nieces—sweating in the thick heat. Next to the other women, Darshon looked like a refugee from some cruel Middle Eastern war. The dress had shrunk lopsidedly and appeared to have been bleached, then smeared with tar. Even from where she sat Bella could see the paint dribbled on those satin pumps. Todd crushed the glass beneath his heel and everyone clapped. The couple kissed.

"Get the hose!" shouted PJ.

Todd's nieces squealed with laughter.

"Please," said Mr. Rosenblum, looking up with a frown from his camcorder. "Not around the children."

While Todd's brother played "Blackbird" on a cheap acoustic guitar Bella watched Darshon approach Sage. "I'm sorry about the outfit," she whispered, "but I used a stain stick and it still—"

"Don't bother," said Sage. "In fact don't even talk to me at all. What does it take with you?"

"I said I was sorry," said Darshon. Bella saw in her face how deeply she was wounded. She'd failed her daughters, failed them both. Why had she never found the path of a virtuous woman? She hadn't even known where to look. It was like spending your life trying to fake a convincing British accent. She'd paid for every mistake but it would never be enough. Her conscience would never be clear. And now she was getting old. Soon she too would follow Mom and Dad and Hub, all of Sage and Darshon's friends who'd OD'd or died in drunk-driving accidents, into the realm of the forgotten. Would she see it coming? Would she know? Would she be frightened? It came to her with a little flutter that just about everyone here would still be alive—buying houses, having kids—when she was gone. Years from now someone would watch this video and point to a dumpy gray-haired woman in a purple dress. *Look— there's that weird old Bella. Remember her?* Her eyes filled with tears and she looked up through the maple branches at a jet arcing lazily across the sky.

The afternoon passed in a blur. Just past sunset PJ floated up behind the chair and put her hands on Bella's shoulders. "Hey," she whispered, "you were always my favorite grown-up." Then she walked away, barefoot, in the twilight, holding her sandals.

Next to the garage Rabbi Margolis was giving Shirley a fly-casting lesson with one of the new rods the Rosenblums had presented the newlyweds. Todd's brother strolled up to Bella with his guitar over one shoulder. "I wanted to read from 'Song of Songs,'" he said, "but I couldn't find it on the

Web. I figured you'd enjoy one of those tunes from the hippie days."

It was cooling off and the air was thick with the smells of perfume, talcum powder, and crushed grass. Under the grape arbor Vern and Luanne were helping Todd's nieces light paper lanterns. Bella was trying to sneak a Sno Ball out of her purse when the photographer called everyone together for a last group photo. Sage and Darshon helped her to a chair beneath the grape arbor. "Here they come," said Mr. Rosenblum. "Here come the Kippers." The others arranged themselves around the family.

"Do you think," Bella heard Sage ask Todd in a whisper, "that she's getting frail?"

"Smile," said the photographer.

"Hey," said PJ. "Does anybody else smell rancid fish?"

THE FOLLOWING MORNING Darshon and Bella drove into Cambridge in a smoking Camaro with rusted-out wheel wells. Darshon paid ten dollars to park a block from Vern and Luanne's hotel. She matched her pace to Bella's and they made their way slowly out of the parking lot. Bella's chest and arms were sore from the crutches. She'd worn blisters on her thumbs. The hotel stood next to the headquarters of McLaughlin & Rotary, and in the courtyard pathetic knots of smokers gathered in the shade. Consultants sat beneath the dogwoods, staring at their laptops and yammering into cell phones. Bella waited on a bench with her foot propped up while Darshon went to get Vern and Luanne.

On the drive to the airport Bella kept sneaking looks at the couple in the backseat and she could see their features eroding into the anonymity of age—grotesque lampoons by a mean-spirited sculptor. Vern kept ranting about Eddie. "I don't mind telling you," he was saying, "that I'm still boiling—excuse my French—about that joker having the nerve to approach you in the hospital. Did you hear the way he said your name? *Bella Kipper*. Didn't it sound like he was affecting some kind of accent? Absolutely no remorse."

"Vern—let it go, OK?"

"Sure. Let it go. Everyone thought he was so *enlightened. Oh, you just don't know him,*" he went on in a shrill mincing voice, "*he only treats me like a sack of garbage because he's so sensitive.* And that ponytail. What did he used to call himself? Raphael? Do you realize that he actually had the unmitigated *gall* to call me up once—looking for you?"

"Vern," snapped Luanne, "will you lighten up?"

Darshon double-parked in front of the terminal. While she unpacked the trunk, Bella hugged Vern and Luanne. "Listen," she said. "Thanks for being so good to us. Both of you. And the wedding—I would have been lost without you."

Vern cleared his throat. "Well," he said. "They're nice kids. They'll do OK."

"You have two lovely girls," said Luanne.

Bella watched the couple carry their baggage inside and knew that she would never see them again.

Darshon hit sixty-five as she headed back toward the interstate. Just past the tollbooth she careened around a corner, grinding sparks off the guard rail.

"Take it easy," said Bella. "What's the big rush?"

"I'm running late. I've got an appointment at Madame Dixon's."

"Who?"

"My psychic." Darshon got off the interstate just north of the harbor. She parked at the bottom of a hill in front of Madame Dixon's Fortune Telling Parlor. The psychic, a tiny black-haired woman who smelled of sweat and coriander, tried to sell Bella what seemed to be the parlor's entire inventory of oils: Black Cat Oil, Cast Off Evil Oil, Come to Me Oil, Do As I Say Oil, Just Judge Oil, Luck in a Hurry Oil, Follow Me Boy Oil, Hot Foot Oil, Kiss Me Now Oil. Bella would never have guessed there were so many available. When she refused, the old woman tried to interest her in tickets to a pancake breakfast in Lynn. Finally accepting defeat, Madame Dixon shuffled into a back room with Darshon behind her.

Bella sat with the crutches on her lap and gave herself over to the warm rushes of the pain meds. She went tumbling down the funnel of years, back to California, when she'd split up with Vern and moved in with Eddie. For a long moment she teetered over the memory of a sailboat ride years and years ago—God, she could smell his hair, see the bluffs along the shore blazing with poppies. Late one night she'd found him standing in front of the refrigerator, grabbed him around the waist, and tickled him till he fell on the floor. For a second his eyes were naked and they were both right there next to it—so close she knew nothing could ever make her feel shabby about following her heart. Well, she'd been wrong about that too. It was absurd. And it had been such a long time since she'd been with anyone. Such a long long time. She wished Darshon would come back. Between bursts of a pneumatic hammer down the block she could hear Bob Seger singing "Still the Same" on someone's car radio. From the stairwell came what could only be a cat gagging up a hair ball. Presently another old woman with a shawl over her head dragged a retching striped cat across the floor and tossed it out the back door. She reappeared a moment later, leading a group of silent dark-haired girls with bouquets of wilted roses. "Hey," she said confidingly, "how about a piece of money for the children?"

"I don't think so."

Darshon and Madame Dixon returned. The old woman took out an appointment book and looked at Darshon. "Same time next month?"

Darshon shrugged. "Sure."

"And you," said the psychic to Bella. "What you look for?"

"Me? Nothing."

The fortune teller laughed. "You lie," she said. "Your face tell you."

THE RIGHT REAR tire was flat and Darshon sheepishly admitted that she didn't have a spare. "Well, my Triple-A card is expired," said Bella. "Do you know anyone who lives around here?"

Darshon lit a cigarette and spat out a piece of tobacco. "Yeah." She nodded toward the Video Nirvana sign down the block. "So do you."

Pulp Fiction was on the monitor when they stepped inside. Behind the counter stood a burly harassed-looking version of Eddie. He watched the two women over his bifocals as they explained their predicament, then smiled. "I've seen you," he told Bella. "Eddie has your picture on his dresser." The movie went off and Bella could hear the crackle and hum of the overhead fluorescent lights. Eddie's brother asked a bored-looking girl of about fifteen with short purple hair to run the register. He brought out a chair for Bella. He made a phone call and ten minutes later Eddie pulled up out front in a tired-looking Escort. His father was with him.

Bella took off her glasses and slipped them into her bag. "Nice to see you again," said Eddie. "How's your foot?"

"Ankle. And it hurts."

He stood for a while, grinning at her and shifting from one foot to the other. "You still smell the same," he said.

"I'm not sure how to take that."

"You know, patchouli."

Finally he asked Darshon for the keys. She handed them over without a word and Eddie went out the door. "Is this going to be expensive?" Darshon asked his brother.

"Probably not," he said. "Eddie knows a lot of people."

His father looked down at Bella. "You're the gal in that picture Numb-Nuts keeps on the dresser."

"Pop," said Eddie's brother, "please?" He turned to the girl behind the counter. "Ruthie, could you run next door and get us a couple of iced coffees?"

The girl gave a disgusted click of her tongue stud. "Are you going to force me to do that too? It's *hot* out, Dad."

"It won't kill you." He took some bills from his wallet. "Get something for yourself too." As she stalked from the store he sighed and turned back to Bella. "You have to admit that it's kind of a miracle—you and Eddie running into each other again. What are the odds? As long as you're in town couldn't you get together with him—just to talk? It would mean a lot to the guy. What can it hurt?"

"Use your imagination."

Eddie's father licked his lips. "I'll tell you what, woman —you're looking *good*."

"Sage and I agree," said Shirley. She and PJ, having stopped at Darshon's apartment on their way to the airport, were sitting in front of the window fan. "We're both concerned about your involvement with this Casanova. From what Vern told me the man is evil incarnate."

"If he was evil incarnate I wouldn't have invited him over. Come on, Shirley. It's been a long time. And it's not like I was totally blameless. Anyway I warned him that nothing's going to happen."

Fireworks boomed out over the harbor and the windows rattled. The buzzer rang. A few minutes later Todd and Sage stepped out of the elevator. Sage had been crying. "What are you two doing here?" said Bella. "Aren't you supposed to be in Maine?"

"Todd talked me into coming back," said Sage. "To apologize." She grabbed Darshon and began to weep. "I'm so sorry," she said. "The wedding was the happiest day of my life. And I had to screw it up by yelling at you. I don't ever want anything to come between us."

"Nobody screwed it up," said Darshon.

"And the present," said Todd. "It was totally awesome."

"What's weird," said Sage, "is I always found that view totally vomitacious." She wiped her eyes with the back of her hand. "Now I can't stop looking at it."

The buzzer rang again. This time it was Eddie, carrying a shopping bag. Behind him stood his brother, niece, and father. "TV shit the bed," said Eddie's father. "And it's pretty near time for our program." He held up a *TV Guide*. "National Geographic? Hope you don't mind." Bella's eyes kept returning to the front of Eddie's T-shirt, where the label was boldly stiched to the outside of the collar. He gave her a chagrined smile as his family moved past him into the loft and arranged themselves around the television. "Well?" said the old man. "Who's sitting on the remote?"

Darshon gave Bella a wry look and clicked through the channels until a bellowing elephant appeared on-screen. *One morning,* intoned the narrator, *a solitary bull awakens with a primal stirring in his massive loins. The blind worm of desire. The appetite that cannot be denied. Yes, for this amorous pachyderm it is the time—the season—of wooing.*

"Now," said Eddie's father, "this is where it gets good."

"What is that *smell?*" said Bella. "It's driving me nuts."

Still watching the TV, Darshon reached into the pocket of her blazer and pulled out a petrified sandwich. "Oops," she said. "Anchovy and jalapeño."

Sage, Darshon, and Bella looked at one another. *"Nastacious,"* they said in unison.

FIREWORKS ERUPTED OVER the harbor, and the brassy spangles silhouetted the skyline. Bella sat on the sleeping bag, her foot propped on the edge of the roof. How many years had it been since they'd been alone together?

"Is it my imagination," said Eddie, "or were you all staring at me?"

"Maybe," said Bella, "it's because you've got your shirt on backward and inside out."

With a sigh of disgust Eddie put down the shopping bag. Turning his back to her, he stripped off his shirt, inverted it, and struggled to pull it back over his head. "I might have known," he said, his voice muffled by the fabric. "I only seem to pull this kind of thing around you." He finally yanked the shirt down to his waist.

"What are you *doing* here anyway?"

"Visiting you," said Eddie.

"I mean in Boston."

"Oh, my brother was in a jam when he started the video business. And then my dad moved in with him. As you can imagine, he's kind of a handful. Anyway I was working construction in New Mexico and I decided to come back and help. You know, I'm still wearing the *I Ching* coin you gave me. You've probably forgotten about it."

"I didn't forget."

"For years I tried to come up with what I'd say if I ever ran into you again. Now that you're here I don't see the point. I can't offer you anything. I manage a video store, for God's sake. I run poetry workshops at the Center for Aging. I owe everybody money. Everything else in my life was . . . unsatisfactory. Except being with you. And I let it go."

"I don't know that it makes a lot of sense to beat up on yourself about it. Another three months and I might have walked out on you." Come on, I was twenty-eight and you were—what—twenty-one?"

"Twenty-two. Did you ever think about me?"

"Well, yeah. Every so often I'd wonder if you were still ticklish. Hey, would you mind putting something under my foot? My ankle is killing me."

Eddie sat beside her. He lifted her foot gently and slipped a rolled-up blanket beneath it. He left his hand on her ankle. "I tried to find you."

"I know." She felt light-headed and for the first time in more years than she could remember she wanted a cigarette. "That's awfully nice. But I'm through with all that. We had our moment and we screwed it up. Why not just leave it at that? I mean, don't you find the idea of trying to pick up where we left off a little creepy?"

"What's creepy about it? We could plan things together. We could wear big wool sweaters and walk down to the post office to check our mail."

"That's a *plan?* Come on, I've got a business to run. And I'm too old for this . . . this sort of thing."

"Bella, if we walk away this time we'll never stop wondering. Maturity means trusting your romantic impulses."

"No, it doesn't."

"Well, I want to do something for you." He stood up and pulled three onions out of the shopping bag. One by one, he tossed them into the air. One by one they slipped from his fingers and bounced on the tar paper. "This roof isn't level."

"Oh, bullshit. Why should that make any difference?"

"It's simple physics. Look it up. You have to be centered. You have to feel the Tao." He tried again. This time the onions blurred beneath the fireworks into a yellow oval. "You know what? My memories of you have faded into the sad pastels of the tango. Each moment a damp petal. How's that?"

"Awe-inspiring," said Bella. She patted a space beside her on the sleeping bag. "Sit down." She took a fresh package of Sno Balls from her bag and tore off the plastic. "Want to split these?"

"I guess," said Eddie.

They sat there in silence, sharing the pastry, as the fireworks sputtered overhead and the smell of the harbor rose around them. Somewhere in South Boston church bells were chiming the hour. Bella could hear Strykor drumming. From the open window below came the girls' laughter and then the trumpet of a lovesick elephant.